T5-DHD-589

CRISIS
AT THE MEDICAL CENTER

DR. OSCAR KLEMENT
The wealthy G.P.'s charming bedside manner obscures his actual incompetence—at least as far as his patients are concerned. But his colleagues are tired of covering up for him. This time he has gone too far.

DR. AARON KRUEGER
With a shameful secret concealed in his past, the psychiatrist has buried himself in sleep research. But just as he's on the brink of a dramatic breakthrough, one of his patients dies—and it appears that his project has been sabotaged.

JOAN KLEMENT
Frustrated in her career as a psychologist by a husband who insists that she play the role of "the little woman," she is ready to kick over the traces, when fate steps in and hands her the solution to her problem.

A dramatic novel of suspense in a major medical center where life-or-death struggles are everyday occurrences, where doctors are larger than life or all too human, where emotions are hidden behind a professional mask, ready to surface at the first sign of trouble.

DREAM WATCH

JOHN H. WAY, M.D. & DAVID C. MILLER

PLAYBOY
PAPERBACKS

Author's Note

Although this is a work of fiction, the passages on REM
(rapid eye movement) dreams and on the physiology
and study of sleep are factual. Several sleep laboratories
throughout the country are engaged in the study of sleep
disorders, and there have been dramatic results obtained
in alleviating drug and alcohol addiction.

Chapter I

"Is it pulsating?"

"What?"

"Doctor, is it pulsating?" The question came as a controlled scream from a petite nurse known for her shyness.

Can't remember her ever raising her voice before, Dr. Oscar Klement thought as he squatted on the small obstetrics stool and stared numbly at the gray blob of tissue. Hanging grotesquely from the vagina, the loop of umbilical cord swayed rhythmically from side to side. He grabbed for the cord and missed. It was annoying how these damn women could continue to move even though their arms and legs were strapped down, he thought.

The nurse almost knocked Klement off his stool as she brushed by him and grabbed the umbilical cord with a small gloved hand. "Oh shit, it isn't!" Her voice carried through the delivery room.

"Nonsense," Klement said airily. His face seemed paralyzed, and he felt himself moving languidly, as if trapped in a bowl of jelly.

"Here," the tiny nurse commanded, "see for yourself," and she thrust the slimy rope into his hand. He rubbed it twice between his slippery gloved fingers, but it slid from his grasp each time.

The patient's moans now turned to piercing screams. Klement couldn't stand that noise. He stood up. "Now, Mrs. Olney, just calm down," he barked. "Everything is going to be just fine." He looked around the room over the pregnant belly of the screaming woman. The eyes above the surgical masks showed cold contempt.

Klement sat back down and began fingering the cord. The veins bulged, swollen by the trapped blood, which meant that none was getting through the artery. No, he guessed it wasn't pulsating.

"This is ridiculous," he heard a nurse say behind him. "He's not doing anything. Somebody call the chief." Klement turned around in time to see the floating nurse at the dial phone on the wall. *What is that bitch up to?* he wondered vaguely.

"Dr. McCallister," he heard her say into the phone. The name galvanized him into action. Grasping the prolapsed umbilical cord with his left hand, he pulled it taut and began to run his right hand along its length, through the vagina, and into the cervical canal of the uterus. He came into contact with a tiny foot. A breech. Of course; he remembered now! Prolapsed cords almost always occur with breeches. *Now, if I can only find the other foot . . .* Through his mental fog, Klement groped around the interior of the uterus. The woman screamed again. If Klement had been looking, he would have seen the floating nurse place one hand against the wall to steady herself.

"Blood pressure seventy over fifty," a nurse at the head of the table said.

"Start some Levophed," Klement ordered.

"Levophed?"

"That's what I said," he snapped.

"Doctor, don't you want her cross-matched?" the nurse asked.

"Damn it, if I wanted to give her blood, I would have said so. Now, start that Levophed. That will raise her blood pressure."

The floating nurse looked over at the head nurse, then shrugged and began mixing the I.V. solution.

Klement swore under his breath as his hand searched

for the other foot. He realized, as fuzzy as his mind was, that the lack of pulsations in the cord meant that it was caught between the baby's body and the mother's pelvis. The baby was being deprived of oxygen. He had to get that kid out of there, he knew. McCallister was on his way. How much time did he have? In his almost dream-like state, marking the passage of time was beyond comprehension. The hell with the other foot! He began pulling on the one foot, hard.

And then there was a sea of red. Later, of all the vignettes of this frenzied evening, he would remember the gushing blood most clearly. It covered everything. The floor was slippery with it.

Dr. Brian McCallister suddenly materialized beside Klement. From his height he looked down on everyone. Thick reddish-brown hair on a leonine head leaked from beneath his cap. The short, squat neck rested on massive shoulders that seemed to strain the surgical garb. He literally pushed Klement from his stool as he surveyed the disaster in front of him. Although McCallister's face was crimson, his voice was soft, and the nurses had to strain to hear his first order over the screams of the woman strapped to the table.

"Stop this woman's suffering; put her to sleep," he said with a quiet authority.

"Yes, sir. What anesthetic?"

"Sodium pentothal."

"Do you want an anesthesiologist called?"

"Yes. She'll need an operation," McCallister said, "but for God's sake, put her out. Now!"

Within a minute the screaming was reduced to moans, and finally to steady deep breathing, as the pentothal oozed through Mrs. Olney's brain.

"What's her pressure?" McCallister asked.

"A hundred and forty over ninety," he was told.

"That's awfully good for this mess down here, all this bleeding." He spied the I.V. bottle. "What is that?"

"Levophed."

"God," McCallister said, his voice now rising, "no wonder her pressure's up. She needs her blood volume replaced, not a vasoconstrictor. Stop it, and get the blood started."

"There's no blood ready."

"What?" McCallister looked around, seeming to notice Klement for the first time. "Cross-match four units stat," he told the nurse while still looking at Klement. "What have you got for a blood-volume expander?"

"Dextran or plasma," came the nurse's reply.

"Stop that damned Levophed and start dextran. And start a second I.V. of normal saline in the other arm. Run them both wide open until the blood is ready." McCallister continued to stare at Klement as the nurses bustled to carry out the new orders. "I have never in twenty-seven years as an obstetrician seen anything handled this badly," he said in a low, controlled voice. "A blacksmith could have done as well." His condemning words were lost to the busy nurses.

Klement had retreated slowly out of the glare of the overhead light, away from the center of the action, and now stood rooted about ten feet from the table. "I thought I'd better get it out," he mumbled, "before, uh, before anoxia, brain damage."

McCallister, having already turned back to probe the woman's vagina, didn't hear him. "Suction," he ordered.

"Yes, sir."

"Sutures, lots of them."

"What size?"

"Big ones—two-0 or three-0 catgut." McCallister began taking large stitches in an attempt to bring the gaping tissues together. Slowly the bleeding began to subside.

"Her pulse is irregular," the nurse anesthetist said.

"How fast?"

"A hundred and eighty a minute."

"Get the cardiac team in here with a monitor right away."

The floating nurse picked up the phone and dialed the operator. "Code MAX," she said hurriedly into the mouthpiece. "Delivery-room three." The paging system immediately echoed her words.

There was silence in the green delivery room, the only sounds the hissing of the oxygen at the head of the table and the clicking of the instruments at the other end as McCallister worked frantically to stop the bleeding. Klement stood unmoving, biting the inside of his lower lip.

"Blood pressure?" McCallister asked again.

"Eighty over sixty."

"Pulse?"

"Two hundred."

There was a commotion outside the delivery-room door. The voices engaged in a heated argument finally forced McCallister to look up from his work. The floating nurse was blocking the swinging doors with her body.

"What's the matter?" McCallister shouted impatiently.

"It's the cardiac team," she answered, "but they're not scrubbed. They're in street clothes."

"Oh, for Chrissake, let them in!" McCallister bellowed.

The nurse stepped aside, and another nurse, pushing a crash cart, burst into the room. She was followed by five more nurses, their starched white uniforms and caps contrasting sharply with the green scrub suits of the delivery-room team. The physician, the chief cardiology resident, was wearing a white shirt and a necktie beneath a long white hospital coat on which the name "Dr. Burns" was stenciled.

The cardiac team started hooking Mrs. Olney to a monitor and doing endotracheal intubation. Burns stepped to McCallister's side and peered over his shoulder. He paled.

"My God," he said quietly, "I've never seen a placenta like that."

"It's not the placenta," McCallister said cryptically.

Burns's eyebrows shot up as he looked sideways at McCallister. "You're kidding. What else would be hanging out like that?"

"Her uterus. It was pulled out."

"Wow!" Burns exclaimed. He felt slightly nauseated. "I've never seen anything like that."

"In twenty-seven years, I've never seen anything like it, either," McCallister said dryly. He jerked his thumb over his shoulder. "If you want to see the placenta, it's over in that basin, with the baby." As he turned to Burns, he caught Klement's eye again.

Klement caught the malevolence in McCallister's stare and seemed to shrink from the intensity of it. His brain still operating at only about half speed, he sought a diplomatic withdrawal from the field of this bloody battle.

McCallister's words did not prepare chief cardiology resident Joe Burns for the sight that greeted his eyes. In the basin, Burns saw the placenta; but also, floating face up in a pool of clotted greenish-red slime—a mixture of amniotic fluid and blood—was a fully formed male infant. The eyes were closed and the face wore a strangely peaceful expression. There was a projection above the left shoulder of the infant that Burns first thought was an extra upper extremity. A mutant, he supposed, possessed of a malformed extra left arm. But, on closer examination, he saw that it was a foot. The left leg, he realized with revulsion, had been ripped from its socket and bent backward behind the dead infant. It was only tenuously attached to the body, hanging by a few threads of skin and tendons where it should have been joined firmly to the torso. The open hip socket revealed clean white bone.

Burns saw the blotches of black start to cloud his eyes in the first stages of unconsciousness. His self-image of toughness was undergoing its most severe test. It had survived countless bloody medical emergencies. He had eaten lunch while carving up cadavers. His specialty of cardiology dealt with the most common cause of death. Yet nothing had prepared him for this. To his embarrassment, he was about to pass out for the first time in his life. Nausea clutched his abdomen.

A familiar hand touched him on the shoulder. "Joe," a voice whispered, "don't pass out; we need you." It was Stephanie, one of the nurses. "This woman is in some kind of tachycardia, and none of us can tell if it's atrial or ventricular. No one else can read the monitor."

Burns had lowered his head, bending to look at his shoes to allow the blood to flow back to his head. From this position, he looked up at the nurse and nodded slowly. Her words had served to distract him from the contents of the basin. His head began to clear. He forced himself to walk to the head of the table and look at the monitor.

"It's just sinus tachycardia," he announced. "She doesn't have a cardiac problem. The problem's the blood loss. She's in hemorrhagic shock." He walked to the other end of the table. "Got the bleeding stopped yet?" he asked McCallister.

"Just about," McCallister answered. He was taking huge stitches through what appeared to be the last of several lacerations.

Burns now noticed that the woman's entire bottom was a mass of stitches. "Those are some tears," he observed to no one in particular.

"Her perineal area is ruined," McCallister muttered. "If she survives, she'll never have decent bowel or bladder functions."

"I guess you heard me say she didn't have a cardiac problem," Burns said.

"I wouldn't expect so," McCallister said, "not in a previously healthy twenty-nine-year-old female."

"Yes," Burns said hesitantly, mindful that he was a resident and was talking to a professor of obstetrics. "Well, then, if you agree that the problem is hemorrhagic shock . . . uh, I mean, I was wondering why blood isn't running."

"Blood wasn't ordered," McCallister said. "It's being cross-matched now." Although there was still a small laceration oozing blood, McCallister put down his suture instruments and looked sternly at Burns. "Doctor," McCallister said slowly, "what are you thinking? Let me tell you right now, this isn't my case. Do you think I would ever do anything like that?"

Burns's eyes followed McCallister's, which had settled on Klement, now standing mutely against the wall close to the double doors of the delivery room, and a flash of understanding crossed his face. "I'm sorry," he said quietly, turning back to McCallister. "I didn't know. I mean, when I walked in, you were sitting on the stool and . . ." His voice trailed off into an embarrassed silence. Self-consciously, as McCallister turned back to his suturing, the cardiology resident looked again at Klement, who looked back at him like some petulant child.

When McCallister had first shoved him unceremoniously aside, Klement had stood behind the chief of obstetrics for a while before walking backward in a series of small steps. He hadn't wanted to stay, but he had been afraid to leave. When the cardiac emergency team entered the room, the added frenzied activity had allowed him to retreat even farther from the delivery table.

He glanced longingly at the delivery-room doors. His senses had gradually become more acute. He suddenly became aware of his accelerated heart rate, the running sweat, the abnormal breathing. And, with them, a familiar need began stirring within him. He looked at the second hand of the delivery-room clock. He started to time his respirations, allowing himself only twelve breaths a minute. No time for hyperventilation, he told himself. He controlled his shaking hands by clasping them together in front of him.

As the others swarmed around the patient, Klement realized that no one took notice of him any longer. The desire to flee was overwhelming, and relief was only feet away in the doctors' locker room. He suddenly got his chance when the doors banged open and two lab technicians came through at a dead run, each carrying two bottles of blood. In three quick steps, he took advantage of the opportunity. Before disappearing through the still-swinging doors, he heard a voice knife through the babble of emergency orders and the clanking of medical instruments:

"My God," a nurse shrilled, "she's *arrested*."

Klement headed directly for the doctors' locker room. Opening his locker, he pulled his money belt from his pants and unzipped it. "Damn," he said aloud. There were only two of them. He had been doing that lately, trying to limit his intake by carrying only a dozen or so with him to work each day. Oh, well, two would hold him, though barely. After the traumas of tonight, the sweats and tremors would come breaking through in full force, and soon.

Earlier, he had planned to spend the night in the doctors' sleeping quarters at the medical center. Now his plans had changed. He wanted to talk to the husband, to stop any legal trouble before it started. Then he would get the hell out of here.

He swallowed both pills and walked to the waiting room reserved for fathers. He poked his head in the doorway, screwing up his face into an expression of confident concern, and called, "Mr. Olney?"

Of the three expectant fathers in the room, a tall blond man in a leisure suit rose and came forward.

"Mr. Olney, there's been some trouble with your wife. I've called in a consultant."

Olney turned pale. "Trouble? What kind of trouble?" He searched Klement's face as though trying to read the diagnosis in his expression.

"Well, it seems your wife has developed some bleeding— hemorrhage, actually. I managed to control that, but I thought it best if we had a consultant, just as a precautionary measure. You don't mind, do you?"

"Oh, no," Olney answered quickly. "Whatever you think is best. I want Irene to have——"

"Good, good," Klement said warmly. "Dr. Brian McCallister is in there with her now. He's an excellent man, a professor of obstetrics. Chairman of the department, in fact."

"That's good, Dr. Klement. I appreciate everything you're doing. Has the baby been born yet?"

Klement looked unwaveringly at Olney. "Why, I wouldn't be at all surprised."

Olney smiled with relief. "Then, everything will be all right?"

"Mr. Olney," Klement said reassuringly, "when I left the delivery room, everything was fine, just a little extra bleeding. Now, Dr. McCallister will be out soon. I'm sure he'll want to talk to you." He smiled at Olney before wheeling away down the hall.

"Thank you, Doctor," Olney called after him.

It was almost five A.M. when Klement pulled his year-old Continental into the driveway. He was exhausted, but the pills had relaxed him. There would be an inquiry into the night's events, he was sure. He was concerned but confident. Hell, he had dealt with death committees and tissue committees before. They were officious and made veiled threats, but most of the time it was just so much bullshit, he told himself. He could handle them—and McCallister, too, the pompous bastard.

Klement let himself into the house as quietly as he could. He did not switch on any lights. The first rays of the sun were filtering through the windows, so that he was able to distinguish the outlines of the expensive furniture in the living room. Walking on the balls of his feet, he went directly to the bookcase next to the fireplace, pulled two books from a shelf above his head, removed a small wad of tinfoil from the cavity, then made his way to the kitchen. There he took a half-filled bottle of bourbon from a cabinet above the sink and poured two fingers into a water glass. Popping two pills from the tinfoil into his mouth, he washed them down with the whiskey, swallowing the bourbon in a couple of gulps. It forced a small cough from his throat, and his eyes watered briefly. He washed out the glass and replaced it in the cabinet.

Easing open the door to the master bedroom, he entered the room and undressed quickly, throwing his clothes haphazardly over a chair. His wife, Joan, stirred in bed, coming to the last level of sleep. Her long hair, black as carbon and devoid of any gray, was fanned in wild profusion against the white pillowcase. Her young girl's body, curled up now like a small animal, had hardly changed since the day she had sat in front of him in that college classroom where they had met.

He sat on the edge of the bed to remove his shoes. He envied his wife's sleep. Sleep was something he was getting only in spurts. The nightmares, the sudden awakenings, and then trying to recapture sleep . . . God how he hated obstetrics—those screaming, groaning women with their legs in the air, the defecating, the blood. The pills helped, and now they were putting him down. Klement lingered in that twilight zone for a minute, more asleep than awake. The image of his father came to him, as it often did at such times. It was always the same: stern, unspeaking, hands on hips. Through flaccid lips, Klement tried to say something, but nothing came, and soon he was asleep.

Klement looked numbly at the pear. That's what it looked like, a bloody pear—a rotten, bloody pear—but not fallen from a tree. The uterus looked like a pear trembling in the wind. And Klement was trembling, shaking. No, he was being shaken. His eyes snapped open. Joan had her hand on his shoulder, her face just inches from him.

"Oscar, wake up! Oscar!"

He closed his eyes. He wanted to drop off into oblivion, to dreamless sleep, this time without the pear.

"Oscar!" Joan was insistent. "It's Brailey. He's on the phone again. It's the third time he's called. I told him you were still asleep, but he insists that you talk to him."

She propped the receiver on the pillow next to her husband's ear, and he heard the voice of the hospital's chief of staff. "The meeting will be in my office at twelve-thirty."

"Meeting?" Klement mumbled the question. "What meeting?"

Brailey spoke slowly, as though measuring his words. "The special executive-committee meeting. Really unique, Doctor. We have so few maternal-mortality conferences these days."

It was the first time Klement could remember Brailey addressing him by his formal title.

"The infant-mortality conference," Brailey continued. "You'll have to attend that later on, too, of course. I'll see you this afternoon."

Klement heard the click abruptly breaking the connection. *Oh, Christ,* he thought, *it's almost eleven o'clock.* He could barely make out the hands of the clock on the nightstand. Every nerve in his body jumped.

"What's this about, Oscar? What's happened now?" Joan said.

He swung to the side of the bed and stared at the floor between his knees. "Last night. A breech. We lost the mother, too."

He looked at her. Her smoky gray eyes, accented by high cheekbones, were noncommittal. The face coloring held the faintest hint of copper, an Indian hue that he had once found passionately stimulating.

"There's a mortality conference this afternoon. Routine," he muttered. He held her eyes a moment longer before returning his gaze to the floor. *Get the hell out of here,* he implored her silently. He heard her feet cross the thick carpeting and sensed that she was gone.

He clenched and unclenched his hands and almost vomited as nausea rode in over the top of his anxiety. He rose, almost fell, and groped his way to the bathroom off the bedroom. His body seemed apart from him. He sipped some water, breathed deeply, and felt the nausea subside. He took a Seconal and washed it down with another drink of water.

It took him twenty minutes to dress and leave the bedroom. The smell of brewing coffee was almost overpowering. Breakfast was unthinkable. Joan looked up as he walked quickly through the kitchen toward the porch door leading to the garage.

"You're not going to eat?" It was almost a statement.

He paused at the door. "Not hungry. Anyway, it's a luncheon meeting."

She said nothing, but she watched him walk to his car, amazed at his composure, the look of confidence on his boyish face. Distressed as he was, he had still taken care to dress in his usual impeccable manner. The tailored suit and color-coordinated shirt and tie, along with the styled haircut, gave him an ordinary appearance—a banker or businessman beginning a routine day.

Joan thought of the long-ago day when she had

brought him home to meet her parents. They were ecstatic. Their only child was going to marry a doctor. A doctor in the family! He was a "catch," in the days when mothers still used that word. Joan had inwardly agreed without qualification. Although she had told herself she had not gone to college only to snare a husband, her aimless academic drifting suggested otherwise. Her graduation was merely the routine culmination of faithful attendance.

She remembered now the quality that had most impressed her parents. It was Klement's apparent concern for others. Joan stared out the window for long moments, even after the car had left her view.

It was almost noon when Klement drove his car into the doctors' parking lot. He still had some time to get his act together, he told himself. With that knowledge, some of his confidence returned. His pace quickened as he approached the medical center's main entrance. Who would be on the committee, and what would they ask? Bronson, his partner, would know the answer to the first question. Klement's hands no longer shook as he dialed the phone in the doctor's lounge. *Good old Bronson,* he thought; *he'll cover my ass.*

Chapter II

The sandy-haired, chunky man in the spotless doctor's tunic walked back and forth in short, agitated steps within the restricted office space. He felt put upon, betrayed. His normally placid features, benignly undistinguished but for a receding chin, were twisted into whorls of anxiety. He could have wept. Though the city was large, the medical community was small enough so that Dr. Tyron Bronson had heard all the details of the delivery-room debacle as soon as he had entered the Klement-Bronson Clinic that morning. Nancy, the chief office nurse, had filled him in blow by blow. Nancy's sister-in-law, an O.B. nurse, had called her that morning.

Bronson, though feigning disdain over gossip had hung on Nancy's every word. He was probably one of the last to hear, he thought, so efficient was the medical community's verbal telegraph service. Thus, Klement's late-morning phone call was expected. Bronson closed the door to his office before picking up the receiver. "Yes, Oscar?" he said pleasantly.

"I'm going to be a little late for office hours this afternoon, Ty, and I wonder . . ."

"Any trouble, Oscar?"

"No, no; no trouble. I just wonder if you'd see a few of my patients until I get there. I'll probably be only an hour or so late, two o'clock at the latest."

"There's no problem, is there, Oscar?" Bronson asked. "I mean, you're not sick again, are you?" Bronson knew there was no need to elaborate on the question.

"No, no, I feel fine. I, uh, I'm going to an executive-committee meeting."

"Oh?"

The line hummed momentarily before Klement resumed speaking. "It's routine, just routine," he said.

Bronson was anxious to know more but was unsure how to elicit it from Klement. "The executive committee, huh? That's pretty heady company. They didn't appoint you chief of medicine while my back was turned, did they, Oscar?"

The droll approach did not make Klement laugh. "I just have to clean up a little matter, Ty," he replied.

"Had a problem in the delivery room last night, a breech. The baby died."

"They're not calling a special executive committee for that, are they? A lot of infants die in childbirth." Bronson wondered if Klement knew the word was all over by now. Probably.

"Well, it's a bit more than that, Ty. The mother died, too, so there's the usual fuss. You haven't heard anything about it?"

"No," Bronson lied, "not a word. Just got in the office myself, as a matter of fact." He also professed ignorance as to the makeup of the committee, and after a few more words Klement hung up.

Bronson held the dead receiver in his hand for some time before finally placing it in its cradle, and buzzed the intercom. Nancy appeared so quickly, he wondered if she had been listening at the door, "Seems your sister-in-law was right," he told her.

The look on Nancy's face was expectant, even eager. "Is he in trouble?" she asked. A tall, leggy blonde with a slight oriental slant to her vivid green eyes, she had so far successfully fought off the appearance of advancing middle age.

"I think so. They've called a special executive-committee meeting, and they don't call those just to pass the time of day." Bronson swiveled his chair and looked out the window at nothing in particular. Almost to himself, he said, "The last one was that outbreak of meningitis in the nursery almost four years ago." He rotated his chair to again face the nurse. "You know, Nancy, I think it's time we started counting pills again."

She nodded crisply and said, "I'll get the pharmacist."

Twenty minutes later, Bronson was thumbing through the charts of the half-dozen people he had been calling. It was so easy to trace Klement. He was not even a clever criminal. He had filched the Seconal the way most physician addicts did. He had written prescriptions for legitimate patients who never received the drugs. For Klement, it was even easier than for most doctors, since he and Bronson had their own pharmacy and dispensed medication themselves. It was unethical and frowned upon by the medical society, but it was legal. And it was profitable: a cut of the drug sales in addition to the fee for office visits. It was so profitable, in fact, that even after Bronson had realized what Klement was doing, getting out of the pharmacy business was unthinkable to him—at least, until now. *God, that Klement's become just too damn heavy to carry.*

Bronson was making his sixth phone call of the afternoon. He drew a deep breath as he dialed the number. This would be the last one. Six were enough, and he couldn't take any more time out of office hours. "Yes, hello, there. Mrs. Decker?" he inquired cheerily. He had learned his phoneside manner from Klement.

"Yes?"

"This is Dr. Bronson, Mrs. Decker, Dr. Klement's associate at the clinic. We're doing some routine checking on appointments, and it seems our office girl lost the appointment book. Now, let's see." Bronson made an act out of noisily shuffling some papers in front of him. "Yes, here's your record. Dr. Klement saw you on May fifth, is that correct?"

"Yes, that's right, Doctor."

"Fine," Bronson said in his most soothing tone. "Now, could you tell me when your return appointment is? Do you have one of our cards?"

"Yes, Doctor, it's marked on my calendar. Just a moment." A few seconds later she came back on the line. "My next appointment is June eighth at two o'clock."

"Fine, just fine, Mrs. Decker. Now I can put it in the new appointment book, and we'll both have the same date. Oh, say, Mrs. Decker, since it's over a month, I wondered, did Dr. Klement give you enough medication?"

"Medicine? He didn't give me any, Doctor. Said my blood pressure was just fine and I didn't need anything."

"I see," said Bronson. "No medication at all? I mean, no sleeping pills or anything? No pills of any kind?"

"None, Doctor. I don't take any pills at all. Is there something wrong?"

"Wrong? Oh, heavens no, Mrs. Decker," Bronson said quickly. "Just making sure. You can never be too sure when you have responsibility for someone's health, you know."

"Well, thank you, Doctor. I understand. Thank you for calling."

"You're very welcome, Mrs. Decker. Take care of yourself, now. We'll see you on the eighth of June. Good-by."

Bronson double-checked Mrs. Decker's chart even as he hung up on her. The last entry, dated May 5, said, "Seconal, 100 tablets dispensed." The other five phone calls had been in the same pattern. Klement had signed for one hundred Seconal capsules of one hundred milligrams each from the pharmacy for each of the six patients—and then had simply kept them for himself.

Bronson looked up to see Nancy staring at him intently. She was efficient—he conceded that much—but it bothered him sometimes that she was privy to so much that went on at the clinic. The nature of her job, of course, made much of that unavoidable. Even so, he felt that she was deriving just a bit too much inner pleasure from Klement's troubles. Bronson was almost positive she would feel the same if it were he, and not Klement, who was squirming. Just a perverse pleasure at catching the boss, any boss.

"We're getting to be old hands at this, aren't we, Nancy?"

"Yes," she said, pouting, "and it's such a shame. Dr. Klement is such a fine man."

"How many Seconal did he sign out for during April? What are those figures again, Nancy?"

"A little over five hundred, nearly all one hundred milligrams. Another five hundred in March."

"That's more than fifteen capsules a day," Bronson said. "Unbelievable. It's unbelievable that anybody could take that many."

"It's too bad," she clucked. "I'm afraid it's beginning to show in his work."

"He's missing work, that's what he's doing," Bronson snorted. "All that calling in sick."

"It can be downright embarrassing, poor man. Sometimes his speech is even slurred."

"Yes, but even worse is the money we're losing. I see our accounts receivable were down again in April."

"Have you talked to him about it?" Nancy asked.

"Twice. I mean, I tried to. Dr. Klement is not an easy man to talk to, to accept criticism."

"What did he say?"

"He denied it. Said he wasn't doing it, wasn't taking anything, that he really was sick those days he called in."

"The pharmacist is very worried," Nancy said.

Bronson looked up quickly. "Really?"

"He's concerned about the FDA. He's worried about an investigation."

Bronson sighed wearily. "Yes, I've thought about that. Does he think that's likely?"

"Yes," Nancy replied. "As a matter of fact, he thinks it's inevitable."

Bronson slapped his hand on the desk, rose, and walked to the window. He looked out over the parking lot of the clinic and fell silent. Nancy took the hint, turned quickly, and left the office.

Can you believe it? Bronson asked himself. *Murphy's law: Just when you think things are going well, something—or somebody—screws it up. Damn Klement; he's wrecking everything!* The clinic had been just what

Bronson had wanted, what he'd dreamed of. He never thought he'd be making this kind of money. Shut out of American medical schools by poor grades, he had trained in Italy, though he had never acquired more than a passing knowledge of the language. He had anticipated problems in setting up a practice; so he had barely believed his good fortune at hooking on to this clinic. He'd had to buy his way into accounts receivable, of course, and pay for half the equipment and the building; but that had been amortized over five years, and beginning the first of July he would be an equal partner. Half a million a year, all for himself.

And now this. Why in hell did Klement have to turn out to be a dopehead? Why couldn't he have been a drunk or chase women, like everybody else? An alcoholic doctor could butcher patients and get away with it. A womanizer could be somewhat of an embarrassment, but the habit was not professionally fatal. But a doctor who messed with drugs was running a definite risk of being finished as a physician. The feds were uncompromising. They held a brief hearing and quietly took away your license and that was it. And Bronson could be washed with the same brush unless he did something—now. Just knowing about it made him a party to the deception. Yet he didn't want to call the FDA himself, or the cops. Someone else had to know, someone in a position of authority who could testify in his behalf, if it came to that, someone who could say that Bronson had been alert to Klement's crime.

Bronson picked up the phone and dialed the medical center. "Could I have the chief of staff, please." Bronson felt a little better just knowing he was taking some kind of positive action. "Hello," he said after a moment, "Dr. Brailey?"

Chapter III

God, Klement thought, it was ten minutes before the start of the meeting and he hadn't learned anything. Either no one knew or they weren't talking. Even Bronson was dry; he had pleaded ignorance. "No one really knows, Oscar," he had said before Klement hung up the phone. "I don't think they even have a regular committee for maternal mortalities. It's kind of an *ad hoc* executive-committee thing."

Well, Klement thought, he'd just have to wing it—be cute, not volunteer too much, and make them commit themselves. It was so much simpler when he started practice ten years ago, in the days before the lawyers got into the act. Now they had committees for everything. You were watched by administrative hand-wringers, worried about hospital accreditation.

Klement paused at the door of the office of the hospital's chief of staff. An edge of anxiety stayed his hand as it reached for the doorknob. The tension had been submerged most of the morning by the Seconal he had taken at home, but now it was surfacing again. He made an about-face and walked into the men's room just across the hall.

Grateful to see that he was alone in the room, he entered one of the stalls and locked the door behind him. With his back to the commode so that he could see over the stall to the top of the outer door, he quickly removed his money belt. Folded inside a wad of tissue were the pills. He selected two and popped them into

27

his mouth. They lay on his tongue like bricks, and he realized they would need some help. He replaced the money belt around his waist and walked quickly from the stall to a washbasin.

Ah, he thought, just washing the pills down with water seemed to have a quieting effect. He stared at himself in the mirror. Unconsciously, he found himself washing his hands, a doctor's ritual. He dried them hurriedly, now ready to face the committee. *Can't have the bastards waiting any longer,* he thought.

Klement crossed the hall again, back to Brailey's office. Brailey would be his main worry. Unlike most hospital administrators, he was a top-notch clinician, a board-certified cardiologist. Couldn't bullshit him. Klement straightened the lapels on his cashmere suit and the knot in his Countess Mara tie, took a deep breath, and opened the door.

He quickly surveyed the room, somewhat surprised at the formality of the setting. Brailey's conference table had been converted to a dining table, complete with tablecloth and silver and china. Two waitresses were serving fewer than a dozen people. Each one had shed his white hospital coat. Vested suits prevailed. Klement wondered if the executive committee always met amid such splendor.

He knew everyone by first name, but on a day-to-day basis he mentally cataloged them by title: Dr. Pathology, Dr. Pediatrics, Dr. Obstetrics, Dr. Surgery, and so forth. They were the department chiefs, the colonels of their respective regiments at the medical center.

He searched their faces for some clue to the mood of the room at this moment. Their faces betrayed nothing. Rogers, Dr. Surgery, looked bored as he toyed with his food. Rogers, as chief of surgery, and Brailey, as head of internal medicine, ran the two largest and most powerful departments at the hospital. They were also bosom buddies.

Seated next to Rogers was Hanson, the chief of pathology. "Doctor," he said, greeting Klement pleasantly enough. The others merely nodded, while Brailey did not even acknowledge his entrance. Brailey's middle-weight boxer's body sat stiffly in its chair. The square head was bent over, a quarter-size bald spot revealed at the center of the coarse, rusty hair of a military cut that grew low on the forehead, just above expressive eyebrows. His shirt collar cut into a double chin. His muscular forearms detoured around a coffee cup as he shuffled through some papers. Klement noted that Brian McCallister, at the far end of the table, was staring straight ahead.

All in all, Klement thought, it was a disarming scene for what was supposed to be an adversarial encounter. He folded his hands in his lap as a waitress slipped a plate of chicken and biscuits in front of him. His eyes focused on a picture hung on the opposite wall, and he became aware of the low babble of voices of the committee members engaged in the small talk of the trade. He glanced sideways to catch Brailey refusing lunch as he waved the waitress aside. *Now,* he thought.

"Gentlemen,"—Brailey cleared his throat—"you all know why we're here. I apologize for the haste with which this meeting was called. However, I'm sure you recognize the necessity of settling this matter very quickly while it is still fresh in our minds.

"Let me begin by briefly reviewing the hospital bylaws. There is supposed to be a maternal-mortality committee that meets regularly. The bylaws, however, were written in the 1920s, when infection and hemor-rhage were the common causes of maternal death. With the advent of antibiotics and blood-banking techniques, maternal deaths have become such a rarity that the official maternal-mortality committee is now defunct." Brailey paused, a little too long for Klement's liking. "Actually," he went on, "we haven't lost a mother at this hospital in over eleven years."

Klement, who was slowly chewing a bite of chicken,

could feel Brailey staring at him, but he didn't look up. Out of the corner of his eye, he noted that McCallister hadn't shifted his gaze from Brailey at the opposite end of the table. No time to panic, he told himself.

"Dr. Klement," Brailey continued. Klement now shifted in his chair to confront Brailey. "Dr. Klement, in fairness to you, you should know that this committee has discussed the events of last night with the obstetrical nursing staff and with the cardiac resuscitation team and that the purpose of this meeting now is to discuss the matter with you and Dr. McCallister."

Was McCallister on the carpet with him? Klement asked himself. He brightened inwardly. As Brailey proceeded with the customary verbatim account from the hospital chart, his mind raced ahead to consider any possible change in strategy. If McCallister was also on the pan, Klement might be able to turn it to his advantage, but he must follow acutely what Brailey was reading from the nurses' notes. Much of the report was a revelation to him; memories of the night were disjointed.

"Two thirty-four A.M.," Brailey intoned. "Following membrane rupture, patient went to bathroom to urinate. Complained of 'something hanging from vagina' to nurse's aide.

"Two thirty-seven A.M. Checked by floor nurse and found to have approximately two feet of umbilical cord prolapsed.

"Two thirty-eight A.M. Dr. Klement awakened from the doctors' sleeping area and informed of prolapsed cord. Dr. Klement ordered patient taken immediately to delivery room and put up in stirrups."

"Was the cord pulsating?" McCallister interrupted. He was still staring straight ahead as Brailey looked up sharply.

Klement was ready for the question. "It was," he said quickly to Brailey, shooting a glance in McCallister's direction.

"I wasn't asking you, Doctor," McCallister said. "Dr. Brailey is chairing this meeting. Dr. Brailey, is there anything in the nurses' notes that indicates whether or not the cord was pulsating?"

"Well, as a matter of fact," Brailey replied, "there is no notation one way or the other."

"It was pulsating." Klement leaped at the opening. "I told the scrub nurse that it was. Didn't she put it down?" He was looking at Brailey and heard McCallister's derisive snort over his shoulder but ignored it.

"It wasn't noted," Brailey said, "but in talking to the nurses this morning, they said that *you* said it was."

"Yes, of course it was pulsating," Klement said. "Everything at that point was fine." This time he directed himself to McCallister.

"Gentlemen, let's get on with it, please," Brailey said. "Two forty-five A.M. Dr. Klement examined the patient and stated that it was a breech delivery and the cord was prolapsed." Brailey frowned. "At this point the ensuing events are not very clear."

"They're clear to me," McCallister blurted out, "damn clear. Labor should have been stopped with Demerol. She should have had an immediate C section."

"Then, why didn't you do it?" Klement asked somewhat heatedly. "You were called in, weren't you?"

"Because, by the time I got there, you had been pulling on that baby like a longshoreman. It was too late. You tore that baby apart and pulled the mother's insides out doing it."

"That's a lie," Klement retorted.

"Enough," Brailey said. "We're not here for personal incriminations. That will not establish the facts. We want to determine first if any hospital rules were broken and second if bad judgment was exercised to the point of malpractice. As regards the first point, the hospital rules state clearly that general practitioners are allowed to do only routine, uncomplicated deliveries, certainly not breeches and prolapsed cords. For these a specialist is to be called. In reviewing this record, it's obvious that Dr. McCallister was called at the first sign that there was a complication. In that sense Dr. Klement broke no hospital rules. What happened before Dr. McCallister arrived only Dr. Klement can say." Brailey turned to Klement.

"Well, as you say, I followed the rules," Klement said. "I had a consultant called in. Now, there was a certain amount of time before Dr. McCallister arrived; I can't say just how long. In these kinds of crises, you don't have much time to check a clock." He made a quick survey to check the reaction. "In view of the prolapsed cord, which was still pulsating, I thought we should get the baby out from below."

"Why from below?" Brailey asked. "Why a vaginal delivery instead of a Caesarean, as Dr. McCallister suggested?"

"Simple, really. She was dilated, was ready. The baby had started down the canal. Its legs and buttocks were presenting out the vagina. I'll admit the head wasn't shaped, wasn't molded to the pelvis yet— breeches never are—and I had to exert some, well, pressure from below."

Klement shifted his gaze from Brailey to each of the faces in the room. They stared back at him. McCallister glared. There was silence, and Klement realized the committee members were waiting for a further explanation. He didn't know what to say. "I might add," he began hesitantly, "that Dr. McCallister was a great help when he finally got there."

"Bullshit!" McCallister exploded. "That baby was way the hell up in that uterus, and you panicked. You reached up and grabbed a leg and started yanking on it like some goddamn nineteenth-century midwife. You wrenched out that damn fetus, you bumbling——"

"Hold it, hold it"—Brailey held up his hand—"that's enough, Dr. McCallister. You weren't there," Brailey reminded him, "not yet, anyway. No matter what you believe, Dr. Klement was the only doctor there at the time. You simply can't say where the fetus was."

"Damn it, Brailey," McCallister countered, "I've got two good O.B. nurses who'll swear he had his arm in that vagina up to his elbow. If that fetus was presenting out the vagina, what the hell was he reaching for, her gallbladder?"

"That's pretty much hearsay," Klement cut in. "Where are these nurses? I tell you, that fetus was halfway out of the pelvis. It was too late for a Caesarean." For the first time, he felt that it was going his way. He was going to get out of this; his instincts told him so. The chronology of events was going to save him, he was almost certain.

"What about fetal monitoring?" The question came from Dr. Pediatrics. It was the first comment of any kind from any other committee member. "Since the baby died," he continued, "I assume the monitor showed some fetal distress somewhere along the line."

In the heat of the emotional exchange between Klement and McCallister, nobody had thought to ask that obvious question except the diminutive, normally quiet chief of pediatrics.

"It's not here in the nurses' notes." Brailey thumbed through the charts once more. "Must be on a separate sheet," he said almost to himself. "Yes, here it is. It was checked at two-thirty A.M. The fetal pulse then was a hundred and forty per minute, perfectly normal." He paused for what seemed to Klement an interminable length of time, then continued: "Apparently it was never checked again. There is no notation that——"

"I sure as hell would like to know when fetal distress began," McCallister demanded, "to know exactly when that umbilical cord stopped pulsating."

"I told you," Klement replied calmly. "That cord was pulsating until you got there." Things were going so well, he had almost convinced himself he could reconstruct the entire evening precisely, when, in fact, even now it seemed like a blurred nightmare. "Where on that chart does it say that the cord wasn't pulsating, that the fetal heart slowed?"

Brailey leaned forward in his chair, his arms straddling the official charts on the table. "It doesn't say anything one way or the other," he said. "It simply wasn't noted. Why wasn't it noted, Dr. McCallister?"

"What do you mean?" McCallister asked. He seemed startled by Brailey's question.

"I mean that from two-thirty A.M. until three twenty-five A.M., there was no fetal monitoring. Almost an hour."

"Well, uh, I don't know," McCallister answered.

Klement was pleased to see that the chief of obstetrics looked flustered.

"Look," McCallister went on, "at two-thirty A.M., when they found the prolapsed cord, they moved her from the labor room to the delivery room. Isn't that what it says in the chart?"

"It does," Brailey replied.

"Well, they had to detach the fetal-monitor heads when they moved her. Then, after they moved her to the delivery room and got her in the stirrups, well, that's when all hell broke loose. I wasn't there, but I suppose with all the excitement they . . . well, they probably forgot to reattach——"

"We can't blame Dr. Klement for that," Brailey said. "They're *your* nurses; their training is *your* responsibility."

There was a heavy silence in the room. Klement, his chin cupped in his hand, looked expectantly at Brailey. Behind him, he could hear McCallister clear his throat. *Fuck you, McCallister,* he thought. He suppressed the urge to smile.

"Dr. McCallister," Brailey continued, "being an internist, I may not be all that familiar with this, but my understanding is that there are only two ways to tell if the artery in a prolapsed cord is compressed. One is to feel the cord itself for pulsations, and the second is to note the slowing of the heart by fetal monitoring. Is that correct?"

"Yes."

"Well," Brailey said, "since it wasn't noted, and since the nurses forgot to recheck or reattach the fetal monitor, we really have only Dr. Klement's word about the cord pulsations. . . . Other contentions," he went on, "would seem to be moot points. Further discussions would be purely academic and, I'm afraid, repetitive."

With that, Klement mimicked Brailey's relaxed posture. McCallister said nothing but continued to glower in Klement's direction. Klement ignored him. Instead, he pointed a casual finger across the table at Dr. Pediatrics and stage-whispered, "Good point on the fetal monitoring."

Brailey shot him a look of disapproval before saying, "I think that concludes our discussion, gentlemen. If there is nothing further"—he raised his bushy eyebrows to McCallister, who chose to remain silent—"I'll let you know if we should meet further on this case. Thank you for coming."

Chairs were being pushed back even before Brailey had finished, and the committee members began straggling out singly or in pairs. Klement lingered, making a show of sliding his chair back under the dining table. He did not particularly care to leave the room shoulder to shoulder with McCallister. He glanced over at Brailey, who had lit a cigar and was once again studiously contemplating the hospital charts, and thought briefly of going over and shaking hands with him. No, that would be too much, he decided.

Leaving well enough alone, Klement walked briskly, almost jauntily, from the conference room.

Chapter IV

Brailey leaned back expansively, savoring the aroma of the burning cigar. He smoked infrequently—too much on the go—but in rare moments of solitary contemplation, such as now, sucking on a cigar had a soothing effect on him. He blew a smoke ring almost the length of the conference table and watched it wreathe a sugar bowl. That goddamn Klement! How in hell had he gotten as far as he had? Brailey sighed. He knew perfectly well what the answer to that question was. There were far too many like Klement picking their way through the minefields of medicine and miraculously surviving. Klement just happened to be an extreme case.

Brailey could remember when he was an associate professor and Klement an intern. At first the teaching staff had handled him as they would have any other intern: they embarrassed him. Since an intern no longer took exams, you couldn't flunk him, so you humiliated him in front of his peers and prodded him to better performance. You sarcastically reminded him in public of the importance of his work. The shame was usually sufficient incentive.

Not for Klement, though. The entire teaching staff quickly became aware that they might have to set new measurements for incompetence. Brailey recalled how he had carefully examined Klement's cases. He had been a hard man to humiliate. The mismanaged cases were almost too numerous to recount.

By the end of Klement's internship, a peculiar thing

had begun to evolve. They had all stopped trying to discipline him. He was no longer even the butt of incessant jokes. Slowly, unconspiratorially, the jokes were replaced by concern for the patients. The concerns were never voiced openly; just as a matter of course, backstopping Klement became part of the normal hospital routine. On nights when Klement was working, the chief floor resident would make a point of coming back late to check on patients Klement had admitted. Even other interns found themselves hovering protectively over them. Brailey had watched the phenomenon unfold and remembered that he had witnessed it in the cases of only two other interns. Both had been disasters as physicians and both had lost their licenses. And that, Brailey knew, almost never happened.

During the last month of Klement's internship, Brailey had been pleased to see him spending more time with his patients. He seemed less abrupt and showed more concern. Other staff members had commented on the change. Only later, when Klement had completed his internship, was it discovered that he had been passing out engraved business cards informing his patients of the address of his future office. The unabashed solicitation drew *déjà vu* groans from the medical-center staff.

The groans came not so much because Klement was wooing other doctors' patients, but because of the realization that he was going to practice nearby and would be using the medical center to hospitalize his patients, for the hospital always kept its word: physicians who trained there would be given hospital privileges—the traditional medical-center nepotism.

Klement's years as a practitioner had been about what Brailey had expected: countless mistakes, but always managing to sidestep open assaults on his professional conduct. He had been at least smart enough to mistreat patients only as long as it took to charge a significant fee and then refer them to a medical-center consultant before disaster struck. The hospital's cover-up had, until now, always salvaged Klement. It had worked often enough to allow him to build a practice of considerable scope. The smooth bedside manner, coupled with the natural healing ability of the human body, built his reputation among the hypochondriacs, who in turn lured the genuinely ill to Klement's waiting room.

Early in his career, Klement's willingness to work had filled a void in a community with a shortage of doctors. His seeming dedication carried him along. And he did a lot of tests: electrocardiograms, electroencephalograms, blood studies, urinalyses. He X-rayed everything. He had his own lab to do these and, while virtually all of the tests were unnecessary, it gave the impression of being thorough. He became what Brailey called a "reflex practitioner." Patients were treated without diagnosis: for shortness of breath, digitalis; for fever, penicillin; for ankle swelling, diuretics.

Now Brailey realized that Klement had done it again in the executive-committee meeting. Remarkable how circumstances, a combination of events, and the lack of positive information on the charts had allowed him to escape once more. Brailey blew the next mouthful of cigar smoke disdainfully at the ceiling.

"Christ, call an air-raid warden. Those cigars are the most evil-smelling things in God's own creation."

Brailey, jarred from his reverie, looked up into the grinning face of Charlie Rogers. Short and crew-cut, Rogers had a soft, responsive face that belied the stereotype of the tough, formidable surgeon.

"What're you doing, Charlie, coming back to hold my hand?"

"Not exactly; but it was obvious that the meeting bothered the hell out of you."

"It was, huh?"

"Yeah, Jim. Your agitation level is exactly com-

parable to the number of cigars you smoke. Five bucks
says 'you're on your third one right now."

"No bet, you bastard," Brailey said affectionately.
Charlie Rogers was the one confidant he could turn to
when the pressures of running the medical center
seemed unbearable.

"Three cigars," Rogers mused. "That's a buck and a
half, and one hour's deep thinking. I guess you got
your money's worth."

"I'll be damned," Brailey said, looking at his watch.
"I wouldn't have believed I've been in here that long."

"I figured you would be. Only an internist could get
that introspective. Goddamn, it's smoky in here! You're
a lung-cancer plague all by yourself." Rogers lit a cigarette. Brailey grinned.

"I take it you're here to complain about the way I
conducted the meeting."

"Who me, boss? Complain? I mean, just because our
resident genius slipped out of the noose again while
you hung McCallister, who, incidentally, is probably
one of the best obstetricians in the state. Now, why in
hell would I complain?"

"Come off it, Charlie," Brailey said. "What in hell
could I have done differently?"

Rogers shrugged. "Not much, I suppose. But McCallister came out looking like he was the one who botched
that breech. Klement never got a drop of blood on
him."

"I know, Charlie, I know. I feel as bad about it as
you do, but I couldn't give it to him the way I wanted
to. The evidence just wasn't there in those charts. And
no matter how you cut it, Klement was the only doctor
in that delivery room. Goddamn it, Charlie, I'm the
chief of staff. I've got a job to do. I'd have handled it
the same way if you'd been sitting there instead of
Klement."

"I believe that, Jim," Rogers said quickly.

Brailey rolled the tip of his cigar around the rim of

a saucer, depositing a long ash in a pool of spilled coffee. He looked at Rogers. "I've about decided to go after the bastard, Charlie. I'm going to get him cold. He's got to be stopped."

Rogers gazed at his friend a long time without speaking. "You really mean that?" he asked finally.

Brailey nodded firmly. "Yes, Charlie, I really mean it. I've had it. I'm sick of covering up for him, and so is the rest of the staff. They've probably been wondering why it's taken me this long to pull his chain. Well, it's time. Hell, it's past time, and you know it." Brailey's voice dropped almost an octave. "It's long overdue, as a matter of fact."

"How are you going to do it?"

"I'm not exactly sure, but I'm going to do it. I'm going to get his hospital privileges pulled, his practice, his license. Yeah, even his license." Brailey studied Rogers for his reaction, his approval. "You with me?"

Rogers looked at Brailey at length before answering. "Look, Jim, I came back here now to talk to you about doing something about the guy. But I was thinking about only denying him hospital privileges."

"No, it's got to be the license. We have to go the full nine yards on this one. By God, if ever it was justified, it is in this case."

"Hell, Jim, sure. I mean, I'm with you. But, you know, I think we could manage to get him thrown off the staff. The license thing, boy, that's another story. I don't know about that one."

"I know what we're up against, believe me, Charlie. Jesus, the state board of registration, a lot of fighting. The lawyers will be in it up to their asses, and ours. But it's got to be his license. There's no other way. You know as well as I do that if we just kick him out of the medical center, he'll be even more of a menace. At least now he's referring his mistakes to us—uh, most of the time. We have some control of him. We kick him out of this hospital and he'll find another one, the osteopathic maybe, someplace. The bums always land on their feet in some new haven. He'll drive thirty miles to a country hospital to do deliveries, or do them at his office, or start his own hospital. And nobody will be around to stop him, not McCallister or you or me."

Rogers spread his arms and let them slap noisily to his sides. He sat down heavily in a chair next to Brailey. "OK, you've convinced me. But how in hell do we get his license?"

"We document it, that's how. We watch the bastard like a hawk and make notes of everything."

"Well," Rogers began slowly, "I can document thirteen cases for you right now."

"What?"

"Yeah, he's had thirteen wound infections. That's the reason I came back here to see you after the meeting, to tell you about them."

"But he doesn't have major surgical privileges," Brailey said.

"Who in hell said they were major? Christ, they were hernias, vein strippings, cysts, lipomas. They were nothing, little cases. We let the interns do most of them."

Brailey settled slowly back in his chair and puffed on his cigar, regarding his friend through a cloud of smoke.

Rogers suddenly ground his cigarette out in the ashtray. "Yeah, you're right. He's been worse lately. He seems out of it, vacant. He's to the point where he can't even follow sterile technique."

"Do you think the hospital board's got the stomach for a license fight?" Brailey asked.

"No."

"Why not?"

"Face facts, Jim. They're going to be queasy. Klement's from a well-known medical family. His father trained here, became one of our most illustrious graduates. He was some sort of medical missionary, a small-time Albert Schweitzer."

"Well, you're close," Brailey said. "He was in the

Public Health Service. Did you know he published some papers on leprosy that are classics?"

Rogers's eyes flared. "Leprosy? Klement's old man worked in a leper colony?"

"More than one. The Public Health Service has got them all over the place. It's like the army. Those guys change jobs every couple of years. If you volunteer for the messy jobs, you sure as hell get 'em. Old man Klement apparently was one of those driven guys always helping the down-and-outers. Kept volunteering for leprosariums and Indian reservations, that kind of thing. Ended up down and out himself. Died broke working his ass off for the Indians during some tuberculosis epidemic, right after Klement finished medical school. Frankly, if it hadn't been for his old man's reputation, we probably would have flunked him. A lot of the older board members remember his father."

Rogers lit a fresh cigarette. "Another thing, Jim: I don't think the board wants to air all that shit in public, including the times we covered up for the prick. We'd probably end up getting sued ourselves. And you know that state licensure board. A guy has to spend ten or twelve years becoming a doctor, and they just don't want to yank licenses, that's all there is to it—especially for incompetence. Have you read the regulations? You have to be a convicted felon or some goddamn thing."

Rogers was not looking at Brailey, and when he heard no response, he raised his head, to see the chief of staff's face surprisingly in repose and the start of a smile working at the corner of his eyes.

"As a matter of fact, I read them just this morning."

"OK, what is it?" Rogers asked.

"What it is is an ace in the hole, Charlie." Brailey paused for a moment. "Just this morning, before the meeting, I got a phone call from Bronson, Klement's partner."

Rogers stuck out his tongue in ridicule. "Bookends!"

"Let me finish," Brailey said. "It seems there's been some Seconal missing from Klement's office."

Rogers let out a low whistle. "Well, now, that puts a different light on things, doesn't it? So some dope is missing."

"Yeah, it looks like a *bunch* of it is missing."

Rogers straightened in his chair with renewed interest. "And Bronson thinks it all went for home consumption, is that it?"

"Yeah, that's what he thinks," Brailey said. "But what's the difference where it went? It went, and not to the patients. That's all the feds are interested in."

For a moment they regarded each other without speaking. Brailey leaned forward and reached for the phone. "Well, life doesn't stop just because of Klement. Business as usual. I've got to call security," he told Rogers. "On top of everything else, it seems there's some nut invading the hospital and playing doctor."

"Huh?"

"Yeah. Apparently no harm done, yet. Just some kook who got hold of a white coat and is running around holding hands and listening to heartbeats. But you never know. Gotta round him up. Talk about the newspapers—they could have a peachy time with that one."

Rogers got out of his chair and waved. "That's how you earn your money, chief of staff. I'll see you later."

Brailey, one hand over the mouthpiece, signaled Rogers to a stop. "Uh, Charlie, about the Klement thing: Keep it to yourself, until the ducks are in line."

"It's your show, Jim."

"What's this *you* shit, Tonto?" Brailey said. "Us Indians are all in this together, right?"

"Right," Rogers said with a wry smile.

Chapter V

Joan Klement sat on one of the overstuffed sofas, her eyes dispassionately surveying the "fireplace" room of the country club. It was one of those secluded cocktail areas intended to mimic someone's private den, only the couches were placed with Euclidean precision to accommodate the most people, and the fireplace conveyed its light by way of a gas jet and fake logs. A bar shielded one wall.

It was the monthly bash of the medical-society members and their wives. When Oscar first began his practice, she did not miss a one; but for the past few years she had attended rarely, pleading headaches and colds. Then she had even stopped looking for an excuse. That had brought on a colossal argument, which led to a compromise of "at least three meetings a year." He went to the rest alone.

Her gaze moved from group to group. She knew them all and could almost reconstruct their dialog verbatim as they registered openmouthed surprise at one another's pedantry. Clusters of smartly dressed men and women chattering about the same things they had chattered about the last time they met.

Oscar was standing at the bar with several other doctors. He was by far the most attractive man in the room—handsome, even, with his curly hair and quick smile that revealed movie-star teeth. The white turtle-necked sweater and light-blue blazer contrasted with a sunlamp tan that left him just shy of being swarthy.

Though his overall image was one of leanness, he was beginning to show a little flesh in the wrong places. A tinge of fatigue in the face, the heavy-lidded eyes. Working too hard? He had always worked hard. Other problems, maybe. He formed one link of a conversational circle, rocking back and forth on his heels in that curious mannerism that was almost his trademark. Curiously, Joan seldom noticed his physical appearance anymore. She had developed a faculty for detachment. Hearing but not listening. Thinking nothing, watching everyone and bathing in the sensation of the place—floating.

"Hi, there, stranger."

Startled out of her introspection, Joan looked up into the face of Mary Beth Merrill, the wife of Grayson Merrill, a successful surgeon. The ubiquitous, slightly overweight Mary Beth was the self-appointed mother hen to the doctors' wives. She had been wooed and brought North by her husband more than twenty years ago from her Georgia home. It had taken her that long to lose her southern accent, and then she had hurried to recultivate it when someone had mentioned that it sounded charming. She had been diphthongizing ever since.

"Mah, but you're a hard woman to find. Ah've been callin' and callin'."

"Well, I'm working full-time, you know." Joan tried to be pleasant. While she had never made friends among the wives, she supposed she was as close to Mary Beth as to any of them.

"Yes, Ah know. It must be frightfully excitin' workin' with psychiatrists, delvin' into a person's inner thoughts and all. It must be nice not to be tied down at home with a lot of——"

"Why don't you sit down, Mary Beth." Joan hoped this wasn't a prelude to a monolog about Mary Beth's four kids.

Mary Beth lowered herself gracefully onto the couch

and smoothed her dress over her knees. She was really quite attractive, Joan thought. She had magnificent green eyes, if one were not distracted by the horrible silver mascara that she wore round the clock. *Don't be bitchy,* Joan told herself.

"Ah'm so happy, Joan, that you're finally goin' to be workin' with us in the auxiliary."

"Working with you? I don't understand."

"Why, the Pap-smear project, of course." She looked at Joan for a moment; then her hand flew to her mouth as though to stifle the high-pitched giggle. "Oh, mah, that rascal Oscar. He must not have told you about it yet."

"No," Joan said slowly. "What was that rascal supposed to tell me?"

"Well, it's quite simple, really. We're startin' a publicity campaign to get all the women in the county in for their Pap smears. It's goin' to take the efforts of all of us to make it a success. Ah'm in charge of the campaign."

"Of course," Joan said flatly.

"In the next few days Ah'll be distributin' lists of people we're goin' to have to call. Since you're gone durin' the day, Ah'll have to drop it off in the evenin'. What night are you goin' to be home, deah?"

"I'm sorry, Mary Beth, I can't do it."

"What?"

"With my job and all, I'm just too busy to get engaged in any kind of project like this."

"But Oscar was sure you would be happy to volunteer. He——"

Joan felt herself losing her tenuous grip on civility. "Oscar should have asked me first." There was an embarrassed silence, and Mary Beth looked out over the room full of laughing, chattering people. Joan wanted to say something that would soften the refusal but was afraid it would only give Mary Beth encouragement.

Mary Beth put a hand on her arm and leaned toward her. "Joan, there's somethin' Ah've been meanin' to say to you. For your own good, understand? Uh, and Oscar's. You've got to become more involved. I mean, deah, you owe it to Oscar's career. It's up to us wives to give our hard-workin' husbands all the support we can. The more visible you can become, the better Oscar——"

"Mary Beth"—Joan stopped her sharply—"I do not need a lecture from you, or anyone, about my familial obligations."

Mary Beth recoiled. "Ah only meant that——"

"I know exactly what you meant." Joan fought to keep her voice steady. "But I feel that's a very personal thing, and I resent your intrusion."

"Joan, Ah——"

"You don't know me that well, Mary Beth."

Joan noted the shock on the other woman's face, the lifting of her silver eyelids. Mary Beth's hands toyed nervously with the collar of her dress, and her head moved spasmodically from side to side. She opened her mouth as though to speak, but no words came out. Then she got to her feet and walked quickly away. Joan watched her disappear, wounded, into the crowd. Her anger mounted; it felt cathartic. Her eyes bored into the back of Oscar's head.

Almost as though by telepathy, Klement turned toward his wife. Seeing her arctic stare, he lost his smile and his brow knitted in puzzlement. He moved toward her. "Now, what was *that* all about?" His eyes were still on the route of Mary Beth's retreat.

"Apparently I've just disappointed one of the devotees of George Papanicolou."

"Who? What in hell are you talking about, Joan?"

"Professor George Papanicolou. He developed the Pap smear."

Oscar's face became wooden. "Damn it, Joan, why

must you constantly work to prove you're the biggest smartass in the room?"

"Why must you constantly try to push me into worthless, time-wasting projects with these shallow country-club matrons?" she retorted.

"You think the project is worthless? You think you're cute knowing the name of the guy who invented the Pap smear—which, incidentally, saves thousands of lives every year."

She was silent, and he sat down beside her. "OK," she said finally, "OK. Pap smears are the greatest thing since ice cubes. I just don't want to start up with the whole medical auxiliary thing—phone calls, luncheons, make-work ego trips. The whole volunteer thing is an incredible waste of time."

"Time? It's always your goddamn time. You spend it either working or reading, which——"

"Which I also don't need to do? Look, Oscar, *I'll* decide how I spend my time."

"Oh, yes, I know. You'll spend your time just the way you want to. No regard for me or someone like Mary Beth Merrill, who's trying to help others. Very self-centered, Joan."

The fight, like all their quarrels, was a bitter yet controlled contest, outwardly civilized. The laughing people around them took no notice. One would have had to read lips. Oscar was silent, and Joan knew he thought he had won.

"Well, answer me, Joan," he demanded, not looking at her. "Don't you think Mary Beth believes in the project? Don't you think she's sincere?"

Joan remained silent. No more, she thought. At one time she would have succumbed to Mary Beth's so-called sincerity. She had once been powerless around dedicated people. It was just that trait—dedication—that had first attracted her to Oscar. He had been the first man she had known who seemed to have direction, to be so sure of what he wanted. She had met him in a biology course. Oscar, the pre-med student, had been deadly serious about it and made the clumsy dissecting of a frog seem an act of great import. There had been an innocence, a naïveté, about him that she had found refreshing. An unworldly ingenue from a poor family—with the wrong haircut and the wrong clothes. Despite her own casual approach to study, she had ended up virtually tutoring him, which, in a way, added to his attractiveness. It had been accepted by most of her friends that they would be married. Only her roommate had expressed misgivings: "Sure, he's sincere. So was Hitler. So is Nixon. It's not just dedication that counts; it's motives. And why is he so hellbent on being a doctor? Does he want to go back home and help the poor—or get away from them? And serious! He never laughs, just flashes that toothy grin at the right time."

Joan turned her face to Oscar. There was no toothy grin there now. His features were hardened, the skin pulled back from his cheekbones, his angry eyes narrowed to chocolate splinters.

"Now, you're going to walk over there and apologize to Mary Beth," he said, "and you're going to tell her you'll be happy to help her with this project."

Joan's voice took on a deadly lightness. "No, Oscar, I'm not going to do that." She was prepared for whatever might come.

His words came as a pout, his voice trying to control the trembling. "In that case, you can just find your own way home."

"Fine."

She watched as he walked away. She saw him lurch slightly, then stop to steady himself. She noted that he had nursed only one drink all evening.

Chapter VI

There was a patient in every examination room and standing room only in the outside offices of the Klement-Bronson Clinic. Oscar Klement let them wait while he smoked a cigarette in his private office and finished a minor debate on the phone with his accountant, John Keesler.

"But, Doctor," Keesler was saying loudly into Klement's ear, "I can't understand why you want to take those real-estate options out of your corporation and put them with your private investments."

"Trust me, John," Klement answered, "I know what I'm doing."

"But you'll have to pay income tax on the amount they've appreciated."

"Which isn't very much," Klement snapped.

"Now, look, Doctor, when I put you into that land deal six years ago, we both knew it wouldn't increase in value unless they went through with that spur for the interstate. And I've recently heard from a pretty reliable source that it's going through. Hell, that's going to turn out to be your best investment by far. If it's not sheltered in your corporation . . ." Keesler's voice trailed off to nothing as he heard Klement give an impatient sigh.

"John, I want this in my personal account. I also want all the airline and gold stocks transferred. And, oh, yes, what's that gambling stock that's moving so well? The one that's hitting it big in Atlantic City?"

"Resorts International," Keesler said.

"Right, that's the one. It's really turning into a winner. Put it in my private account."

Keesler started to interrupt, but Klement had anticipated him:

"Yes, John, don't say it. I know it's gone up in value. I'll pay the goddamn taxes on the appreciation."

"That isn't what I was going to say," Keesler said. "I was going to ask just why you're taking your most promising investments out of your professional corporation. I could understand if you wanted to get rid of Chrysler or American Motors or some of your other dogs."

"John, believe me, I know what I'm doing."

"I'm sure you do, Doctor. You've got the best business sense of any professional man I've ever dealt with."

"Well, I work at it," Klement said with some pride. "I read a lot and——"

"Tell me," Keesler interrupted, "isn't your associate, Dr. Bronson, coming in with you as a full partner soon?"

"Well," Klement said, hesitating, "yes, he is—in a year or so."

"Hmmm, I had thought it was this year."

Klement continued guardedly, "Uh, I'd have to look it up. What about it?"

"Well, it's just that if it's soon, you know, as your corporate accountant I, uh, will be Dr. Bronson's accountant, too."

"So?"

"So, since I'm the corporate accountant, I should be doing what is best for your corporation."

There was a long moment of silence during which Klement could hear Keesler breathing into the phone. Time to knock off this bullshit, he told himself. "Look, John," he said sharply, "you let me worry about that. You're my personal accountant, right? You handle my books. You do my income tax. Do you want to continue in that capacity or don't you? I certainly respect your advice, but, believe me, I'm doing the right thing."

"Of course, Doctor, whatever you say," Keesler capitulated. "I was merely bringing up significant details I thought you should be aware of, to protect your interests."

"Yes?" Klement drew out the word with a touch of sarcasm.

"So whatever happens," Keesler continued, "you will have been assured that I had done my job properly." When Klement didn't respond, he added, "I'll begin right away to carry out your wishes, of course."

"Yes, John," Klement said bitingly, "you do that. Good-by."

Klement hung up the phone and looked down at it for a moment as he mentally replayed the conversation. The son of a bitch had come very close to accusing him of cleaning out the corporate account before Bronson was due to become a full partner. It was essentially true, of course; nevertheless, Keesler had a nerve. Klement paid him handsomely to look over his financial holdings and had even let him in for a piece of the action on occasion. John was too damn timid, anyway, he told himself. Typical accountant's mentality. You could never make a killing thinking small. You could dabble and be comfortable, maybe, but that wasn't big money, and big money, Klement believed, was the only way to go. He might have to think seriously about dumping John, he told himself, as soon as he got a big enough stake here. A few more years should do it.

"Doctor"—the interoffice squawk box interrupted his thoughts of riches and high finance; it was the voice of Nancy, the chief nurse—"Mr. Olney is out here and would like to see you. He said he'll only take a few minutes."

Startled, Klement was abrupt. "We've got a clinic

full of patients, Nancy. I'm extremely busy right now.
It's impossible—— Wait a minute." The name suddenly
rang a bell. Olncy, Olney . . . Of course, damn it!
The husband of the dead breech! How could he ever
forget that name?

"Hold it, Nancy. Of course I'll see him. Send him
in." What the hell did the man want? Klement hadn't
talked to him since that night. He had let McCallister
break the news. Why not? McCallister was the one
who had muscled his way into the delivery room. For
all anybody knew, he was the one who had screwed
it up.

Klement was on his feet and around his desk when
the door opened, one hand extended in greeting, the
other coming paternally around Olney's shoulder. "Sit
down, please, Mr. Olney," he said, guiding the man to
a chair.

He did a quick study of his visitor as he returned
to his own chair behind the desk. A blond man of
about thirty-two, casually dressed. Olney didn't seem
as tall today as he had that night at the hospital. Steady
eyes, though—level gaze, no-nonsense eyes. Klement
had never met the man until that night, and he vainly
sought some clue to the man's character by trying to
recall casual conversations with his wife. A factory
worker, had she said? Low intellect? Vindictive? Klement's brain raced through the possibilities.

"What can I do for you, Mr. Olney?" he asked
gently. "First, I want to tell you how saddened I am
by your loss. May I say that your wife, while we
knew each other only professionally, was a warm, generous person. If you'll permit me to say so, I feel I've
lost a friend. You were indeed a lucky man." Klement
took a breath and waited. Across from him, the eyes
of this stranger, this widower, filmed over slightly; but
his voice, when he finally spoke, was strong:

"I'd like you to tell me, Doctor, what happened that

night." Olney swallowed once, but his eyes never left Klement. "Dr. McCallister explained it to me the best he could, but he said I should talk to you, since you took care of Irene most of the time."

What in hell did McCallister tell you? Klement wanted to ask. Instead he said, "Mr. Olney, a breech delivery is a difficult thing at best. And there's something none of us knew, or that medical science could know. Your wife was not a strong woman." He paused a moment and looked at Olney, waiting.

"But she was," Olney finally said.

"Was?"

"Was strong. She had never been sick a day in her life."

"Ah, but that can be misleading, Mr. Olney. It's that kind—that is, someone who appears to be strong—that often, uh, fails. Every day we see patients who claim they feel fine. They want the rest of the world to think they do. But we can tell. Yes, we can tell. Their health is not what it——"

"But you said she was strong."

"I did? When?" Klement was caught off guard.

"During all her checkups. You checked her every month while she was pregnant, every week the last month. She always came home and told me that she and the baby were doing just fine. She never said nothing about the baby being in backwards."

Klement looked down at his hands cupped in his lap and silently, deliberately counted to fifteen. He raised his eyes to Olney. "Yes, that's the problem. I see now why you have these questions. It's a problem I often have, a problem most physicians don't have. I've been criticized for it before."

"Your problem? I don't understand, Doc."

"My problem, Mr. Olney, is that I try to take too much of my patients' burdens on myself, try to spare them the worry, the anxiety. It's all too human, I suppose, but I guess those are feelings a doctor can't afford." Klement spoke slowly, constantly checking Olney's reaction, ready to change tactics instantly if necessary. "These young, pregnant ladies, God bless 'em, they're scared, uncertain. Mr. Olney, I should have told Irene that this was a breech delivery. I just didn't have the heart to do it."

Olney blinked several times and swallowed back his grief. He dropped his eyes. "I see. Yes, I guess I understand. What you're saying is that you didn't want to worry her."

"Yes, yes," Klement said quickly, hoping Olney did not see his relief, "exactly. I have her record right here in front of me." He also hoped Olney could not read upside down. He tipped the manila folder more toward himself. "We had said all along that it was going to have to be a breech delivery."

"But when the baby's turned around like that, don't you take an X ray?"

Klement, who had momentarily relaxed, raised his guard again. He had thought that Olney was buying the whole thing. What the hell was this about X rays? No matter. He was already committed. "Oh, no. We can tell by palpitating, by feeling the uterus. X rays would only be harmful—the radiation on the baby, you know."

"Oh, sure, sure," Olney replied.

Klement felt as though he had just jumped a very big hurdle. All he had to know now was what McCallister had told Olney. "I would have called you, Mr. Olney, or talked to you, but Dr. McCallister said he had explained everything. He did tell you exactly what happened, didn't he?"

"Yes. He said the womb fell out"—Olney frowned—"and there was a lot of bleeding and Irene went into shock and . . ." Olney stopped.

Klement could have cheered. The womb *fell* out,

McCallister had told him—not that it was pulled or prolapsed or even that it came out, but that it fell out, like the apple from Newton's tree. An act of God. Knowing Olney was watching him, Klement rose, looking at his watch. "Yes, yes, those things do happen."

Olney got the hint and also got to his feet, his hand outstretched. "Dr. Klement, I want you to know that I feel you done everything you possibly could to save my wife and baby. I've taken a lot of your time, Doctor. I want to pay you for this. I mean, I came in without an appointment and all and——"

"Not at all. I wouldn't hear of it," Klement said, grasping Olney's hand with both of his own. "I only wish to God it could have been under different circumstances."

Olney's eyes were moist as he paused at the door. "Doctor, I want you to know that you're still our family doctor. Nothin's changed that way as far as I'm concerned."

"I appreciate that, Mr. Olney," Klement said with what he holped was a look of sincerity. "If you have any problems, call me—anytime, day or night."

"Thanks, Doc. Good-by."

Klement closed the door behind Olney, then turned and leaned against it. *Shit, I don't need this kind of confrontation, not with everything else that's going on.* It had gone off all right, though. McCallister could have messed him up, but he hadn't. McCallister was still in the fraternity, and for that Klement was grateful. He could feel the perspiration dampening his shirt at the armpits. He slumped into his chair and reached almost absently for the Seconal bottle. Disdaining the use of a water wash, he moved his tongue inside his mouth until he gathered enough saliva to run the pills down his throat. He had been trying to hold the pills down to nine per day, one before each meal, three when he went to bed, and three more when he was awakened by the nightmares. Damn Olney! And damn his stupid, dead wife!

In another office, spartan by comparison, Joan Klement was trying to hide her impatience. She craved a cigarette. Intermittently she scribbled a few notes as familiar words came to her from the distraught woman across the desk. The interview had already lasted some twenty minutes and was dragging to its predictable conclusion. The folder in front of Joan told her the woman was only twenty-seven. It was hard to believe. She was short and thin, with tired eyes and that sallow, beaten look. Her neck was creased with aging wrinkles, the kind that fifty-year-olds had surgically removed. Probably had lost weight recently, Joan thought. *And now, damn it, she's going to cry.*

Without looking down, Joan opened a lower drawer and extracted a box of tissue. The unspoken acknowledgment of the woman's emotional state was a signal that unleashed heaving sobs.

Joan leaned back, concealing her boredom as best she could. She had long ago abandoned any pretense of open sympathy for these women. Anger, though outwardly suppressed, overruled any other feelings. She looked away, waiting for the weeping to subside. When she looked back, the woman's shoulders still shook, but the interval between the wracking sobs was lengthening.

"And what were you thinking about when he struck you?" Joan asked.

The woman looked up, fighting for control, her eyes still awash. "I kept telling him . . . I just said it wasn't true."

"That's what you were telling him, but what were you thinking?"

"Well, I was thinking how unfair he was, accusing me. And I never did, never thought of doing such a thing."

"How long has your husband acted this way?" Anticipating the answers, Joan asked the questions more quickly now. The script seldom varied.

"Ever since we were married."

"Not before?"

"Well, yes, in a way. He would always hover around, watching me. Like if I was talking to another man, at a party or something."

Joan's pen was idle. "And you liked it." Perfunctory now.

"Yes, I guess I did. He seemed so attentive, so protective. It made me feel important, special."

"And when did you stop feeling so special?" *And stop your goddamn simpering,* she wanted to add, to shout. Joan knew she was being abrupt, almost contentious. The woman looked wary.

"When . . . when he began yelling at me all the time for no reason, accusing me of fooling around. And then the hitting. It got so I was afraid to even say hello to a man."

"But your husband never accused you in public, did he?"

"No, it was always later, when——"

"When you were alone."

"Yes, always."

"And you would proclaim your fidelity, tell him how wonderful he was, how much you loved him. And you'd often end up having sex."

The woman lowered her eyes and only nodded. Joan knew she was supposed to direct the conversation in such a way that the patient said all these things; but that would take forever. It suddenly made her question whether she had chosen the wrong line of work. Such antipathy after only two years? A jaundiced view from seeing only women? Her boss had insisted on that when he hired her. ("Too threatening to have a female psychologist do the testing and pretherapy interview of men their first time at a psychiatric clinic.")

Joan looked directly at the still-trembling woman. "Tell me, why is it you're here seeking help?"

The woman blinked uncomprehendingly for a moment. "Well, for my nerves. My nerves began bothering me. I was having stomach pains. Got an ulcer. It wouldn't heal. Finally my doctor said I should——"

"Yes, I understand. But what about your husband? He seems to be, well, at least part of the problem. Did he refuse to come?"

"Yes. Said he didn't need a psychiatrist. Said he feels fine."

I'll bet he does, Joan thought; *like a million, even though he's the one with the problem. Feeding on her like a leech . . . He can always refinance his bankrupt self-esteem by falsely accusing her of adultery.* She almost laughed at the image of this plain, whipped woman making a cuckold of her neurotic husband.

Joan rose, shuffling the notes on her desk. She managed a smile. "I think that's all we need. We've finished the testing. You'll be starting next weeek with Dr. Samuel Morrison. He'll be treating you."

The woman sniffled. "How long will it take?" she asked softly. "I mean how long will it take for me to feel better?"

Joan wanted to tell her no longer than it took her to stop being a psychological tackling dummy. Instead she said, "Perhaps not long. It depends on several factors. You have to get to know why you react the way you do, get some insight into your problems. And," she couldn't help adding, "your husband's."

Joan sat back and drew gratefully on her cigarette. There was another patient waiting, she reminded herself, but she continued to sit and stare out the window. *Is this job starting to warp me?* After a while you could begin to believe that the whole masculine world was populated only by assholes, grown boys still searching for their mommies. Her thoughts went immediately to Oscar. *I'm getting out from under that one,* she thought, smiling at her own metaphor.

Oscar had just gone through his paces before the mortality committee. He'd lost the baby, too. Joan felt her eyes fill. She was stunned to find herself crying—not the deep sobs of the patient who had only recently left the room, but the tears of soundless grief. "Stop it, damn it," she said aloud; but the disobedient tears kept coming. She reached for the box of tissue. She hadn't wept in years. The last time was when she had miscarried her own child. She (he?—she hadn't wanted to know) would have been a teenager today. Then Joan had walked the house for days, pausing here and there to sob. She would curl up in the chair before the fireplace and will her mind to go blank, only to break out in another weepy indulgence. Oscar had blamed the pregnancy on her, reminding her that they had agreed on no family until they could afford it. He had raged for days and gone into a sullen funk. She had carried the child only a couple of months.

She reached for another tissue. *God, a patient is waiting and the counselor needs counseling!*

Chapter VII

Dr. James Brailey was intimidated by the board of trustees of the medical center. It was a fact he conceded to himself, though he would never admit it to anyone else.

He knew it was irrational. He had arrived at a stage of life where his self-confidence had never been higher. He had often reflected that as he grew older, he cared less and less about what other people thought of him. And with good reason. He had risen steadily to his present position by nicely balancing intelligence, honesty, and hard work. Not that he lacked aggression. From the day he started his residency, he knew he would stay in academic medicine, disdaining the big money of private practice. He had pursued the medical center's unwritten code, making his way through the labyrinth of research, teaching, and publishing, excellent at all three. The promotions had come on time, from chief medical resident to graduate fellow in cardiology to assistant professor of medicine. Associate and full professorships had come ahead of time, and by the age of forty—somewhat to his surprise—he had become chairman of the Department of Internal Medicine.

As often happens, through a series of capricious events—the sudden, unexpected deaths that occurred higher in the pecking order—Brailey then found himself chief of staff of one of the largest medical centers in the country. Pure serendipity, he thought. Or was it? Had he really been that lucky? he asked himself. Had he remained that true to his beliefs? How many worthless papers had he written for the sole purpose of lengthening his bibliography? And, he admitted to himself, he had sought out honors and actively campaigned for promotions. He had just recently been appointed a member of the national advisory council for the American Heart Association. It had been his ticket into *Who's Who in America.*

On a day-to-day basis at the medical center, he had quickly learned the one-upmanship of an inbred academic institution. Only last week he had received credit for diagnosing an atrial myxoma—a rare heart tumor—when, in reality, Joe Burns, his chief cardiology resident, had first mentioned it as a probability. Brailey had done nothing to change the staff's impression that he had diagnosed it himself.

All of this, he told himself now, perhaps explained why he had difficulty dealing with Oscar Klement. It was very easy to dismiss Klement as a medical charlatan chasing the almighty dollar. But Brailey had power over Klement, in a way, and didn't the psychiatrists say that pursuit of power and pursuit of money were psychologically synonymous?

Brailey told himself that his discomfort with the hospital board probably was tied directly to the feeling that he really didn't deserve it all. Did the hospital board sense his insecurity? he wondered.

The medical center's board of trustees, like most hospital boards, originally had been composed of those whose major qualification for trusteeship was personal wealth. Boards were set up at a time when American society equated money with brains and leadership ability. It was also hoped that they might repay the honor by remembering the hospital in their wills.

In recent years, however, boards had become representative of their communities. Organized labor, then racial minorities cracked the membership, to be followed most recently by women. Established "old" money still dominated, however, and Brailey was uncomfortable in its presence. Businessmen and community leaders were outside the circle in which Brailey had climbed. His successful power play had been within the medical center.

His appearance before the trustees had been a special ordeal this time. He needed their backing. It was a fact of life that he couldn't carry this off on his own. They had to lend more than moral support. It was imperative that the state licensure board believe that the impetus for Klement's license revocation came from the trustees. Lacking that support, it would just appear to be the case of one disgruntled physician out to get another.

Knowing this, Brailey had spent two weeks carefully preparing his presentation. He and Charlie Rogers had reviewed hundreds of Klement's charts in the record room. They took voluminous notes, which Brailey had painstakingly typed. He had intended to limit his report solely to Klement's incompetence, not raising the drug issue. It hadn't worked out that way, however. In fact, it worked out in a way that Brailey had never imagined.

At first pointing out minor yet significant mistakes, Brailey had quickly moved on to more serious errors. He recounted Klement's misinterpretation of lab values, his wrong diagnoses, the unnecessary wound infections treated with the wrong antibiotics. Nervously but unequivocally he had built the evidence, malpractice by malpractice, and ended with the most recent fiasco—the disaster in the delivery room.

"Mrs. Olney was the only mother to die in the medical-center delivery room in over eleven years," he told the board somewhat melodramatically. "It was this unforgivable obstetrical blunder that moved me to take this unpleasant but necessary action, ladies and gentlemen."

Satisfied that his case was solid, Brailey had been stunned by the board's reaction.

"Wasn't Dr. Klement exonerated of that woman's death by a special executive committee?" was the first question. The rest of the interrogation followed the same pattern, a challenge to Brailey's administration. Why hadn't the hospital system of checks and balances worked to red-flag the problem before it became serious? he was asked. Where was the infection-control committee? And so on. It had become ludicrous without being funny. A disinterested third party would have thought that it was Brailey who was being censured.

A few of the trustees had even commented on Klement's reputation as an "outstanding citizen" active in community affairs. Brailey heard him described as a "nice guy" at least twice, and there were several references to Klement's father. Brailey, knowing he had failed, had thrown away his prepared script and in desperation brought up the documented evidence of the missing Seconal, saying flatly that Klement was a drug addict. That statement had at least brought a silence to the room. The chairman had whispered something to the trustee on either side of him, and there had been a nodding of heads.

Clearing his throat—somewhat awkwardly, Brailey thought—the chairman had then announced, "Well, thank you, Doctor. Of course, we would like to have some time to discuss this very serious matter." Brailey's hopes had risen slightly with the chairman's remarks. "We will call you as soon as possible with our decision." The chairman had favored Brailey with a tight smile, his signal that he was being dismissed. Brailey had only nodded and walked from the room, heading for his office.

The phone rang several times, and Brailey had to fight the impulse to pick it up before his secretary did. But the call was not from the board. He took a cigar from his shirt pocket, started to unwrap the protective cellophane, then decided against it and shoved it back in his pocket. Not knowing what to do with his hands, he started drumming his fingers lightly on the desk.

There was a knock at the door, and Charlie Rogers entered.

"Hi, Jim." Rogers greeted him. "Thought I'd sweat it out with you. Heard anything yet?"

Brailey shook his head.

"Cheer up," Rogers said. "The board will do something. Hell, it has to. You're the chief of staff. They have to listen to you."

"I don't think so, Charlie. I think I blew it. You should have heard them in there. Klement's record was almost beside the point. I——" The jarring ring of the phone severed Brailey's sentence. He looked at Rogers for a moment before picking up the receiver.

"Brailey," he identified himself calmly into the mouthpiece. There followed a mostly one-sided conversation. "I see," he said twice. And once, just before hanging up, "Yes, sir."

In all the time he had known Brailey, it was the first time Rogers had ever heard him speak with such deference. Brailey hung up the phone deliberately, his face expressionless. Rogers waited in vain for a comment.

"For God's sake, Jim, you gonna sit there all day? What the hell is it? What'd they say?"

"Charlie, you'll never believe it."

"Don't play games," Rogers said impatiently. "What in hell did they do?"

"They won't go after his license. They want Klement to see a psychiatrist."

"What!"

"You heard me. They want him to see a psychiatrist. We are taking steps to reclaim the career of the good Dr. Klement."

"Christ almighty," Rogers said. "I'll be a son of a bitch." He slapped his forehead with his open palm. "Those assholes. You were right, Jim: You blew it. I knew they wouldn't go after his license, the stupid bastard feather merchants. They just can't relate to this thing. Worried about the hospital image. I told you you should have gone for getting him kicked off the property or putting him on probation."

"Charlie," Brailey said sternly, "I told you what I was going to do, and I still think it was the right thing to do."

"Sure," Rogers said sarcastically, "but a hell of a lot of good it did. Jesus, that butcher will spend a month or so telling a shrink about his fixation for his mother's tit; then he'll be right back with us. Back, hell—he never left. He's still got hospital privileges."

"Yes," Brailey said wearily. "They said he's obviously a sick man, needs help. I'm to say nothing to the narcotics people or to anyone about the Seconal business until Klement has undergone psychotherapy."

Neither man said anything for a moment. Brailey stared down at his desk, his chin resting on his clasped hands. Rogers's face glowed hotly.

"That's just dandy," Rogers sputtered. "Nobody's bad anymore. Nobody's evil. They're just sick. Poor Klement. He can't help himself. He's just a poor junkie. Shit!" Rogers was walking in tight little circles in front of Brailey's desk. Brailey was forced to smile.

"My, my, Charlie, do I hear the bleatings of an existentialist?"

Rogers stopped pacing and looked at Brailey. "You're damned right you do," he replied.

Brailey raised his eyebrows. "So you do know what the word means. You get a smattering of Camus or Sartre in college, Charlie?"

"Hell, I don't read those twentieth-century assholes."

"Oh? What *do* you read?"

"Nineteenth-century Germans mostly," Rogers said. His early rage had left him now. Resignedly, he had plopped into a chair. "Nietzsche, Hegel, Schopenhauer. Mainly Schopenhauer."

"You read those tough guys, huh?"

Rogers nodded.

"I didn't think surgeons even knew how to read. And Schopenhauer, you believe him? You believe you have the right to decide who should live and who should die?"

"Well . . . yes, I believe him," Rogers said intensely. Rogers was usually intense, in varying degrees. "I mean, I believe him to the extent that we all have choices and we make them with a free will. If you're corrupt or immoral, it's because you choose to be. And if you make the wrong choice—when it catches up with you—you don't crawl into a bottle of booze or swallow pills or cry on the shoulder of a psychiatrist. You stop doing what you're doing or you get stopped." He paused to gaze across the desk at Brailey. "Sounds more like Hitler than Schopenhauer, doesn't it?" he said sheepishly.

"It's where Hitler got his ideas, Charlie."

Rogers put both hands above his head in a gesture of surrender. The muscles in his face had stopped jumping. "OK, OK. Hell, Jim, you did your best. I'm pissed at the board, and I'm taking it out on you." He rose to leave. "Who they sending Klement to?"

"Krueger," Brailey replied.

"Krueger? You're kidding. Why him?"

"Because he's the chief of psychiatry. The board specified that it be Krueger. Guess they want to keep it in the family."

Rogers, who had almost reached the door, turned and walked back to Brailey's desk. "But, hell, Jim, Krueger's a research man. Doesn't the board know that? He does all those weird sleep experiments, spends all his time at the neuropsych building, a sleep center or something."

"Sleep laboratory," Brailey corrected him.

"OK, sleep laboratory, where he tortures cats or some goddamn thing. Puts people to sleep. He's no practitioner, Jim. I don't think he even sees patients."

"Yeah, a few," Brailey said, "one afternoon a week."

"Hell, Klement will bury him. He'll absolutely dazzle him," Rogers said, his anger returning. "You know how he can bullshit his way out of tight spots. He'll have that shrink eating out of his hand."

"Look, Charlie, it's obvious the board wanted somebody from the hospital treating him, someone who could watch over this drug thing. Krueger presumably is the one who would have the most clout if Klement doesn't get off the pills."

"And how in hell will we ever know that?" Rogers asked. "Who'll ever know if he gets off the pills? I never even see Krueger. I have trouble remembering what the guy looks like. The board may think he's part of the medical center, but he spends all his time over at that sleep lab. He doesn't even bother to attend the executive committee meetings. When's the last time you saw him?"

Brailey shrugged. "It's been a while," he conceded. "The annual staff meeting, maybe. Don't worry, Charlie, I'm sure Krueger will be sending us full reports."

"Yeah, big deal," Rogers muttered. He had been leaning with both fists on Brailey's desk, and now he straightened up. He shook his head. "I'd hardly know the guy even existed. He came in here, after you hired him, with a splashy reputation for developing tranquilizers, and he hasn't done a damn thing since."

"He may be making a comeback, Charlie. Did you see a few weeks ago where he made all the papers?"

"Yeah, yeah. Got some goddamn rapist off the hook by hypnotizing him or something."

"He didn't get him off, Charlie; he got him convicted. The guy admitted he beat up the girl but claimed he didn't rape her. Said he couldn't because he was impotent. Krueger proved that the guy could get a hard-on."

"You kidding?"

"Nope. He hooked a wire to the guy's cock while he was asleep and proved he was a liar. The guy got ten years."

For a moment Rogers was silent while he contemplated Krueger's mystical powers. "Well, maybe so," he said finally, "but that's a hell of a long way from treating a junkie doctor. A little time on the couch with Klement telling the shrink just what the shrink wants to hear and——"

"Give it up, Charlie. There's not a damn thing either one of us can do about it, at least not yet. Now, get the hell out of here. I've got some thinking to do."

Chapter VIII

The pediatrics oncology ward was at the crook of the elbow of the L-shaped pediatrics wing of the medical center. It was once a playground for children recuperating from anything from tonsillectomies to open-heart surgery. To most of the young patients, it had been only an adventurous interlude before returning to their homes and adulthood, but with hospital stays shortened in recent years for many of the treatable afflictions, what was once a nursery had been set aside for the untreatable. The atmosphere was considerably subdued. The patients were now nearly all victims of catastrophic illnesses. Many were repeat visitors, returning time after time for some advanced treatment as doctors fought delaying actions against the inevitable.

Parents visited their doomed offspring in an ambience of painted cartoon and nursery-book characters, games, and stuffed animals. Some of the children wore a mad hatter's variety of headdress to conceal the baldness that resulted from chemotherapy. The play was often desultory. There was an occasional squeal of delight, testimony that for some, at least, there had been an innovative treatment that had temporarily checked the inexorable march of the saboteurs within their bodies. The nurses were special. How could they be otherwise? They wept at home. It was the only catharsis that allowed them to smile the following day.

Dr. McCallister's eyes traversed the room. These visits were not part of his job, and he couldn't explain to himself what drew him back here regularly. Some of the children were his friends. He had been present at their births, and he raged unprofessionally at the unfairness of the death sentence imposed on those who would never fully taste of life. It left him coldly depressed for days afterward.

He stopped beside Gwendolyn Miles. He sensed a crisis. The seven-year-old girl was staring, expressionless, as her mother talked to her earnestly. Both looked up at him, the girl's face still retaining the false flush of health. McCallister knew it would not last long. He noticed the tear-streaked face of Mrs. Miles, the features pulled taut by the two years of her daughter's illness. The strain of being constantly around the sick worked its ravages on the healthy. Mrs. Miles's face showed hollows not there before.

"Hey, Gwen," McCallister said, "how we doin' today?" God, the inadequacy of it all!

The girl's huge brown eyes regarded him somberly. "I'm going to die," she announced reflectively. It was a statement of fact, a recitation.

McCallister shot a stunned look at the mother, who turned her head quickly so as to hide fresh tears. "Whoa, wait a minute. Who told you that? Why——"

"The doctor," the girl interrupted.

"What?"

"Doctor," Mrs. Miles said sharply to McCallister. She got off the chair in front of her daughter and walked away. A backward tilt of her head told McCallister to follow.

"Mrs. Miles," McCallister said out of earshot of the girl, "what——"

"Yes, a doctor. I didn't know him. I was talking to Gwen when he walked up to her and patted her on the head. Seemed pleasant enough." A small sob stifled the rest of her words, and she reached into her purse for a handkerchief to wipe her eyes.

"And?" McCallister had to wait for the woman's composure to return.

"He said . . . he told Gwen that the pain would be over soon. He told her, 'You'll soon be with God.' "

"You didn't know him, didn't know his name?"

"I never saw him before, Dr. McCallister. He may have told me his name. I wasn't paying any attention. He just said he was making his regular rounds. He talked to Gwen, asked her how she felt, listened to her heart; you know." The woman was biting the corner of her handkerchief. "I've been here for an hour talking to Gwen. What would possess any doctor, any man? It took me by surprise. I didn't think to question him. It's been hell on earth these past two years, Dr. McCallister, and now this doctor. We haven't tried to keep anything from Gwen. We told her from the start it was serious, but . . ."

McCallister took her by the arm and steered her to a couch in the corner of the room. "Come on, sit down," he commanded gently. He saw the little girl staring at them. Anger rose to curdle his compassion. His voice was low, a controlled fury. "Now, tell me, exactly what did this doctor look like?"

"He was tall. Well, no, not really. I think he looked taller than he was because he was so skinny."

McCallister mentally clicked down the roster of ectomorphs he knew on a staff that numbered over a thousand. Doctors, male nurses, and nurses' aides, orderlies, janitors, security people.

"He had kind of, oh, I don't know, brownish hair. He had sleepy eyes, like turned down at the corners. He *looked* like a doctor—you know, white coat and everything."

Hell, why should he necessarily be a staff member? McCallister reasoned. Probably an outsider, one of those unordained religious nuts that haunt hospitals— this one just a little nuttier than usual. "Mrs. Miles," he said, "I don't think that man was a doctor. I can't conceive of any physician doing such a thing."

The woman's eyes were vague, lifeless. She worked the handkerchief with both hands, her look directed unwaveringly on her daughter.

"Mrs. Miles, I apologize on behalf of the hospital. I can assure you we'll do everything we can to see that there is no repetition . . ." McCallister bit his lip on the hollow assurance that was of no consolation to the Miles family. He got to his feet. "Uh, I'll say good-by, uh, say a few words to Gwen on the way out, see what I can do." He bent over to pat her hand. "Would you like me to get the nurse to give you something?"

Mrs. Miles shook her head numbly.

McCallister walked toward the girl, completely at a loss for words. He should probably tell Brailey about the incident. That should brighten Brailey's day.

In the hospital pharmacy, pharmacist Donald Bradshaw made sure the attention of the other two pharmacists was elsewhere engaged. Then Donald Bradshaw, medical-school dropout, slipped the stethoscope from the pocket of his white coat and into the back of his personal drawer beneath the counter.

Chapter IX

Brailey could not recall ever being in a similar mood. He was angry, and his anger angered him. He had remained reasonably pleasant to those around him, though he had become quieter and more preoccupied.

Oscar Klement. That damned Klement had been in

his thoughts almost constantly, whether Brailey was making rounds or at home with his family. He had tried but failed to put the trustees' meeting out of his mind; it had always returned like the ache of an abscessed tooth. Even while he was lecturing, an irrelevant question from a medical student would somehow trigger an image of Klement—and of Brailey's frustrating experience before the board. Lately he found himself unduly agitated over life's petty annoyances. He was especially furious with himself for having promised the trustees that he would do nothing about Klement's drug addiction.

He was reminded of his old psychiatry professor's lecture on hate, the man's statement that hostility was the most difficult emotion to handle. Fear, jealousy, lust—all could be dealt with better than anger. The hater turned out to be more emotionally crippled than the hated. And Brailey knew enough psychiatry to realize that his anger was compounded for its being "free floating." There was nothing to which he could attach it. Nobody was to blame. His anger at the board had gradually dissipated. The trustees were not really at fault. As disappointed as he had been at their decision, he knew they were acting as best they could, however naïvely. To someone outside the medical center, their action would seem responsible, even humane. They were, after all, expeditiously correcting the problem by sending Klement to a psychiatrist. One would have to have the inside perspective of Brailey to know that, in Klement's case, psychotherapy would be about as effective as putting a bandage on a virulent malignancy.

Besides, would Klement consent to seeing a psychiatrist? Brailey doubted it. Klement would probably bluster his denials in the face of everything and refuse to go. And knowing the trustees, Brailey thought, they would probably back down.

He pulled a second cigar from his shirt pocket.

Klement probably knew the temperament of the board as well as he, Brailey told himself. It would be strength against strength, and the board had little stomach for fighting. Klement would probably surmise that the trustees were bluffing, that they didn't really want to pursue a licensure revocation—or even to lift his hospital privileges, for that matter.

Wait a minute. The match burned down to his fingers as the cigar remained unlit, clamped between his teeth. *Wait a goddamn minute! How in the hell would Klement know the board's reaction? He wasn't at the meeting. I was at the meeting,* Brailey told himself. Klement would have to accept his version.

Brailey sprang from his chair, which rotated two full circles on its swivel base, and hurriedly divested himself of his white hospital coat, throwing it on the clothes tree and grabbing his suit coat in one motion. In a half-run, he jammed a hand into one sleeve and used the other to fish for his car keys.

Only minutes later, Brailey killed the engine of his car in the parking lot of the low, modern Klement-Bronson Clinic. Unlike most private clinics, this one had no traffic congestion despite a steady stream of cars. Designed for efficiency, it featured a special "in" and "out" driveway. Klement had built the clinic at the junction of a lower-middle-class neighborhood and a slum: between medicaid and welfare, Brailey thought. Klement knew his clientele. The clinic was an architectural island in a sea of clapboard houses.

As he walked through the automatic doors, Brailey's eyes were assailed by a myriad of signs. To his right was the laboratory; to his left, the pharmacy. He followed the arrow that pointed straight ahead to the receptionist and the waiting room for physicians. He passed another waiting room, outside of which a sign pointed left to the X-ray department and right to the area for "injections and shots." Brailey smirked: *And all this time I thought injections and shots were the same thing.*

He passed by not one but two injection rooms. The first had about six booths, each with a nurse administering shots as fast as she could. And people were standing in line awaiting their turn. It reminded Brailey of his army days. The second room was a small amphitheater-like area where the patients waited for thirty minutes after their injections as two nurses watched for adverse reactions.

Brailey entered the physicians' waiting room. As he walked into the handsome offices, his ears were caressed by classical instrumental music wafting from the clinic's stereo system. Every few paces patients passed him soundlessly on the luxurious carpeting. He confronted a beautiful brunette seated at the reception desk. She gave no sign of recognition as he announced himself but flashed him a dazzling smile as she pushed a hidden button under her desk.

Within ten seconds Klement's chief nurse, Nancy, materialized as though through a wall. She recognized Brailey immediately. "Why, Dr. Brailey, what a surprise. How nice to see you again."

"Hello, Nancy, how are you?"

"My, how many years has it been? Let's see, I left the medical center fifteen years ago. Time certainly does fly."

When you're having fun and making money, Brailey almost added. She had been the best intensive-care nurse at the hospital, and Brailey had been sorry when Klement had lured her away from him with a huge salary increase. It was amazing how people like Klement knew how to surround themselves with such pros. He wondered how many times Nancy and that gorgeous receptionist had bailed Klement out of trouble.

"Are you still the chief of staff?" Nancy asked him sweetly.

"Yes, I am, Nancy."

"I see," she replied. Brailey didn't know what in hell that was supposed to mean. "Dr. Klement's office is right this way," she said.

Brailey followed her, noting that she had immediately assumed he was there to see Klement. Nor had she bothered to ask the nature of his business. As she was showing him to a chair, Brailey had a chance to admire his surroundings. First class, he thought somewhat enviously.

Klement suddenly entered the room by another door and stopped abruptly, surprise washing his face. It was a reaction one was not often privileged to see, Brailey thought. It was obvious that Nancy had not had time to alert her employer to the identity of his visitor. Gone was Klement's glib prolixity. He recovered enough, however, to mumble a greeting and force a small smile before taking his seat across the desk from Brailey.

"Well, well," he said, then paused. Clearly he had not yet completely regained his composure. "This certainly is a surprise. That is, it's unusual seeing you out here—at the clinic, I mean."

"Yes, it's the first time for me," Brailey answered soberly. He studied Klement closely. Brailey felt a certain injustice that Klement's face still retained a rather youthful, if somewhat dissipated, look for someone in his late thirties, while his own, he knew, showed all of his fifty-six years.

"You sight-seeing, Dr. Brailey, or are you thinking of going into private practice?" Klement chuckled awkwardly, the laugh catching somewhere in his throat.

Brailey did not alter his noncommittal expression. "No, this is business," he answered, his eyes never leaving Klement.

"Oh? Medical-center business, I presume?"

"That's right," Brailey said slowly, now starting to savor Klement's discomfort. He fell silent, refusing to elaborate.

"Well, now," Klement said finally, "what can I do for you? Is there any . . . some problem?"

"Yes, there's a problem. There's definitely a problem." Brailey realized that his laconic manner was pointless, but he did nothing to change it, so satisfying was the long-overdue spectacle of Klement actually squirming.

"Well, what is it?" Klement asked. He probably was unaware that his mouth still held the tight, sickly smile it had adopted the moment he saw Brailey seated unexpectedly in his office.

"You, Doctor," Brailey said, "you're the problem, and I've been delegated to tell you of the steps that are being taken to resolve that problem. You see, Dr. Klement, I've just come from a meeting of the hospital board of trustees."

Klement swallowed, one sweat bead now following a meandering course down the side of his face. "And?" he asked. He had suddenly lost patience with Brailey's game of cat and mouse. "What was it about?"

"You, Doctor," Brailey answered. "It was about you." He was pleased to see Klement stiffen and straighten up in his chair. "The meeting centered on your capabilities as a physician." Brailey continued to talk slowly, enunciating each word precisely. "It has come to the attention of the trustees that you have been having repeated problems, that you have manifested shortcomings in several cases admitted to the medical center."

Brailey was a little surprised to find himself using such pretentious language. He awaited the shrill defense he was certain was coming. But Klement said nothing.

"The most recent incident, it was decided, forces the trustees—using their own words—to take some action," he continued. "They feel that it is their responsibility, that the most recent case leaves them no other recourse than to——"

"It was that goddamn breech delivery!" Klement exploded. "I'm going to get it after all. They're sticking it to me. Somebody's sticking it to me." His head lowered noticeably toward Brailey, who ignored the implication. "I thought the executive committee cleared all that up. Didn't you tell the board about the findings of the executive committee? I mean, you said yourself that McCallister——"

"There were several options open to the board, of course, Dr. Klement. They examined all of them."

Klement had unknowingly grasped one hand tightly over the other and was furiously kneading his knuckles. His anger was building, Brailey could see, and he was ready for it. "The board looked at the options," Brailey went on, "and discussed each thoroughly. They included loss of hospital privileges and——"

"OK," Klement said suddenly. He thrust one palm toward Brailey in a stop gesture. "I'm kicked off the staff. You can tell your trustees that there are other hospitals in town. I know you guys look down your noses at the little private hospitals, but at least they don't have a bunch of tin-god professors constantly breathing down everybody's neck. Your medical staff can go to hell, Doctor."

The curled lip and confident, disdainful look were back. It was vintage Oscar Klement, Brailey thought, on the attack. Klement's eyes lit up as he took the initiative, but Brailey had anticipated it.

"You misunderstand me, Doctor," Brailey said softly. "The final decision of the trustees was not to suspend your hospital privileges."

"What?"

"No. As I said, the board considered several options. One of them was loss of privileges; the other was to petition the state licensure board to have your license revoked." Brailey stopped and let his last words hang heavily in the now-silent room.

Klement's shoulders sagged. "On what grounds?" he asked.

"Drug addiction, Doctor."

"Drug addiction! Me? Why, there's not a shred of evidence that I——"

"They know about the Seconal."

"Seconal? What about Seconal?"

Klement's voice remained steady, but he was betrayed by cheeks turned scarlet. Brailey even now marveled at the unique coolness of the man.

"It's no use, Klement. You're wasting your time. I know. The board knows. Everybody knows."

"Well, just a minute, Brailey, that's a serious charge. It seems to me that——"

"No, *you* wait a minute, Klement," Brailey's voice now assumed a sharp edge. "You don't want the trustees to start counting pills, do you?" He leaned back, thoroughly enjoying his little game.

Klement's face was now mottled, and he opened his mouth several times, but nothing came out. Brailey bit the inside of his cheek, successfully hiding a smile. Finally, Klement stopped shifting in his seat and cleared his throat:

"Suppose, Dr. Brailey, you tell me exactly what it was the board decided."

"Well," Brailey said, leaning back in his chair, yielding to the temptation of prolonging the scenario, "the board decided, before taking any more drastic action, that they would give you one more chance—with a stipulation, of course."

"Stipulation?"

"You're to see a psychiatrist," Brailey said emphatically.

"I'm *what?*"

"To see a psychiatrist."

Klement stared at Brailey for what seemed like several minutes.

"I think, Doctor," Brailey said, "that you'll agree we let you off quite easily. You'd be well advised to cut your losses now. Do I make myself clear?"

The tight lines in Klement's face gradually softened, and he shifted his gaze to the top of his desk, nodding ever so slightly. "OK, OK, you're calling the shots."

"Right away," Brailey answered in his best administrator's tone. "You'll be seeing Krueger, Dr. Aaron Krueger, chief of the psychiatry department. You know him?"

"I've seen him around," Klement mumbled almost inaudibly. "Short guy, uh . . ."

"Yes. Well, that's settled. I'll arrange it right away and let you know when you are to begin treatment. You will keep your appointment." It was not a question.

"Yeah, sure," Klement said. "I'll see your psychiatrist." He was no longer looking at Brailey. He was now slumped low in his chair.

Brailey left the room without another word. Walking to his car, he recreated the satisfying encounter. It couldn't have gone better, he complimented himself. Had he not bent the truth, had he given Klement a true characterization of the board's timorous reaction, the worm would have wiggled off the hook again. It was the implications—the things Brailey had left unsaid—that had brought results.

Turning the key in the car's ignition, Brailey smiled to himself. God, that was good. To hell with the petty annoyances of life; they could be canceled, he was pleased to rediscover, by the small, sweet victories.

Chapter X

"Yes, I'm certain he received the message." The voice in Brailey's ear was plainly irritated, and so was Brailey.

"But I've called five times in the past two days, and he hasn't returned any of my calls."

"Dr. Krueger is a very busy man, Dr. Brailey."

"So am I," Brailey said gruffly into the phone.

"You might try him at the sleep lab here in the neuropsychiatry building, extension 481," the secretary suggested. "He spends most of his time there on his research project."

"I've called there twice," Brailey said impatiently. "He's always in the animal lab or someplace else and can't be disturbed."

"Well, I'm sorry, Doctor, but he does get so involved with his work that he sometimes forgets. I can assure you that I've relayed every one of your messages to him."

"Look, Miss . . ."

"Green."

"Miss Green. You track down your boss, wherever the hell he is, and you tell him that Dr. James Brailey, the chief of staff of the medical center, wants to talk to him. You tell him it's urgent, and if he doesn't call me back today, he won't have any animal lab to hide in. You tell him that!" he shouted and slammed down the receiver.

Brailey fumed. The bastard's cavalier attitude bordered on insubordination. Jesus, the hotshot came here twenty years ago with that big reputation and promptly dropped out of sight. Brailey didn't even know what in hell he was really doing in that lab of his. For that matter, he hardly ever saw him. The job of chief psychiatrist had become almost a sideline with the guy. And now the chief of staff of the medical center had to request an audience with His Highness.

The phone rang. "This is Dr. Aaron Krueger," the voice at the other end announced. "To whom am I speaking?"

"This is Dr. Brailey, Krueger. Well, I finally got hold of you. I wanted to talk to you about a problem that——"

"Dr. Brailey," Krueger interrupted, "I'd like to know what you meant about closing the animal laboratory. You know I don't receive any financial support from the medical center. If it weren't for the drug companies, I——"

"Yes, yes, I'm aware of that, Doctor," Brailey said.

"My secretary led me to believe you had implied that the hospital was threatening to close the neuropsychiatry building."

"She must have been mistaken," Brailey lied. "Dr. Krueger, I called you at the request of the board of trustees on a matter of utmost importance. We—rather they, the board—want you to treat a certain patient, a doctor."

"That's impossible," Krueger said brusquely. "My practice is limited to a few patients related to my research."

"But this is a special case. As I said, the patient is a physician, here at the medical center, and the board specifically requested that you personally undertake his treatment."

"No. I'm too involved in my research right now to see any private patients."

Brailey's satisfaction over the other day's conquest

of Klement was giving way to frustration over the intransigence of this little man. "Dr. Krueger, the man is a drug addict. Now, you are using medical-center facilities for your research, and the board feels that——"

"An addict, you say?" Krueger's voice betrayed a sudden interest. "You're certain he's addicted? To what substance?"

"Seconal."

"Really? Interesting. Not very addictive as a rule."

Brailey waited through several seconds of silence while Krueger considered his decision.

"All right, Doctor," Krueger said finally. "I'll see him. Have him come to my office at one o'clock next Monday. I'll treat him right here at the sleep lab."

"At the sleep lab?" Brailey was confused. "I mean, that's not very conducive to psychotherapy, is it?"

Krueger chuckled softly. "We're having some really remarkable results with drug addicts in sleep therapy," he told Brailey. "I must send you some reprints of my articles. I've written over thirty of them on just this subject."

"I have enough trouble just keeping up with the internal-medicine journals, Doctor."

"Yes, well, most people at the medical center aren't aware of what we're doing over here."

"I guess, Doctor, that we feel we have our hands full just trying to keep people alive," Brailey said somewhat sarcastically. "I assumed that your research concerned itself mainly with narcolepsy, insomnia, bedwetting, that sort of thing."

"Yes, of course," Krueger said condescendingly. "We still treat the common sleep disorders. But we've developed some rather successful techniques for altering sleep patterns in drug abuse. I think you'll be quite surprised at what we can accomplish. Ah, tell me more about this doctor of yours. How long has he been using Seconal?"

"I don't know. Frankly, it's hard to tell."

"That would not be unusual," Krueger replied. "It's

quite difficult to tell when they slip over the edge. I'm sure that's the case with your man, what's his name?"

"Klement—Dr. Oscar Klement."

"Klement. I don't believe I know him. And his addiction has grown to the proportions that it now interferes with his professional performance, correct?"

"That's correct. Something's got to be done."

"And he was such an incompetent doctor before he became addicted that it is now impossible to tell exactly when the problem began, is that correct?"

"Right again," Brailey said. "That's a pretty good long-range composite you've put together, Doctor."

"Not very difficult, actually, Dr. Brailey. Fairly typical, as a matter of fact. Physician addicts are like most addicts—self-centered, with an uncaring kind of greed —but their training takes so long that their lack of values isn't manifest for a few years. Your man is comparatively wealthy, I'd wager."

"The local medical Midas," Brailey answered. He found himself gaining new respect for Krueger.

"Yes, yes. The trouble usually doesn't start until they've finished amassing their wealth. Accumulating money obsesses them up to then, and that obsession postpones the realization that they don't like themselves. Then the drinking and pills start."

"Very interesting, Doctor. I'll be watching your progress with Klement very closely."

Krueger paused, then said, "As long as you understand, Doctor, that I can only return the man to you the way he was before he became an addict. I cannot give you back a new man—a good doctor."

"I understand," Brailey said. "I'll be waiting to hear from you. Good-by."

Brailey dialed Klement's number next, to notify him of his appointment with Krueger. *Maybe it will work out after all,* he mused. *The guy talks like he knows his business.* Brailey was too involved in the day-to-day hospital administration ever to have paid much atten-

tion to Krueger, but he had an impression of a purpose-
ful, driven little guy, short but somehow imposing.
Krueger's resolute, intelligent face with its intense black
marble eyes seemed to add inches to his height. *Klement is going to have to play it straight. He isn't going to
be able to shit that little man. Stubborn maybe, but
Krueger isn't the fool some people think he is.*

At the other end of the line, Dr. Aaron Krueger hung
up the phone as Brailey was saying good-by. *Well,
well, the big man needs me,* he thought. *He is actually
acknowledging my presence by asking me for a favor.*
Krueger spun slowly in his chair to look out at the vast
expanse of the medical-center grounds. His office window reflected a bright yet weak spring sunshine. He
could see the top of the multistructured hospital where '
a hundred noisy life-and-death battles were being
waged. That was not at all the atmosphere of the
neuropsychiatry building. Here it was quiet, the noises
of the animal laboratory muted by the three floors that
separated it from his office. *The man who hired me,
who brought me here only to ignore me, now comes
to me for help.* Krueger was pleased by the irony. He
looked at the clock. He was late for Riley's party.

Chapter XI

"Come on in, Doctor. Welcome!"
Krueger was able to generate a vestige of a smile. He
looked over the shoulder of his greeter, Frank Riley,
and into the hazy din of the cocktail party. The dozens

of people crammed into the small motel suite gave the room the appearance of a well-lighted cave.

"Hello, Frank," he said. "Good to see you again." Actually, Krueger was engaging in hyperbole. An honest answer would have been that he was seldom eager to see Riley. Fortunately, Riley came to town only three or four times a year. His first order of business—always—was to throw a cocktail party, and Krueger hated them. For one thing, he didn't drink. Generally he stood uncomfortably on the fringe of the party, his nose twitching distastefully at the smoke, sweat, and whiskey odors. But tonight it would be a little different.

"What can I get you?" Riley asked, already knowing the answer.

"Maybe a cola, Frank, or some tomato juice would be fine."

Riley guffawed. "Comin' up, but take it easy. You're driving, you know."

Krueger tried tactfully to disengage himself from Riley's grip on his elbow, which hadn't loosened, but finally allowed himself to be half dragged across the crowded room to the bar. Riley used the glass in his free hand as a pointer to call out the names of other guests by way of introducing Krueger.

Riley, Krueger thought, was the stereotype Irishman. He was fleshy, almost rotund, and red-haired. Capillaries dilated by alcohol formed tiny red tributaries around his nose. In probably no other situation, Krueger thought, would he and Riley be thrown together. But Krueger needed him. Riley was the research coordinator of the Monarch Drug Corporation, upon which Krueger was entirely dependent for money to continue his study. Despite the optimistic blandishments of Brailey when he had hired the psychiatrist, the hospital had never backed Krueger's professorship with any cash other than his salary. Without Riley and the drug company, there would be no sleep laboratory. And with no sleep laboratory, there would be no Aaron Krueger of any consequence.

Riley had been impatient with the pace of the research. On his last trip he had pointedly asked Krueger how the corporate funds were being used and what progress was being made. The question had nettled Krueger, inasmuch as he had regularly filed detailed reports to corporate headquarters and had faithfully mentioned the company in the footnotes of his medical-journal and magazine articles.

Riley thrust the glass of tomato juice into Krueger's hand and then left him to fend for himself. Krueger watched his host lumber like a garishly cloaked circus elephant from person to person, tossing off a quip here, another there. Riley was dressed in a cream-colored linen suit, the coat unbuttoned to reveal a shocking-red vest.

Krueger took off in pursuit of Riley. "Uh, Frank," he called out, "I've got something to tell you."

Riley turned to face him, his eyes cheerily out of focus. He threw his arm around Krueger's shoulder. "What is it, Doc?"

Trying not to wince at the contact, Krueger said, "I've got forty-nine cases without a failure, Frank."

Riley looked down at Krueger, tilting his head to the side. "Huh?"

"That's right, forty-nine cases. Not one single failure."

A light of comprehension crawled slowly across Riley's face. Miraculously, the eyes cleared; the jumbled speech became coherent. "Over here, Krueger." Again Krueger was held captive in the big man's grip. Riley backed him into a corner and put his face down close to the psychiatrist, who blanched at the slipstream of Jack Daniels that came from Riley's mouth. Riley beamed. "Well, now, Krueger, that's more like it. What about FDA approval?"

"Now, Frank, not so fast. You know I have no idea

what the Food and Drug people will do. As I said, the cases all responded. The drug had no side effects and——"

"When will it be approved, Krueger?"

"Frank, I just can't say."

Riley wheezed disparagingly. "Shit, Krueger. You know the company is on my ass to get this drug approved."

Krueger smiled. His pause was calculated. "Well, Frank, then you'll be interested in this. I've sent an abstract of a paper to the World Health Organization. It's been accepted for the Stockholm meeting. It will be a report of fifty cases of drug addiction cured by amitrypton. I had a case referred to me just this week by the chief of staff. That will be number fifty."

The congratulatory slap on his back came with such force that Krueger almost lost his balance. Tomato juice slopped over the rim of the glass.

A broad smile cut a dozen valleys into Riley's red face. "Well, now, great! Well, well, well. How about that?" Riley grabbed Krueger's hand and began pumping it so vigorously, the doctor's glasses slid to the tip of his nose. Riley turned and boisterously shouted the news to a tall man in a brown pinstripe suit who had been introduced earlier to Krueger as a manufacturer's representative. The man came over to add his congratulations.

Riley's joy was infectious, and Krueger realized he was smiling foolishly. He had forgotten the irritant of the cocktail party. He was looking past his well-wisher, when his eyes stopped at a woman standing against the opposite wall. She was dressed plainly, her dark hair pulled back severely from her temples, and was regarding him without expression, her bony face fixed like that of a statue. Krueger's smile left him and he swallowed hard. It couldn't be! No, but the resemblance was remarkable. He experienced a light-headedness that had him swaying. He felt a weakness in his legs; they were trembling.

"Hey, Krueger, old buddy, you OK?" Riley said.

"Uh, yes, certainly." He looked at Riley, trying to resurrect his smile. "Maybe I'll get a little air," he told him.

"Sure thing," Riley said, grabbing him by the arm.

Krueger allowed himself to be led to the small veranda off the motel suite. There he inhaled deeply.

"Too much of the bubbly, Doctor," Riley said, smiling. "I warned you about that."

Krueger managed to smile back. "Go back to your party, Frank. I'll be all right." Riley nodded, and Krueger watched him return to the room with his rolling gait.

The resemblance to Sarah had been almost uncanny. Krueger was still shaken but convinced now that what he had seen was a rare look-alike. It has been said that each of us has a twin someplace in the world, and Krueger had just seen his ex-wife's. He steadied himself on the wrought-iron railing and inhaled the perfume of the May evening. All the thoughts that had been forced to the farthest corner of his memory bank came flooding back: New York, his childhood, medical school, psychiatry residency, his long-ago private practice.

He had met Sarah while she was working part-time as a lab assistant and pursuing her doctorate in biochemistry. Their romance had begun quite unromantically in the biochemistry lab and continued into late-night study sessions. They had studied and discussed science, often into the early-morning hours. Rumor had it that the tall, angular Sarah had been jilted by an alcoholic divinity student, who had fled to a religious retreat in India.

Krueger had proposed marriage at the end of his sophomore year of medical school. He remembered now how he had wanted those science discussions to go on forever. His mother had been delighted that he was marrying a "sensible Jewish girl." His father had seemed relieved. He had interpreted young Aaron's shyness and fastidiousness as a disinclination for the opposite sex. Krueger chuckled ruefully to himself as the party roared on unabated behind him.

He had been mortified to find out that he hated the practice of clinical medicine. In the first two years of medical school he had been fascinated by the basic science courses, especially biochemistry and pharmacology. He loved the abstract study of the science of medicine. His junior year had brought him into contact with charity wards reeking of urine and cheap wine, of rectal exams and blood-soaked scrub suits. He had thereafter gravitated toward research, which made his parents almost apoplectic. "Aaron, my boy," his mother had wailed mournfully, "we want you to be a *real* doctor."

Psychiatry had been the compromise, and his parents were ecstatic. Through it all, he remembered, his wife had remained neutral, except to remind him that clinical medicine was financially more rewarding. Krueger felt betrayed by the memory that his wife had stopped her biochemistry doctoral studies on the day they were married.

It had been almost painful to admit to himself that he didn't like analytic psychiatry very much, either. The results, if any, were slow. His restless, impatient personality demanded satisfaction that he found lacking in the analysis sessions. He realized that he had never really developed the knack of easily communicating with others.

He had begun rescheduling, cutting down on office hours and leaving early. Then he had stopped working Fridays. The rescheduling soon took care of itself. Patients didn't care for a psychiatrist who didn't talk or listen to them. The bank account had diminished steadily, and Sarah had reminded him of that often. In fact, Krueger's lack of monetary success was about the only thing on which they eventually agreed. The gulf had widened between them until finally their relationship cracked in a way that Krueger could never have imagined.

He would never forget "the incident," as the medical society had called it. Even now he shuddered at its recollection. Standing in the shadows of the veranda, he glanced back into the light at the partygoers, relieved that they could not share his thoughts.

A woman he had successfully treated had phoned, begging him to treat her thirteen-year-old daughter. Krueger had tried to put her off, but she had persisted. He had finally agreed only because the woman, distraught over her daughter, had seemed on the verge of a relapse herself. Would his life have been much different had he refused? he wondered.

A chronic runaway, the girl had come to his office as the last patient of the day, after his secretary had gone home. Despite the frantic mother, Krueger had found the girl remarkably composed and not at all embarrassed by her nymphomania. An intelligent child in almost every respect, she had sat smugly across from Krueger, her self-assurance and vocabulary far outdistancing her age. She had emanated a warmth that had Krueger comparing his wife unfavorably to her. He had found himself admiring the girl's candor. Her quick, revealing answers had left virtually nothing for him to pursue.

"Why don't we just stop these ridiculous questions?" the girl had said suddenly, slowly rising and walking around the desk, unbuttoning her blouse. From that antediluvian time, Krueger still remembered how her girlish blue eyes had vied for attention with a worldly smile.

He had responded to her advances, and the cruel girl had talked. The mother had also talked—to the medical society and, vengefully, to Krueger's wife. Sarah had given him a puzzled backward glance and scurried from his life. The divorce had been final for so many years, Krueger could barely recall what she looked like, until tonight.

So he had fled New York, sublimating his physical urges beneath an extravagant capacity for work. To say he had been driven would have been to minimize his single-mindedness these past years. But he believed that his mental capabilities had become keener as a result. He was more aware, perceptive. Nietzsche preached that resorption of unused sperm into the system enhanced wisdom. Perhaps it was true.

Riley's thunderous laughter jolted Krueger back to the present; it reigned supreme over the other noises of the party. The edge had gone from Krueger's earlier triumphant announcement. He squared his shoulders and moved forward, hoping to enter the room unobtrusively. He wanted to find Riley, excuse himself and leave.

Chapter XII

Klement sat in Krueger's reception room awaiting the summons, as it were, and ruminated on a lifetime distrust of psychiatrists. He remembered the flip definition used in medical school: a Jew who wants to be a doctor but can't stand the sight of blood.

They're not real doctors, anyway, he thought. *Why do you really need any of these assholes?* In all his years of private practice, he had never referred a patient to a psychiatrist. Mental illness had never touched anyone around him, unless you counted Lillian, his mother's baby sister, who went nuts when Klement was just a kid. Didn't everybody have a screwy aunt in his family? He remembered being mildly interested at the time only because the family had talked surreptitiously of Lillian's "sickness," as they called it. Lillian had gone to a psychiatrist, he remembered hearing, apparently to no avail. Her life had ended in an upstate sanitarium, and Klement remembered no funeral.

He glanced around the room. Someone had taken some care to see that this office did not match the decor of the rest of the medieval-looking neuropsychiatry building. It was not ostentatious but warm and comfortable. Burnt-orange carpeting coordinated with the dark-brown furniture. There were even a couple of paintings, well done, hanging on the paneled walls.

Klement seemed to be the only patient. He winced at the word. His admiration of Krueger's office had momentarily allowed him to forget why he was here. His nervousness returned, and a voice, though soft, made him jump.

"Dr. Klement."

Krueger stood in the open doorway to his private office. He was even shorter than Klement remembered from the couple of times they had passed in the hospital corridors—five-four, five-five at the most—a long-faced man with thin, graying hair, tortoise-rimmed eyeglasses, and a beaked nose. He could have come right out of central casting. The vested, dark-blue suit was exquisitely tailored.

Klement rose quickly and strode toward the psychiatrist. He hurriedly dried his wet palms on his trousers and extended one hand to Krueger before he realized that the psychiatrist had turned and was preceding him into the inner office. He took a chair without being asked and saw that Krueger was already looking down at him from across the desk. *Why, the little shit's got an elevated chair,* Klement thought with as much amusement as he could muster under the circumstances. He glanced quickly around an office as comfortable as the one he had just left. He realized that he was looking for a couch. He returned his gaze to Krueger, who was leaning back in the huge leather chair, his hands forming a steeple. Peering over the top of his glasses, he reminded Klement of a Nazi interrogator just before he pulled out the victim's fingernails in one of those corny World War II movies.

Krueger came right to the point. "Tell me, Doctor, what is it that is bothering you?"

"Well, uh, it is probably not as serious as you may have heard, Dr. Krueger. I mean . . ." Klement knew he was stammering. He took a quick breath and started over. "That is, it's true that I probably take more sedatives than I should, but——"

"I was given to understand, Dr. Klement, that you have an addiction problem."

"I don't know that you'd call it an addiction," Klement said sharply. He saw Krueger's eyebrows raise almost imperceptibly. "That is, it's true that I probably take more sleeping pills than I should. Dr. Brailey . . ." He wanted in some manner to convey to Krueger that the chief of staff had steered him here through a misunderstanding or personal vendetta, but he stopped himself. Never mind that bullshit, he told himself. Brailey and Krueger had obviously been all over his personal history in minute detail.

"I do have a problem, I suppose," Klement began again haltingly. *Why doesn't he say anything?* he wondered. Krueger had not changed his expression except for a slight pursing of the lips, and for the first time Klement noticed the strong chin and the eyes that seemed to drill a hole right through him. He hated Krueger for his composure. "It's just that I've been, well, nervous. Can't relax. And the pills, well, they help."

"And the pills help," Krueger repeated. He spoke more to himself, but there was no hint of sarcasm.

"Yes, that's it." Klement was relieved that Krueger had finally said something.

"Have you tried staying off the pills, the Seconal?"

"Yes, Dr. Krueger, I've tried. It's just that, as I say, I get nervous and shaky. The pills relax me. I feel more sure of myself."

"And when you try, Doctor, when you stay off the Seconal as long as you can—a few hours, say—what causes you to, uh, weaken and take them again?"

"Well, when I get upset about something, you know, when things don't go well . . ."

"You get nervous and take the pills, is that correct?"

"Yes."

"What about the times when you're not upset, when you're not working or are on a vacation, when you've had a good day, so to speak? You continue to take them anyway, is that correct?"

Klement slumped in his chair. "Yes," he said softly.

"Now, Dr. Klement, when you've had one of these good days, when nothing in particular has upset you or made you nervous, at what time of day are you most apt to weaken and take the Seconal?"

"At night," Klement answered quickly. "It's always at night. I just can't——"

"Precisely." Krueger had anticipated Klement's answer. "It's mainly the nights, isn't it?"

"Well, I can't sleep. I suppose it started with the night calls. I get keyed up."

Krueger interrupted again. "Dr. Klement, do you feel that if you could sleep well at night, you could become free of your barbiturate addiction?"

"Yes," Klement replied. "Yes, I really think I could."

"Fine," the psychiatrist said, with a slight smile. It was the first time he had shown any animation. "You'll be an excellent candidate for sleep therapy. We'll start tomorrow night, eight o'clock. My secretary will give you instructions and directions to the sleep laboratory. It's here in the neuropsychiatry building, on the second floor." Krueger, who up to this point had seemed studiously bored, now picked up the tempo and seemed anxious to end the interview.

"Sleep therapy?" Klement sat unmoving in the chair.

Krueger sighed. "Yes, Doctor. Certainly you've heard of it?"

"Well, yes," Klement said, none too convincingly, "I've heard of it." *Where in hell did I hear of it?* he asked himself. *Newsweek? The Wall Street Journal?* "Actually, Doctor, I've never paid much attention to the journals—the psychiatry journals, I mean," he finished lamely. He had heard someplace that Krueger was fooling around with something like this. "You've developed some new technique for treating people while they're asleep and——"

"I think I am permitted to say in all modesty that I have been an innovator in the research of sleep therapy, with some others around the country, of course. In fact, I'm presenting a paper on it at the World Health Organization this summer."

"That's wonderful, Dr. Krueger," Klement said impatiently, "but just how are you going to treat me? I gather from what you say that I'll be sleeping here and you're going to give me something so I can sleep better. Is that it?"

"Precisely. Tell me, Dr. Klement, a minute ago you said that you had difficulty sleeping at night. Is it trouble getting to sleep, or is the problem that you awaken *after* you get to sleep?"

"I wake up," Klement answered. "I work hard, Doctor, and I'm exhausted when I get to bed. I fall asleep OK, but then in an hour or so, uh, sometimes less, I wake up. It's awful. I'm nervous and——"

"And you're having a nightmare?"

"Yes, terrible ones. I'm shaking. It's scary. I sweat right through my pajamas. Sometimes I have to change them two or three times a night."

"And then you take more Seconal, isn't that right?"

"Yes."

"How many?"

"Uh, one, sometimes two."

"Sometimes more?"

Klement looked resignedly at his relentless questioner. "Yes," he admitted, "sometimes more. Sometimes three or four."

"Until the next time you wake up?"

Klement paused. "Yeah," he said, "they're only good for one or two hours."

Krueger made a pyramid of his fingers again, propping them under his lower lip. He looked at Klement over his glasses and swiveled his chair, slowly shaking his head from side to side. "Yes, classic," he said finally. "Classic—typical REM pressure."

"Pressure? What about blood pressure?"

"Not blood pressure, Dr. Klement, REM pressure— R-E-M. It stands for "rapid eye movement." REM sleep is one of the stages of sleep. Quite different from ordinary sleep. Your eyes, instead of being rolled up inside your head, dart back and forth as though following objects."

"What happens during this REM sleep?"

"You dream."

"Dream? That's all? You just dream?"

"REM dreams are necessary, vital to your emotional state. And you've been suppressing them."

"I have?" Klement asked. "How?"

"With the Seconal. It abolishes REM sleep. All the barbiturates do, as do Quaalūdes, chloral hydrate, Doriden—all the potent sedatives. Even alcohol, if you drink enough."

"And the sedatives don't allow me to dream, don't allow REM sleep?"

"Precisely." Krueger was pleased that Klement was perceiving the process, but at the same time he was ready to end the interview. He began drumming lightly on the desk with his fingers.

"Dr. Krueger, are you saying that because I take Seconal, I don't get enough REM sleep, that I don't dream enough? It's that simple?"

"It's not simple at all," Krueger said impatiently. He glanced toward the ceiling and began again slowly, as though talking to a child. "I thought you might have known something about it, being a physician, I mean. Perhaps I've been too abrupt. Here, I have these pamphlets that I give to all my patients. They explain sleep therapy and how the medication will alter your sleep patterns. They're probably similar to those from the American Heart Association that you pass out to your heart patients." Krueger stood up.

Klement knew he was supposed to leave, but he couldn't. *Wish I could take a couple of pills right now,* he thought. He had been totally unprepared for the sleep-therapy bit. He had to know more about it. It frightened him. He had come expecting to lie down on a couch and talk, that kind of thing. He knew he could handle that, and very well, but this idea of getting medication while he was asleep, helpless, not in control . . . He saw Krueger staring at him, waiting for him to leave. *Not just yet.* He sat a little straighter in his chair, gathering his reserves. "Dr. Krueger, I'm not sure I want to undergo this sleep therapy," he blurted out.

Krueger's face showed his surprise. "I'm afraid I don't understand."

"Neither do I," Klement replied with some heat. "I don't want to read it in some pamphlet; I want to hear it from you. I mean, this is some sort of experimental thing, and I wasn't expecting it. I'm, well, I'm apprehensive."

"Of course you are, Doctor." If Krueger was upset at Klement's little display of pique, he gave no outward sign, though Klement had the impression that the little psychiatrist was not accustomed to being questioned. "I can understand your apprehension," Krueger continued, still standing, "but, well, Dr. Brailey and I have discussed your, uh, problem, and it was my impression that you were perfectly agreeable to undergoing whatever treatment I recommended."

So much for bluffing, Klement thought. He formed a mental picture of Brailey and Krueger dissecting him and his "problem." "Certainly," he said quickly, "I'm eager to cooperate, to begin some kind of treatment. I suppose I'm nervous, not expecting or understanding this sleep business. That is, sleep therapy is brand-new to me."

Krueger remained standing on his platform looking down at Klement for a few seconds, saying nothing. "Of course, Doctor," he finally said, simultaneously sitting down and reaching into his right-hand desk drawer. He extracted a piece of paper and methodically smoothed it down on his desk top with both hands. "Dr. Klement, this is a sleep-pattern diagram. It outlines the various stages of sleep. As you can see, there are basically two kinds of sleep, REM and non-REM. When a person first falls asleep, he is in non-REM sleep and his sleep quickly becomes very deep. The brain-wave cycles become very slow with very little activity. The person vegetates and during this time obtains his physical rest.

"But, as you can see from this diagram," Krueger went on, "this deep sleep lasts only about ninety minutes. Then the subject's brain wave begins to register more activity. His sleep becomes progressively lighter until he approaches wakefulness. But instead of waking up, he goes into REM sleep and begins to dream for fifteen or twenty minutes. Fascinating, really. During this period of REM sleep, he is in a sense awake. He is seeing objects in his dreams, following them with his eyes. If he's dreaming of a tennis match, his eyes move horizontally. If he's watching a yo-yo, they move vertically. During this REM period, there is tremendous activity in the autonomic nervous system." Krueger looked up at Klement. "You, of course, understand the autonomic nervous system?"

"Controls digestion, heart rate, sex, that sort of thing," Klement mumbled.

"Precisely," Krueger said. "There is tremendous activity in this nervous system, often more than when the subject is awake. The heart rate accelerates, and digestion and stomach acid are at their highest. It's why people have fatal heart attacks and ulcer pain at night. Those always occur during REM sleep. Erections also occur uniformly, even when the content of the dream is not sexual."

"And you say I've been depriving myself of this REM sleep by taking Seconal?"

"Yes, and that is the danger, because you need to dream. We all do. It's our emotional safety valve. If a person is deprived of REM sleep for a while, he becomes nervous, irritable. If you continue to suppress it, you become psychotic. REM dreams allow us to go quietly insane four or five times a night," Krueger said with a smile.

"Four or five times?"

"Yes. Look here at the diagram. The REM periods occur every ninety to one hundred minutes, and each REM period—each dream—lasts fifteen to twenty minutes."

"Is everyone the same?" Klement asked. "I mean, does everyone dream the same amount?"

"Yes, we're all remarkably similar."

"Well, I must be different."

"Why?"

"Because despite what you say, Doctor, I'm dreaming too much, having nightmares all the time."

"Ah, that's the REM pressure," Krueger said. "What happens is that you're able to suppress your dreams for a few weeks with the Seconal, but then those dreams create an enormous need, and they come crashing down on you in the form of nightmares."

"Dr. Krueger, you said a minute ago that people who suppressed their REM sleep with drugs could become psychotic. Could I, uh, that is, could I go crazy? I mean, could these nightmares ever lead to——"

"Yes, we see it," Krueger answered unemotionally, "especially in alcoholics. Surely you've encountered delirium tremens in your practice."

"Yes," Klement said quietly. "It's horrible. They see snakes and bugs. They have hallucinations——"

"Nightmares," Krueger said. "They are in one prolonged and continuous nightmare. These people have been suppressing their REM sleep with alcohol for weeks and months, and finally those pent-up dreams spill over into their waking hours and they become psychotic."

"And this treatment—it will prevent REM pressure? Stop the nightmares?"

"Precisely. You've been awakening every ninety to one hundred minutes during your REM sleep period, taking three or four Seconal to hold back the nightmares. Then, after another ninety minutes or so, you wake up again and take more. The cycle repeats four or five times a night. The Seconal only suppresses the nightmares for a while, allowing them to accumulate. Now, I—that is, we—have developed a new drug. It allows you to dream normally, even when you're an addict. If you take this drug, there won't be any more nightmares or frantic awakenings, yet you'll be able to dream enough to dissipate the REM pressure.

"The drug," Krueger continued, "is called amitrypton. It's a tranquilizer of sorts itself. It works much like methadone works with heroin addicts. It sedates you just enough to keep you asleep; but it doesn't suppress your dreams. You sleep and you dream. After a couple of weeks of dreaming, you'll be calmer. You won't have nightmares. You'll be cured!"

"Have you done this before?" Klement asked.

"Forty-nine times without a failure," Krueger answered proudly. He rose and stepped down from his desk platform. "Eight o'clock tomorrow night, then. My secretary will outline the procedure."

Krueger turned away abruptly and walked out the door, leaving Klement still sitting in his chair. Klement got up slowly and stared after the psychiatrist. He shrugged and started for the outer office. *Eight o'clock,* he said to himself. *Precisely!*

"Damn it!" Klement swore as he stumbled over a pile of trash inside the kitchen door. He had just let himself into the house. Old papers, periodicals and some other crap, he didn't know just what, were scattered all over the floor of the entranceway. It looked as though the goddamn dog had been rutting around in the stuff. No, it wasn't the dog's fault; it was Joan's sloppy housekeeping. The living room, too, was a mess—clothes, newspapers, even dirty dishes cluttering the floor. Mostly there were books—Joan's. They had long ago overflowed the numerous bookshelves in the library and den. Joan, looking as disheveled as her surroundings, was sitting in the center of the debris, her hands propping her face. She didn't look up from her newspaper as her husband entered.

Klement wanted to rage at her about the house, really get pissed off, but he said nothing. He had been in a foul mood since the interview with Krueger, but he needed to talk to Joan, extract some information on sleep therapy. The whole thing was slightly scary.

He opened the liquor cabinet and looked down at the top of his wife's head. She had still made no acknowledgment of his presence. He poured himself a drink and then reached inside a never-used ice bucket for two Seconals. He popped the pills into his mouth and used both hands to lift the Scotch. Some of the liquor spilled over the rim of the glass as he raised it to his lips. Krueger's clipped, haughty word came back to him:

"Precisely." *The Jew bastard.* Impulsively, Klement reached for a third Seconal.

"Uh, how was your day?" His voice was uncommonly loud in the spacious living room.

Joan looked up and studied him for a few seconds. "All right, OK, the same." She returned to her newspaper.

The frigid bitch can't even carry on a decent conversation. "Well," he began again, "what's new? In the paper, I mean."

"Nothing."

He sat down in a chair near her. The silence outdistanced the physical space between them by a thousand light-years. He cleared his throat and spoke again. "I, uh, I was reading one of the medical journals. It was probably more in your line. About sleep. Interesting, uh, REM sleep and all that."

"Uh-huh," she mumbled, a signal that she was listening.

"It said something about what could happen if you don't get enough of it. Have you ever run across any——"

"You go crazy."

"What?"

She looked up. "If you don't get REM sleep, you go crazy. We see a lot of it, mainly in alcoholics and addicts who——" She stopped, and a smile crept across her face. "You're seeing Dr. Krueger at the medical center. He's going to try sleep therapy on you, isn't he?" The smile was a strange counterpoint to the terse, uncaring tone of her voice.

"How did you know that?"

"There was a phone call from Brailey after you left for work this morning. He said I was to remind you of your appointment with Krueger."

"That goddamn Brailey!" he exploded. "Just because he's got a vendetta against me is no reason for calling my home and telling you——"

"He didn't tell me anything, Oscar. I doubt he even realized that I knew who Krueger was."

"You've met Krueger?"

"No, but I've read his stuff in the psychiatry journals." She gave a quick flip of her head to get the hair out of her eyes and returned to her newspaper.

"Well, uh," Klement began slowly, "ah, it just so happens that you're right. That is, I am going to be spending a few nights there." He cursed his wife's perception. Oh, hell, he would have had to tell her eventually. "Just a couple of weeks to, uh, clear up a problem."

"The Seconal," she announced flatly.

He leaned back in his chair. Well, what in hell did he expect? Of course she knew, had probably known all along. He was a complete idiot ever to have deluded himself that she would not know. Son of a bitch, the whole world probably knew!

Joan looked up, her face a triumphant animation. "I'm no fool, Oscar."

He stared at her. "No," he said quietly, "of course not. Of course you're not."

Chapter XIII

Despite Klement's twenty-year association with the medical center, this was only the second time he had been at the neuropsychiatry building; the first had been his interview with Krueger. As he drove into the parking lot, he was relieved to see again that the building was separated from the hospital, with an entrance that couldn't be seen from the doctors' parking lot. He had not told anyone about having to see a psychiatrist, and he had warned Joan to keep quiet about it. She had shrugged noncommittally. Of course, he told himself, hospital gossip being what it was, word would soon get around. Enough people knew already—Brailey and the entire hospital board and no doubt Brailey's buddy, Rogers, since those two chieftains of medicine and surgery ran everything, and God knew how many others. Well, fuck 'em. Fuck 'em all. He'd pull out of this yet. He'd play their little game.

Only a half-dozen cars were parked in the lot. The late-model cars looked out of place next to the dilapidated building, as though they had been transported backward by some time machine. Horses and buggies would have been more appropriate.

Klement walked to the door, picking his way carefully over the cracked and buckled sidewalk. He noticed that the medical center had made one housekeeping concession that the neuropsych building was part of the same operation: The grass had been cut.

The building, stark in appearance, was constructed of red brick that had aged to a dirty orange. Three stories high, it was partially obscured from street view because it nestled in a swale below the level of the medical center, almost a full block away—as though it were an embarrassing appendage the medical center had tried to hide behind its back.

The somber building looked deserted at this hour. He walked past rows of small rooms that more closely resembled jail cells—each with an outside lock on the door. A regular old-fashioned nuthouse, he thought, now rendered obsolete by tranquilizers and liberal laws. Following the directions of Krueger's secretary, he took the stairs to the second floor and came upon a blue-uniformed receptionist at the end of the hall. She was stout, a grandmotherly type except for her light-brown hair. She sat stiff-backed on the edge of her chair, her unrouged lips set for business. Still she smiled as he approached.

"Mr. Klement?" she inquired politely.

He wondered whether she hadn't been told that he was a physician or was merely being diplomatic. "Yes."

"We've been expecting-you. You're late. We'll have to hurry so as not to get behind schedule. Here"— she thrust a paper at him—"you'll have to fill out this questionnaire before we begin." She gave him a clipboard and ballpoint pen, motioning with the pen to a row of classroom chairs along one wall.

He took a chair twice removed from that of a tall, acne-covered teenage boy who was hunched over a paper Klement assumed was also a questionnaire. The boy looked up and greeted him with a cheery "Hi." Klement merely nodded. He was shaking now, so much that his handwriting was almost illegible. He answered most of the questions perfunctorily. To the inquiry "Reason for sleep therapy?" he hedged. "Possible excessive use of sleeping pills," he wrote, unable to bring himself to use the word *addiction.*

He hesitated over the question "Time any medication was last taken?" Krueger had warned him not to take any barbiturates for at least twelve hours before coming to the session because of the danger of mixing the effects of the Seconal with Krueger's drug. Klement had kept his word—barely. He candidly noted on the paper that he had taken two Seconals exactly twelve hours ago, at 8:30 A.M. He had suffered through the day without any more, though several times in the late afternoon he had had to suppress the urge to scream at patients to get the hell out of his office. Now he felt an urgent need to get up and walk around the room.

"Nice evening."

Klement looked up at the smiling boy's remark. He managed a tight smile but said nothing.

"This your first time here?" the youth wanted to know.

"Yeah," he croaked. "Yes, it is." The words came like dust from his dry mouth.

"It's my sixth."

"Sixth, huh?" Klement really had no wish to engage in small talk, but, on the other hand, it served somewhat to get his mind off his withdrawal.

"I knew it was your first," the boy went on. "I can always tell."

Klement didn't know if the boy was perceptive or a teenage smartass. He looked back at the questionnaire, doodling with his pen in one corner of the paper. "How can you tell?" he asked.

There was no answer, and Klement looked up as he heard the boy's pen rattle on the floor. To his amazement, the teenager's eyes were closed, and his upper body was slumping lower and lower toward the writing arm of the chair. His tongue protruded limply from his mouth, and Klement was astonished to hear him snoring.

Klement looked over at the receptionist, who glanced briefly at the sleeping boy, then returned unconcernedly to her coffee cup. She was talking quietly to a white-coated physician, who also ignored the napping teenager. In fact, they were chuckling quietly at some private joke.

"I can always tell."

Klement jumped and looked around at the bright-eyed boy, now fully awake. "What . . . what . . ." he stammered.

"I said I can always tell when it's the first time here," the boy repeated pleasantly. "People are always so nervous about it."

"Oh—oh, yes." Klement stared openmouthed at the boy. Then he got quickly out of his chair and strode toward the receptionist's desk, glancing back at the friendly youth. He handed the questionnaire to the receptionist and was about to ask about the boy, but the white-coated physician stretched out his hand to him.

"I'm Dr. Aldair," he said, "Dr. Kenneth Aldair, the chief psychiatry resident. I'll be looking after you tonight." He was gaunt, with straight black hair, his small head seeming to sag under the weight of huge, thick eyeglasses. His movements were those of a jerky waterbug. The bony shoulder line was straight just below the ears, as though he had forgotten to remove the coat hanger. The strong handshake from the frail body was a surprise.

"Hello," Klement said.

"If you'll follow me, please," Aldair said. As they walked through the door, Aldair called over to the boy, still sitting in his chair, "Are you having as many attacks, Freddy?"

"Nope," the boy answered in a clear voice.

"Good, good," Aldair said. "I'll be back for you in a minute." Aldair's arm directed Klement into the sleep area. It consisted of three doors about ten feet apart. The left and right doors were marked "sleep rooms."

Klement followed Aldair through the middle door into a room that was filled with two sets of every conceivable type of monitoring equipment. Lining opposite walls, the walls adjacent to the sleep rooms, were separate sets of electroencephalographs, electrocardiographs, and other monitors. They reminded him of the instrument panel of a jet airplane. In the middle of each wall was a window that afforded a view of each sleep room. He peered through the windows and found both sleep rooms identical. Despite the shabby decor of most of the neuropsych building, these rooms resembled those of a modern, moderately priced motel.

"We've found this decor most conducive to sleep," Aldair said, reading his mind.

Klement nodded dumbly, unable to comprehend how, in his present agitated state, he could ever fall asleep without a little help.

Aldair motioned to the room on his left. "In there, Doctor," he said, and, acting much like a bellhop, he led Klement out of the monitoring room and into a sleep room. There was a separate bathroom in the sleeping area, and Klement was told to ready himself for bed. Aldair would be back "in a minute."

Klement methodically brushed his teeth and began putting on his pajamas. He wished he had brought deodorant. The sweat of his withdrawal had brought its attendant odor.

Aldair reappeared and asked him to lie on the bed. He began applying the electrodes to Klement's head, face, and chest. He meticulously pasted them in place and secured each with a small strip of clear tape. Klement wondered why it took so many.

There were four electrodes for the eyes: one attached above each eyebrow, Klement remembered, to record the vertical eye movements; one placed at the side of each eye over the temple to register the horizontal eye movements. The fifth and sixth electrodes recorded brain-wave tracings: one on top of the head for the frontal lobe and one at the base of the skull for the occipital lobe. In addition, two more electrode leads were attached to his chest to continuously monitor his heartbeat. The cool touch of the leads felt soothing and acted as somewhat of a balm to his nervousness.

All these wires were gathered together at the head of the bed into a single cord that led through the windowed panel above the bed into the monitoring room. Contrary to expectations, Klement found that he was only minimally restrained and could move almost freely. Aldair handed him a standard hospital-bed buzzer in case he needed anything or had to go to the bathroom.

We'll begin in just a little while," Aldair informed him. "I have to get the other patient hooked up to the monitoring equipment. It's past his bedtime."

Klement did not return Aldair's smile.

* * *

Klement was left alone for almost an hour. He was seething when Aldair finally returned. It was after 10:30 P.M., more than fourteen hours since his last Seconal. His fingernails dug into the sheets, and his pajamas were heavy with sweat. The perspiration had loosened at least three of the electrodes. More than once he had been very close to pulling off the damnable wires and walking out, but the memory of his interview with Brailey had stopped him each time.

The infuriating delay had primed him with a number of sarcastic remarks to be directed at Aldair, but the psychiatry resident never gave him a chance. He walked in talking. By the time he had finished, Klement's angry balloon had lost its air.

"Sorry I'm late, Dr. Klement," said Aldair in nothing resembling an apology. "Had to spend a lot of time with the case next door." He nodded at the wall that separated the sleep room from the monitoring room. "We're monitoring a patient in the other room."

The doctor made a quick check of Klement's electrodes and, not saying a word about his drenched condition, began resecuring the leads. He first dried Klement's skin with a cotton swab. Then he pulled a tube from his pocket and squeezed from it a gluelike substance to reattach each lead, replacing the old tape with four or five larger strips. "Don't worry about these coming loose," he said. "If they do, it will register on the printout in the monitoring room."

Aldair pulled an I.V. bottle from the drawer of a cabinet and hung it from the pole above the bed. Seemingly with the same motion, he swabbed Klement's forearm with alcohol and plunged the needle into the vein.

Klement felt relief as he watched the dripping I.V. solution. "Finally. Maybe now I'll get some sleep," he said to Aldair.

"Not from this you won't," Aldair said breezily.

"It's only five percent glucose in water. A little sugar never put anybody to sleep."

"I thought . . . I mean, I assumed this was that new drug that would put me to sleep. Without using——"

"Afraid not. You'll have to fall asleep on your own. Once you're asleep, we'll add the amitrypton to this I.V. bottle."

"But that's part of my problem: I can't fall asleep."

"Yes, in part," Aldair replied, "but usually the main problem you people have is awakening and then not being able to get back to sleep. The drug will keep you in a light stage of sleep, but just deeper than REM so you won't dream. If you do ascend to the REM stage and begin a nightmare and start to wake up, we'll just speed up the I.V. medication and you'll go back to deeper sleep. You'll get a decent rest for the remainder of the night."

Klement resented being lumped with "you people" but said only, "And what if I can't get to sleep at all?"

"That rarely happens in barbiturate addiction. It may take an hour, maybe even four or five."

Four or five, Klement thought. *My God, I'll never be able to stand it.*

"But you'll eventually get to sleep," Aldair assured him. "We'll let you sleep later in the morning if it takes a long time."

Klement looked puzzled. "One thing I still can't understand is, if the amitrypton also prevents REM sleep, why doesn't it increase the REM pressure? Why doesn't it act like alcohol and, er, pills?"

Aldair arched an eyebrow. "I'd assumed Dr. Krueger told you all of this."

Klement did not reply but continued looking expectantly at Aldair.

"Uh, it would seem that way," Aldair started over, "but for some reason it doesn't happen. The amitrypton freezes you in the lighter stages of sleep, but just short of complete REM, and allows you to dissipate the REM pressure without having the frenzied dreams and nightmares of the barbiturate withdrawal."

Though Krueger and now Aldair had explained this, Klement still did not fully understand, but he was jumpy and anxious to get on with it. Aldair, however, seemed to be in no hurry.

"It's a relatively new technique, of course," he continued, "to supplement the more conventional, proven methods."

Klement eyed the psychiatrist closely. "What do you mean by 'proven methods,' Dr. Aldair?" he asked. "Have you had any problems?"

"Oh, no. No problems. The amitrypton is a safe and simple drug. We've used it forty-nine times without a failure," Aldair said, adding almost to himself, "at least not yet."

Klement, who had momentarily turned his head, snapped around quickly. "Now, what in hell do you mean by that?"

Aldair hesitated for a moment. "Uh, nothing, nothing at all."

"Don't give me that 'nothing' crap," Klement said. Patience had left him under the onslaught of his mounting withdrawal symptoms. "I'm in no mood for enigmatic bullshit, Doctor." He could see he had startled Aldair, who had taken a tentative step toward the door and then stopped. "Look," Klement said quickly, "I didn't mean to blow up at you. I'm just a little nervous right now. I'm sure you can appreciate that. I'm not going to repeat anything you say to your boss, Krueger, and I'm certainly in no position to get up and walk out of here."

Aldair simply looked down at him.

"You do know why I'm here, don't you?" Klement asked.

Having heard the rumor about Brailey and the hospital board, Aldair nodded.

"Then level with me. Is there something about all

this that I should know—something Krueger didn't tell me? Is there some risk that——"

"No, no, definitely not," Aldair said. "There's no danger at all, Doctor, none whatsoever." He paused, and Klement heard him sigh. "Look, Dr. Klement, what you may have interpreted as hesitancy on my part has nothing at all to do with the sleep therapy. It's perfectly safe, and effective, as far as it goes. It's merely a difference in philosophies. Tell me, did Dr. Krueger talk to you?"

"Sure, of course, yesterday, before he set up the sleep therapy."

"No," Aldair pressed. "I mean, did he talk to you about your problems, your anxieties? Did he go into the underlying reasons behind your addiction?"

"Oh, that. No, he didn't bring it up. Neither did I, as a matter of fact. What good would that do?"

Aldair regarded him studiously. "It might just do quite a bit of good, Dr. Klement; perhaps more than this." He gave the sleep room the casual back of his hand.

"But you said yourself that this works, that I'll be able to sleep at night, without pills, and no more nightmares."

"Yes," Aldair said slowly, "but I'm not so sure it will last."

"Well, you said it lasted with the others who have come here."

"Yes, that's true," Aldair conceded. "So far it seems to have worked. But I question whether it gets to the heart of the problem. A person needs to know himself before he can help himself. You have to find out yourself why—that is, what made you addicted, why you started using drugs in the first place. All that takes time, long-term therapy, talking it out."

Klement regarded Aldair a shade contemptuously. *Bullshit,* he thought. *I don't have that kind of time. I'm glad this guy's not my psychiatrist. He'd have me*

*coming back twice a week for the rest of my life.
But then he's young, this chief psychiatry resident,
probably in his late twenties. He's got a lot of time.*

"How about the boy next door?" he asked, interrupting Aldair's monologue on the benefits of psychoanalysis.

"What?" Aldair had to suddenly shift mental gears from the psychoanalytical couch to the sleep lab. "Oh, him. He's a narcoleptic, can't stay awake. Maybe you noticed him. He was checking in the same time you were."

"We met," Klement said. "You using the same drug on him?"

"No," Aldair answered, "we're just monitoring his sleep to confirm the diagnosis. An interesting and quite pitiful disease, usually diagnosed by the time a person is seventeen or eighteen. Narcoleptics have sleep attacks, seizures. Although both your cases are characterized by excess REM pressure, in your case it's because you've suppressed it with drugs and allowed it to build. With narcoleptics the pressure is there for some unexplained reason, probably some mix-up in brain biochemistry. They just suddenly fall asleep and start dreaming, nightmares and so forth. We can make a diagnosis by monitoring them. They have a tremendous amount of REM-dream pressure. They go straight from a wide-awake state into REM sleep."

"Have you tried giving them this drug?" Klement asked.

"We've tried it in a few cases. It doesn't seem to work as well as with addicts or alcoholics. Addicts' brain metabolism is basically normal. They've just temporarily screwed up their sleep patterns with the drugs or booze. Narcoleptics have a brain-chemical disorder that makes them have sleep attacks, so it's more difficult, and it's permanent."

"Permanent?"

"Yes, lifelong," Aldair said. "It's really something.

They go through life fighting against falling asleep,
falling into machinery, getting into car accidents, getting fired from jobs. It's a hell of a life."

"Nothing you can do?"

"Nothing much," Aldair admitted. "Generally about
all we can do is to advise them to plan their lives
around their sleep attacks, if that's possible. They
sleep for only one REM period of fifteen or twenty
minutes. For an hour or two they feel OK, but then
they have to sleep again, because the REM pressure
builds up again."

"I'll be damned," Klement said.

"Yes," Aldair said. "So you see, it could be worse.
Once you get rid of your REM pressure, you'll be
OK. The narcoleptic goes on forever."

Both men fell silent while Klement contemplated the
treadmill life of the narcoleptic. Aldair opened his
mouth again, and Klement had the distinct impression
the psychiatrist would like to expound further on the
subject. In fact, he had the impression that Aldair,
given the chance, would expound on practically any
subject under the sun. Klement looked pointedly at
his watch.

Aldair noticed the gesture and looked at the glass
panel above the bed. "Ready in there?" he called
to the window.

"Yes, anytime you are," came back a female voice.

"Now, Dr. Klement," said Aldair, suddenly all business, "would you look straight ahead, please?"

Thereafter, Klement dutifully followed Aldair's commands to move his eyes from side to side and up and
down while Aldair verbally checked out the monitoring
equipment with the unseen technician.

"Well, that does it, Dr. Klement," Aldair said
finally. "All you have to do now is relax."

Klement spit imaginary cotton from his mouth and
nodded skeptically.

"Pleasant dreams," Aldair said in parting.

Chapter XIV

Joan looked back at herself from the mirror. The cheap glass distorted her nude upper half, but she could see enough to take pride in a body that did not show all of its thirty-six years. The face was remarkably free of wrinkles. A long, delicate throat, almost birdlike, pointed the way to small, upturned breasts. Unlike most women her age, Joan would have preferred to be a little heavier.

It was cold in the motel room, and she shivered. The goose bumps on her breasts were so large, they looked like a thousand small nipples. She felt mechanical. This would be the last time, she told her mirrored clone as she started to dress. Were they all alike? This one was certainly no better than Oscar—arrogant, self-centered. They all had a selfish way of making love that put her somehow outside the sexual act, as though she were looking down on the whole thing. The gratuitous asses.

She jumped as she felt a cold finger slide between her skin and the strap of her bra.

"Here, let me help you," he said, fumbling with the fasteners.

She cringed at his touch, even though she had spent the last half-hour underneath him. She buttoned her blouse quickly. "Let's go," she said, trying to smile.

"So now you're the one in a hurry. That's a switch." Sam Morrison was only slightly taller than she. He had jet-black hair and was the proud possessor of a

116

goatee that Joan thought he probably believed gave him a macho image. He looked at his watch. "Yeah, I guess we better get back to the office. Enough of these desserts on our lunch break." He snickered at his joke. Joan turned her face from him.

Driving back to the Morrison Clinic, he asked her, "What do you think of Mrs. Smythe? I'm seeing her first thing—at one."

He said it casually, as though making small talk, but Joan knew better. She had come to learn that his questions about patients were serious inquiries. The Morrison brothers played it as a game, not wanting to admit how dependent they were on her psychologic testing and initial interviews. She supposed it was their way of keeping her down, of heading off requests for a higher salary.

As psychiatrists, they continued to see the patients at weekly intervals but often foundered and referred them to Joan for "more testing" or "follow-up interviews." They were stupidly transparent, she thought. It had taken her only about six months to realize what was happening. At first it was flattering, and then it was amusing, but it had recently roused her anger when it dawned on her that it was just another exploitation.

She was smarter than either of them, and she took solace in the knowledge. She looked out the side window of the car and thought how it had taken even less time to realize that she was also smarter than her husband. In fact, she had sensed it almost immediately. But it was ten years before she began resenting it, before the impact of the wasted years finally struck her. In the early years of Oscar's medical training, things had been too hectic for her to do much of an analysis. His endless hours at the hospital had the effect of postponing that day of realization. She became angry at herself when she remembered how she had been a willing—even eager—victim of years of patronization, watching Oscar transfer his love from her to money, watching him getting it, hoarding it, being trapped by it, yet craving more.

The realization that he was also a terrible doctor had brought a feeling of relief. It had enabled her to cope with her daily life and deal with Oscar's demands. Her indifference to him had grown, and her job at the clinic was the vehicle she had used to shape an alter existence. Oscar had objected to her going to work, then relented only because it was out of town and wouldn't be an embarrassment to him; so she had not been forced to tell him that she would have taken the job over his objections.

Then the affairs had started. The first ones were intense. She had "fallen in love" with her boss. She now smiled to herself, casting a quick glance at Sam Morrison crouched behind the wheel. Difficult as it was to believe, she had once actually thought that she was in love with this creep sitting beside her. Had there ever been anyone as vulnerable?

Oscar seemed never to suspect a thing. That thought alone had often infuriated her, and more than once she had almost made a sadistic confession just to witness his vulnerability. How she would like to see that again— a vulnerable Oscar, weak and naked, *afraid like the rest of us,* she thought—to see some humanity force its way through that shell of confidence, that bullshit he spread to protect himself from the rest of the world.

She had known enough psychology to believe at first that with Oscar it was all an act. Only once, just once, had he peeled back his defensive layers. One night, in a rare burst of personal insight, he had told her of his confused feelings about his father. He had talked of his shame at the poverty of his parents and of his guilt at that shame. That was the night she had agreed to marry him. She held back a sad laugh. She had believed she could change him.

Well, she was going to end it; it was time. End it

with Oscar, with the Morrisons, leave this town, start over. She owed it to herself.

"Here we are." Sam Morrison's voice intruded on Joan's thoughts. He pulled his car behind the restaurant where her car was parked. Following their pattern, they would now drive separately to the clinic. "Thanks for lunch," he said.

Joan continued looking out the window, not wanting to see his leer. Then she got out wordlessly and walked straight to her car, not looking back.

Chapter XV

Oscar Klement looked through the glass, trying to pick out the familiar face among the dozen or so pathetic figures who sat scattered about the dayroom of the nursing home.

"How's she doing?" he asked deferentially of the licensed practical nurse at his side.

"Why, I think your mother's doing just fine, considering everything, Dr. Klement." The nurse was a dumpy woman in her fifties, with black hair-rinse applied so liberally it rang false at a distance. Her doughy face was marked most prominently by heavy, mannish eyebrows that had been religiously tweezed. A red carnation, slightly wilted, was pinned to the lapel of her starched white uniform. "She has her bad moments, of course, but she seems content. And she's hardly any trouble at all. Not like some of them, I can tell you that, Dr. Klement. She has her friends here, as I've told you, and she seems to keep herself occupied quite nicely."

Klement looked back through the gleaming glass partition.

"She's over there by the window," the nurse said, smiling. Her finger smudged the glass, showing Klement the way. As he moved to the door leading to the dayroom, she laid a hand lightly on the sleeve of his jacket. "We've often said—that is, the staff has said— that it's too bad some of the relatives of our other guests are not as devoted as you are, Dr. Klement." Her voice was secretive, almost a whisper. "Some of these poor souls, you know, they never get any visitors."

He was not sure of the source of his embarrassment, but he knew he wanted to leave this woman's presence. "Yes, ah, thank you." He pulled himself gently from her and pushed open the door.

The room gave off its usual heavy torpidity. In the far corner two women watched a television set as it flicked the hyped bacchanal of a morning game show. The sound was turned low, and one could barely hear the cued glee of the delirious contestants.

Klement made his way across the room to where his mother sat in a straight-backed chair. Although she was next to the window, her attention seemed to be directed at the wall. The furniture was luxurious by nursing-home standards, and a bright yellow paint had recently been applied to the walls. For the fees they charged, Klement thought, maintenance certainly should be no problem. The home was the most expensive in the area, but he paid ungrudgingly. He had vowed that his mother's later years, at least, would make up in part for all she had been denied when he was growing up.

The only conversation in the room was between two aged men who occupied a blue couch. One of them was agitated, making a point with a bony, almost translucent arm that jutted sticklike from an obviously expensive bathrobe that looked several sizes too large. Remarkably, the man's tirade was almost inaudible, though his mouth was an animated disfigurement as it opened and closed rapidly. His companion regarded him stolidly.

For a moment Klement stood looking down at the woman with the gray hair disharmoniously streaked a dirty yellow. "Mother?" he said louder than he had intended. None of the others even looked his way, he noticed. "Mother?" he said again, more quietly.

He put his hand on her shoulder and knelt beside her chair. Slowly she turned toward him, her eyes moving no faster than her head. Her hands lay in her lap. The skin sagged on her forearms, in contrast to her face, where it adhered so closely to the bones as to appear to have been recently waxed. She seemed to look through him, and he smiled hopefully. She tipped her head to the side as though it were a weight she could not support.

A small groan involuntarily escaped Klement. "Mother, it's me, Oscar." Holding the smile had numbed his face. "How are you, Mother?"

Her dry lips came slowly to life. They started to manufacture a smile. Her eyelids fluttered, the blurred movement of an in-flight dragonfly. "Karl," she said, "what are you doing here?" Her eyes took on a flippant coquetry.

"No, Mother," Klement said patiently, "I'm Oscar. Don't you remember? Dad's name was Karl."

Her musical laugh twinkled whimsically. She raised a blemished hand toward him and pointed an admonishing finger. He saw that the gold wedding band now slid freely on her emaciated finger.

"Now, don't you think I know the difference between Karl and Oscar?" She wagged her finger sideways in front of her face, a tolerant scolding. "Oscar is in school, and you should be at work. What are you doing home this time of day, anyway? Are you playing a joke on me?" She threw her head back, and this time her laugh was a sharp report.

Klement sighed and looked away, waiting for the echo of her laugh to die. Then he looked at her again. She was as he had found her, her curtained gaze once again fixed at a cosmic spot on the wall. How many things must she be seeing there? he wondered.

He talked to the side of her face, not at all sure she was hearing any of it. "Ah, Mother, they say you're getting along OK. Uh, I left your allowance at the office. They have promised to call me right away if you need anything."

The words sank into the void she had erected between them. Whatever her fanciful mind was telling her now, it had no place for him, or this room. Maybe this world?

He got to his feet and moved squarely in front of her, then pulled up a chair and lowered himself into it, bringing his eyes down to the level of her timeless stare. "Mother, I'm sorry, but I'm in a bit of a hurry today. Can you hear me? I've got some papers for you to sign. Then maybe you'd better go lie down and rest for a while."

Her eyes searched his face, their coldness a discordant note to her other features, which showed a serene composure. "Oscar, you shouldn't feel bad."

He had to mentally regroup, and he stammered in the process. "I, uh, yes, that's right, Mother." She smiled and seemed pleased. "How are you, Mother?"

Her face turned grave, and she leaned forward. Her fingers suddenly went to his face and cupped his chin. Startled, he recoiled. "Oscar, you mustn't be angry at your father. He's a fine man. He meant to be home for Christmas, but you know he has his duties. He would have been home if he could. You know that, don't you?" Klement would have liked to scream. "Don't you?" his mother persisted.

"Mother," he started. He tried to make his next words

soft, and they came out that way—almost a caress. "Mother, Dad is dead. He passed away a long time ago." Oh, shit, what did he say that for?

She looked at him uncomprehendingly. An hour crawled by in the next minute. Her eyes never left him, and he saw them fill with tears. He cursed himself silently.

"Dead," she said finally, plaintively. Then: "Of course." A tiny smile lit her face beneath her moist eyes. "I know that, Oscar. Dad's been gone a long time." She laid one of her clawlike hands on his arm.

He put his hand over hers and felt a warm film come over his own eyes. The old woman's face turned to the window.

"He wanted to be home," she continued. "I remember, you were so little; you slept in the chair waiting for him to come home that Christmas. I couldn't even get you to eat."

"Mother," Klement said, squeezing her hand in a gesture that was meant to console them both, "don't cry."

"I'm all right, Oscar," she said.

Klement swallowed. "Sure you are, Mother. You're going to be just fine." He loved her. The stone that clogged his throat, he realized, was a regret that he had not told her so more often, that he had not reassured her as she tried, almost alone, to steer him through his adolescent years.

She turned to face him once more. "Well, you will be wanting to get back to your work. What is this about signing something?"

Her voice had lifted, become stronger. He was amazed, as always, at the shift in her awareness, her resiliency. She could remain in the present tense for days, perhaps even through his next visit, but nothing was certain. He unzipped the briefcase.

"Mother, these papers, uh, they have to do with the clinic. They require your signature." He put them in

her lap, using the briefcase as a desk, and handed her
his pen.

She signed each paper unhesitatingly. Her signature
was bold, fashioned with the steady strokes of one much
younger; her movements brisk, businesslike. She looked
at him, her face alive. "We're having a party tomorrow,"
she told him proudly.

"That's nice, Mother." He filed the papers back
in the briefcase.

"Yes, Mrs. Dougherty is coming back to live here.
You may have heard me mention her before. She was
in the hospital for so long. Now she's coming back,
and we're giving her a party. I have to meet with Mrs.
Collins today. We're on the decorating committee." She
was smiling now, her eyes moving and alert.

He returned the smile. "Fine, Mother. I'm sure it will
be a lot of fun." He got up from the chair and stood
beside her, the briefcase held in front of him with both
arms.

She followed his movements. "You have to go so
soon? When will you be coming back, Oscar?"

"In a few days, I promise. I'll have more time. We
can have a nice long talk."

She nodded and raised her face for the obligatory
kiss. He avoided her proffered mouth and kissed her
on the forehead, as usual ashamedly revolted by the
black hairs on her upper lip.

"Take care of yourself," he murmured against her
skin, his hand closing briefly around her shoulder.

Klement looked back as he reached the door. Her
face was turned to the window. The once-agitated man
on the couch was asleep, sitting upright, his head
slumped backward. He was snoring harshly, breathing
through a toothless cavern.

Chapter XVI

Aldair walked into the hospital cafeteria, his ears assailed by the pandemonium. The banging of plates and rattle of silverware competed with the strident bark of the paging system. From the sauna bath that passed for a kitchen came the crash of cooking pans coming together. There was an almost constant scraping of chairs as interns, residents, and students answered the commands of the paging system—often in midmeal. Aldair hated the place. The food all looked the same, and tasted that way, too. Cooks bellowed like lumberjacks. The food was fast and it was filling. It might even have been nourishing, for all he knew, but it was served in a setting that did nothing to nourish the mind. It dampened conversation, and Aldair dearly loved to talk.

Conversation was his avocation. It was more than communication; to Aldair it was a sacrament. It was one of the reasons he had gone into psychiatry. Another, of course, was his own psychoanalysis, which he had undergone ten years ago. At first dreading the thought of someone else probing his mind, he quickly began looking forward in eager anticipation to the therapy sessions. Ventilation coupled with reassurance and the advice of a good analytic psychiatrist had assuaged his tensions each week, and all from talking. His teenage anger and guilt were dissipated through the spoken word.

He made his lazy way through the serving line, practically ignoring the food, his eyes focusing on the dining area, searching out a sounding board for today's philosophical dissertation. It was a daily ritual. If he found no one to his liking, he would eat alone. He had, within his first two months at the hospital, assessed everyone's conversational ability, judging style as well as content. Then he categorized them: "stimulating," "good listener," and "better than nothing." Bores were not tolerated. Aldair would have been shocked to learn that most of the hospital staff regarded him as one.

As he left the serving line, he spied Joe Burns and made the decision to join him. The cardiology resident was a little too flip for Aldair's liking, but he was animated and a good listener.

Burns smiled and waved him over. "How are things going in Krueger's sleep zoo?"

Aldair shrugged. "OK, I suppose." He sat down and stared at his food.

"You don't seem too enthused about it."

"Well, I'm not. Damn it, Burns, his whole project stinks."

"Whoa, wait a minute." Burns was smirking. "That's your project, too, you know."

Aldair clenched his teeth at the remark. "It's not *my* project," he said firmly. "It's not even psychiatry; it's chemistry—psychochemistry, really." He sighed deeply. "Oh, I don't know what the hell it is. Drugging people while they're asleep, manipulating their dreams —it's absurd. You have to treat the emotions, analyze the dreams. The content of the dreams is what's important, not the amount. It's the only way. It's what people dream about that counts." Aldair was warming to his subject.

"You don't buy all that stuff?" Burns asked.

Aldair wondered if Burns was baiting him, expressing sympathy to get him to open up only to cut him down. Burns had that reputation. "To a point, I suppose," Aldair answered warily. "REM sleep is well documented. It occurs. We all dream during it. But he's tampering with it, giving drugs to change the kinds of dreams."

"Is Krueger really able to do that?" Burns seemed genuinely attentive. "Change the content of a dream?"

"Well, sort of. The drug decreases the REM pressure. It diminishes the intensity, the vividness of a dream. It stops nightmares, that sort of thing."

"Hey, that's something," Burns said. "That's really something. I didn't know anyone could do that. And it really works? People really feel better afterwards?"

"Yeah," Aldair acknowledged reluctantly, "it works."

"Then, what are you in a sweat about, Aldair? Sounds exciting as hell to me. You and Krueger could be famous."

"Because it's wrong." Aldair slammed his open hand on the table. The sound was like a rifle shot to Burns and he jumped, but it was lost in the cacophony of the cafeteria. "You shouldn't tamper with people's dreams," the psychiatrist continued heatedly. "Dreams should be analyzed and studied. They are the key to the patients' problems."

"But if it works, Aldair—Christ! Nothing succeeds like success. If it works, they feel better. The patient is cured. Why in hell not use it?"

"Because you could accomplish the same thing with psychoanalysis," Aldair said pompously.

Burns suddenly assumed his more natural pose of studied indifference, the one in which he enjoyed deflating people who took themselves too seriously. He picked up a plastic knife and began toying with the soggy carrot slices left on his plate. "Now, Dr. Aldair" —Burns briefly considered calling him Dr. Kildare, the nickname hung on Aldair by the house staff and one, Burns knew, he detested—"surely you're not talking about analysis—I mean, good old-fashioned psychoanalysis?"

"You bet I am," Aldair said with almost religious fervor.

"Good God, an honest-to-goodness, real-life throwback." Burns chortled. "I didn't know there were any of you left in the world."

"There aren't many, that's for sure." Aldair leaned across the table closer to Burns, his voice dropping conspiratorially. "But it works, Burns, it really works; and it would work on these cases of Krueger's."

"Bullshit," Burns said, dropping the knife in what was left of his lunch. "I'm no psychiatrist, Aldair, but I can read, and I know damn well that analytic psychotherapy doesn't work on drug addicts and alcoholics. Even Freud admitted that."

"It takes a long time," Aldair offered softly. He wondered now why he'd even sat down with Burns, Burns the insouciant. He would henceforth cross him off his conversational list.

"What'd you say?" Burns asked.

"It takes a long time," Aldair repeated. "Freud said it takes a long time to cure alcoholics and drug addicts."

"How long? Burns tilted back, balancing the chair on two legs. His voice was mocking. "Ten years?"

"Maybe."

"Maybe! 'If you're lucky, *maybe* we'll cure you in ten years.' Is that what you'd tell them? Terrific! Hell, Krueger is doing it in fourteen days."

"Yes, but it won't last."

"Have it your way, Aldair, but you'd better stick with your chief. It may be that he has something. You could spend the rest of your life talking mumbo-jumbo to a couch. Haw!"

Aldair was still seething as he mounted the steps to his bachelor apartment three blocks from the hospital. Why had he allowed himself to be trapped by that insensitive Burns? The world, he guessed, was made up of two kinds of people: doers who did irreparable harm and those who did nothing.

Goddamn it, Krueger's approach was too simple, he had tried to tell Burns, too superficial. It was like giving morphine to a person with appendicitis. They'd feel better only for a while. That was just the way the mind worked. Hell, he'd been reading about REM sleep since Kleitman discovered it in 1953. It was interesting, granted, but it was just a passing fad. And cultists like Krueger, while indulging themselves, were postponing meaningful treatment, maybe denying it entirely. It was destined to go the way of Esalen, encounter groups, biofeedback, and primal-scream therapy. He had told Burns all those things, his voice rising to a pitch that had nearby diners staring. Burns, unfazed, had shrugged his shoulders, screwed up his prep-school face, and left Aldair to finish lunch by himself.

Aldair turned the key in the door and stepped into the small living room. "Hello, Ken! Hello, Ken!" came the squawk. Aldair glanced across the room at the caged parrot he had purchased last summer while on vacation. Aldair, the conversationalist, had taught the bird a rather extensive vocabulary. He was proud of that.

He threw his coat across the back of a chair and started for the kitchen. Krueger was merely engaging in chemistry, he had said, trying vainly to penetrate that damned Burns's none-too-nimble mind. "Psychopharmacy"—that's the word he had used. *Shit,* he thought, *nobody talks anymore. Psychiatrists don't talk; they give pills: antidepressants if you're down, tranquilizers if you're up. REM dreams—a bunch of crap. It's not only wrong, it's inherently evil.*

"Hello, Ken! Hello, Ken!"

"Shut your goddamn mouth!" Aldair shouted at the bird.

Chapter XVII

Klement stared at the ceiling while the lead wires were being attached to his moist skin. Aldair had only nodded on entering the sleep room, and Klement was puzzled that this man, who had very nearly talked him into an emotional breakdown the first night, was now going mechanically about his routine without uttering a word.

In fact, Aldair was mentally reconstructing his conversation with Burns in the hospital cafeteria, and it was refueling his anger. He could recall conversations the way some people remember entire symphonies or replay each move of a chess game, and now that it was too late, he was thinking of a brilliant riposte to Burns's deprecatory remarks.

Klement, though not as apprehensive as during the first few nights of sleep therapy, nevertheless was now the one who wanted conversational succor, some reassuring words. He looked at Aldair's bespectacled face for a sign. Aldair seemed to focus on him for the first time.

"Feeling OK?" the psychiatrist asked indifferently.

"Oh, yes, fine," Klement replied.

Aldair cocked his head equivocally to the side.

"Well," Klement amended, "actually just so-so."

"Yes, yes," Aldair now said crisply. "It's much too soon. But you did sleep well last night?"

"Yes, the best in years. No nightmares. I have to admit your stuff worked OK. But," he conceded, "I'm

130

still shaky during the day." He paused for a moment. "Uh, won't that get any better?"

Aldair pursed his lips. "To a point."

"I don't understand."

Aldair didn't answer directly. He laid a finger studiously alongside his cadaverous jawline, one cupped hand supporting the elbow of his other arm. "Why did you begin using barbiturates in the first place?" he asked suddenly.

"Well . . ." Klement began haltingly. The question had taken him by surprise. "Well, uh, it was four or five years ago that I started." He stopped as though that had answered the question.

"Yes?" Aldair prodded.

"I, uh, was nervous, tense—you know. I couldn't sleep. They worked at first, really helped. I don't understand why they didn't after a while."

"We've been all over that." Aldair's voice had an edge of exasperation. "Sleeping pills work only for a few weeks, until the REM pressure builds up. That's not my point, Dr. Klement."

Klement's eyes narrowed, his exasperation matching Aldair's. "Then, what specifically *is* your point, Dr. Aldair?"

"OK, I'll be specific. The best this sleep therapy can do is alleviate the REM pressure and help break your addiction. It will not remove the cause. The best you can expect is to be the nervous, tense person you were five years ago." He stopped, then said bluntly, "The one who became a drug addict."

Klement jerked his head sharply at Aldair and felt the tug of the encephalograph wires at his temples. His frown deepened. "What you're telling me is that even if I go through with this sleep therapy, there's a good chance I'll become addicted again?"

"A very good chance unless . . ."

"Unless?"

"Come, now, Dr. Klement, we discussed this last night, remember?

Klement said nothing. Aldair finished checking out the monitoring equipment, then moved to the foot of the bed and stood in contemplation for a long moment. Klement quizzically followed his movements. Slowly Aldair walked to the chair beside the bed and sat. He cleared his throat:

"Uh, Dr. Klement, you say you were so upset and nervous five years ago that you began using barbiturates. Tell me, what occurred at that time that prompted you to start taking drugs?"

"Nothing," Klement said after a moment's hesitation. "I mean, things were pretty good." He looked over at Aldair. "You know, personally and professionally. My practice was going well. Hell, I was doing fine."

"I see." Aldair's tone implied that he didn't believe Klement.

Klement caught the skepticism. "I mean, I don't know why I became nervous," he finished feebly.

The sleep room was deathly quiet as he waited for Aldair to say something. Klement realized suddenly that he welcomed the interrogation. The distant whine of a siren penetrated the ancient walls of the building. A tapping sound came to him, and his sideways glance took in the sight of Aldair, legs crossed, lightly striking a notebook with a pencil.

"I see," Aldair said again. "There is nothing in your childhood, your background, that could account for it? Your relationship with your parents? Your brothers, sisters?"

"I was an only child," Klement said quickly.

"Uh-huh. What about your parents? That is, how did you get along with them?"

Again quickly: "OK. I mean, fine."

Klement found he was vainly trying to pick up the sound of the tapping pencil, but there now followed long moments when his ears heard only the sound of his own breathing. He started to speak but only brought forth an unintelligible grunt. It elicited nothing from Aldair. Klement's eyes went to their corners again. Was Aldair taking notes? No, he sat there unmoving. Klement could sense rather than see the psychiatrist's mute intensity.

"Uh, well, sometimes I'd get edgy at my dad. He'd get me a little uptight and . . ."

"Yes? What did he do?"

"Oh, hell, you know, yell at me a lot."

"Why?"

"Oh, about my grades, disciplinary things, that kind of stuff. It was no big deal. He was my father, after all." Klement's next words were a vocal shrug, an afterthought. "He was a doctor, too."

"Try to remember, Dr. Klement. When you were young, is that the only time you can recall being nervous or upset—when you were around your father?"

"I don't know that you can say the *only* time." Klement hesitated before continuing. Then he said in a rush, "Most of the time." It came so quickly, it was slurred.

Aldair leaned forward. "Pardon me?"

"I said yes, most of the time when my dad came down on me for something, I would get upset." Klement's voice gained strength. "But I loved him; I respected him."

"Respect is not necessarily the same as love," Aldair said softly.

"He was a helluva guy," Klement said defiantly. "He was the most respected person I've ever known."

"And how about you? Are you respected?"

"What do you mean?"

"I mean, do your patients respect you, Dr. Klement? Do they respect you as a doctor?"

Klement's shoulders hunched ever so slightly on the white sheet. His hand rose slowly off the bed, then dangled limply at the wrist. "I suppose so," he said reflectively. "I mean, some do and some don't; that's the way it is."

"And your colleagues?" Aldair asked. "What do other physicians think of you?"

Klement's voice was softly sardonic: "Who the hell cares? They're jealous. They know I'm making twice what any of them—"

"We're talking about respect," Aldair cut in. "Your father was respected—apparently by most people, certainly by the medical community. Tell me why or, rather, in what way he was such a good doctor."

Klement didn't answer at once. "Well, for one thing, he was conscientious," he said finally. "Read his journals, worked hard; even though his patients didn't pay him, the government did. He'd stay up with them night and day, worry about them—you know, one of those completely dedicated guys." He gave a little snort, almost a frivolous chuckle, but his hands involuntarily curled into fists. "Took better care of them than he did of his own family."

Aldair watched as Klement busied the sheets with his hands. Then Klement went rigid. The movement was almost imperceptible. In a moment he relaxed as though the breath had gone from his body. His face took on a glacial composure, the brown eyes filmed over and distant. Not wanting to shatter the mood, Aldair raised his eyes to the wall clock without moving his head. It was still comparatively early, but he would have to start the treatment soon. It would be just his luck to have Krueger walk in on him. Just a few minutes more . . .

He leaned closer and repeated Klement's words back to him: "Better care of them than his own family."

There was no word or movement from Klement save for the slow blinking of his eyelids—once, twice.

"He took better care of them than his own family," Aldair said.

Again no response.

Aldair used the tip of his pencil to resettle his glasses

on the bridge of his nose and inhaled deeply. Then he asked softly but distinctly, "Dr. Klement, you really don't think of yourself as a very good doctor, do you?"

Klement's face gave no sign that he had heard the question, but he answered at once, his voice a low monotone: "I did at first. I mean, I tried. I wanted him to be proud of me. When I couldn't make it, couldn't be like him, I said the hell with it."

"You couldn't make it?"

"Oh, I made it through school—barely—but it wasn't good enough for him. He had gone to school here, too, and I kept hearing about him from all the professors: how he had been first in his class and had gone out to help the poor, how he was their most famous graduate."

Klement's voice had taken on an almost ethereal quality, as though he were talking to himself. Aldair quietly inched his chair nearer the bed to better make out the words.

"It was easier back then," Klement continued. "They mainly did a lot of mechanical things—taking out gallbladders and appendixes, draining abscesses. You didn't have to know so much. It was more doing than thinking." He was rambling now, the pace of his speech sluggishly decelerated. "Now all these drugs to know, cardiac monitoring, isotopes, committees watching you."

Aldair lowered his voice to Klement's level. "You're saying that when your father was a student and a physician, it wasn't as difficult?"

Klement did not reply but nodded his head slowly.

"And you think he was unfair to criticize you, especially when you were doing the best you could?" Aldair bent forward. His voice dropped to a near whisper, and he said conspiratorially, "Why didn't you just quit medical school?"

"I did. I told the dean I was quitting; but he talked me out of it. I'd already finished two years. He said to stick it out, since I was halfway through. And then he said, I'll never forget it, he said I could be a doctor

without being like my father. I decided right then I
would go ahead and finish."

Klement once again fell silent, and Aldair waited for
him to continue as he watched the long red second
hand twice sweep the face of the clock.

"Yes," Aldair said finally, looking back at Klement.
"You made a decision to be different from your father."

He waited for the denial, but none came. Klement
was asleep. Aldair could hear his soft palate vibrating
as he inhaled.

"Actually," he said quietly to the sleeping man, "you
hated your father, didn't you?"

Aldair was elated. Fantastic progress in such a short
time. He had not taken a note, and now he scribbled
furiously for several minutes. He glanced at the clock
again, then rose and walked quickly to the monitoring
booth. He must add the damned amitrypton to the I.V.
before the first REM dream.

Chapter XVIII

Joan Klement hesitated before pushing on the swinging
door leading to the kitchen. Oscar was in there, she
knew. She didn't know what to expect of him or how
she would react. She had seen him for only fleeting
moments since he had entered sleep therapy four nights
ago. On leaving the neuropsychiatry building each
morning, he had gone directly either to his office or to
the hospital. This morning it had been different. He
had come home just as she was awakening. She had
heard him rattling around in the bathroom off the

master bedroom but had said nothing. And then, to her amazement, she had felt his body slide in next to hers in bed. He had reached for her, running a hand down her bare shoulder and over the mound of one hip. She had feigned sleep, keeping her back to him, and tried to simulate deep breathing. He had eventually removed his hand, and she had heard his footsteps fade from the room. She had lain there for some thirty minutes sorting out her thoughts.

She took a breath, pushed open the door, and entered the huge kitchen, its walls painted a soft yellow that blended harmoniously with the dark wood casings that enclosed the cupboards and appliances.

Oscar looked up from the table in the breakfast nook and favored her with a smile. "Good morning," he said. The greeting was tentative.

"Hello, Oscar." She stood there for a moment saying nothing.

"Uh, I've got to be at the hospital soon," he said, "but, ah, I've got time for a cup of coffee with you."

"All right," she said guardedly, taking a seat opposite him as he reached for the automatic coffee maker and set a cup and saucer in front of her. While he poured, she kept her gaze directed on her cup, not daring to look up at his face.

"Well," he said, "what's new with you?"

Joan allowed herself to look into his large brown eyes. They were clearer than they had been in months. The treatment was restoring his dark good looks—that and the fact that he'd resumed regular racquetball sessions at the club.

"Oh, nothing much. Actually, Oscar, I should be the one to ask that question. How is the therapy going?"

"Good, Joan—great," he said with boyish enthusiasm. "I mean, it looks like it is the best thing I could have done. I'm beginning to feel like a tiger, really. It's miraculous. At first, you know, I thought that little shit Krueger had a screw loose somewhere, but, damn it all, he's really got something. I'm a convert. Hell, a week or so and I'll be as good as new."

She eyed him suspiciously. "No more pills?"

"Right. I've slept better the last week than I have in years."

"You mean, you haven't had one Seconal since you started therapy?"

"Not one, honest." It was said expectantly, like a child's search for approval.

Joan groaned inwardly. "Well, I'd say that's certainly encouraging."

Her voice was flat, the tone impossible for Klement to read. He searched her face for something else. She cleared her throat, her thumb slowly caressing the rim of the coffee cup. The overhead light caught the brilliance of the diamond ring on the third finger of her left hand.

"And how are things at the hospital . . . the office?" she said.

"Good, good," he answered quickly. "Busy as hell, like always. Not enough time in the day." He chuckled hollowly. "You know, Joan, I'd kiss off that medical center right this minute if I still didn't need them. I'm seriously thinking of opening my own place. Year or so, I think I could swing it. Might bring in a surgeon. The market's there. I can't keep up now. I whip this little problem and the sky's the limit. Bronson agrees with me that, hell, we have the facilities and the patients right now. We could incorporate. . . ." His eyes were bright with promise.

Bronson, that ass, Joan thought. She wondered what Oscar would say if she told him that his loyal partner had telephoned a few days ago like a common backyard gossip to tell her of another of Oscar's medical blunders. He had been solicitous, of course, and was only telling her "for Oscar's own good." The son of a bitch. He'd screw Oscar without a moment's hesitation. That snake pit of a clinic, she thought. One needed a scorecard over there to tell who was doing what to whom. For the moment, she felt strangely protective of Oscar.

"Oscar," she said, "I wouldn't put too much faith in Bronson. I mean, you were the one who built that practice to what it is and——"

"I can look after myself," he interrupted, "especially now. Bronson is small potatoes, Joan. I may buy the son of a bitch out. Shit, I don't need him any more than I do that lousy medical center. This is only the beginning."

He got up suddenly, depositing his dirty cup in the sink. The spoon rattled like a tambourine. Joan's wifely concern left her as quickly as it had come.

"Gotta go," he said. He scooped up his raincoat, which was draped over the chair, and started for the door, then stopped and turned. "Hey," he said, "maybe I could come home for lunch. I can break away for an hour or so from the clinic."

Joan looked at his face, colored slightly in what could have been a blush. Her gaze went quickly to the garden outside the window. "I'm afraid not, Oscar. I'll be extremely busy at work."

The red of his face was now that of anger. "Jesus, Joan, that job again. Why in hell are you still working? Working for those creeps!"

She sat straighter in her chair, her combative pose. "Oscar, we've been over this a dozen times. You said you didn't want me working around the medical center. It was the closest job I could find. It's only a thirty-minute drive. I enjoy it."

"I break my ass to make us a damn comfortable living and you have to run out every day to be a secretary to a couple of psychiatrists."

"I'm not a secretary." Her words were cold, decisive. "I'm almost a psychologist. I do their testing. They need me." She continued, her voice never rising. "You are damn well aware, Oscar, that if it weren't for you, I'd have my Ph.D. You're the one who——"

"OK, OK, it's my fault." He stopped talking and looked at his wife's rigid posture. "I just thought that now . . . you know, now that I'm feeling better . . . it would be nice to have you around once in a while."

She turned her head to look at him. "Around? You mean like for lunch today?"

"Well, why not? I mean, we used to."

"That was a long time ago, Oscar." Her eyes left him again. She could hear the floor creak slightly as he shifted his weight.

"Well," he said finally, "things are going to be different now, the way they used to be."

Her gaze stayed at the window.

"You hear me, Joan? Things are going to be different."

She turned to face him. "I heard you, Oscar. Things are going to be different." She knew she was being condescending.

Klement's face was rigidly set. He took a step toward her. "Yes, different, completely different, you and me. You're going to be here, at home, not running off——"

"Oscar, stop it." It was a tired, indifferent command. "This caveman posture is out of character. We've settled this already. I am not going to sit around here day and night knitting doilies and wondering what to wear to the medical-society Christmas dance. For the first time in years I feel like a real person, a person who——"

"Oh, God, that women's-lib shit again. It's OK to be the clinging dependent female while the jerk is out working all hours to get the house, the two cars, the country-club membership—all those comfortable little accouterments. It's——"

It angered her to hear her voice rising. She had not wanted to lose control. "Oscar, if I'm dependent, it's because you tried to make me that way. I've never given a damn about the country club or all the money."

"I didn't hear anybody bitching about it up to now."

"Maybe you weren't listening." How did this start? she wondered. She got up from the chair and spread her arms to her sides. "Look, Oscar, let's stop this. It's beginning to sound like a bad TV soap opera."

His finger pointed at her, only inches from her face. "You're quitting that goddamn job, Joan. I'm resigning for you. I'm calling Sam Morrison this afternoon and telling him you're quitting, effective immediately."

Furious, she grabbed the wrist of his extended arm. "Oscar, you bastard, you're still not listening. You don't own me, you understand? If there's any quitting to be done, I'll do it. You hear?" she shouted.

He had made no effort to pull from her grasp, but his face was angrily contorted. They stood there like the participants in a stalemated tug-of-war. She could feel a pounding behind her eyes. They both breathed heavily. Her voice, when it came, was a slow, guttural whisper:

"You hear me, Oscar? That job at the clinic is my business. It has nothing to do with you."

He wrenched his arm from her. "Yeah, some business. How in hell do I know what goes on over there? For all I know, you're giving the Morrison brothers a lot more than professional advice. What else you giving them, Joan? You must be giving it away someplace. You sure as hell aren't giving *me* any."

The words rushed from her like water from a ruptured dam: "I didn't think a junkie had time for such things."

Her head snapped sideways from the force of his open hand. She began to fall but was stopped by the edge of a counter that cut cruelly into her lower back. Tears obscured her vision. She sprawled across the top of the counter, spread-legged, with only her elbows preventing a collapse to the floor. Oscar hadn't moved. Joan had difficulty speaking around the numbness of her jaw:

"Well, Oscar, this is a side of you I've never seen. You're just full of surprises, aren't you?"

He looked at her fiercely. Was he capable of beating her up, of administering a good old-fashioned wife-beating? He looked ready to advance on her but then appeared to have second thoughts. He walked slowly backward to the door and was gone.

Joan righted herself. She stood for a moment, surveying the breakfast mess Oscar had left. Then she shrugged and walked from the room, one hand massaging the red blotch on the side of her face.

Chapter XIX

Donald Bradshaw was panting as he reached the end of his climb, and he took a moment to steady himself and allow his breathing to return to normal. The tree limb was not a secure perch, by any means, but he had to get high enough to be able to look down into the second-floor bedroom window. The huge elm tree must have been a hundred years old, the leaves and branches so thick as to seem almost impenetrable. He wrapped his legs around the limb, feeling the rough texture of the bark through his denim clothing. He groped for the trunk of the tree, settling his lower back against the crotch. Carefully he parted some smaller branches and looked into the darkness. It was a ritual to satisfy himself that he was invisible from the street.

Tonight he had arrived late at his lofty station. He had taken longer than usual to complete his rounds at the apartment house, where he ministered to his elderly neighbors. He had spent more than an hour with Mrs. Winslow. After examining her, he read Bible passages that were denied her by her sightless eyes. She was over ninety years old, and hearing him recite the Scriptures was comforting. He was preparing her to meet her Maker. He had left some sleeping pills with her with explicit instructions as to the maximum dosage. He was careful that Mrs. Winslow's final sleep would be only in the hands of the Lord.

Mrs. Winslow and his other "patients" were grateful, sometimes emotionally so. He still made house calls. He performed a valuable service. He thought of the arrogant so-called specialists at the medical center. They were more interested in making money and playing God with people's lives. So clinical, so cold. They walked the corridors of the hospital oblivious of the fact that there was only one true Healer. They dispensed no words of faith with their medicines. It was with considerable pride that he remembered Mrs. Winslow's words this evening as he prepared to leave her. "Dr. Bradshaw," she had said, her hand searching for his face, "you are a saint."

The honk of an automobile horn on the darkened street below brought Bradshaw back to the present. He cautiously bent back the branch in front of him to look down into the bedroom of Mrs. Mortimer, the promiscuous Mrs. Mortimer. There she was. He had missed her entrance. She stood in the middle of the room, her red hair a violent contrast to the blue housecoat. The red hair reminded Bradshaw of his mother, but the similarity stopped there.

He watched as Mrs. Mortimer took off her housecoat and sank to the floor. Then, as usual, she started slowly through her nude exercise routine. Arms at her sides, she swung one leg over the other and then reversed the process. Bradshaw saw her lips move as she counted off the required gyrations. This would be followed, he knew, by fifty sit-ups. He assumed the exercises were a nightly routine, although he seldom climbed the tree more than once a week. He had once stayed away longer after a neighbor's dog had noisily detected him. A quarter-pound of drugged meat had permanently silenced the dog a few nights later; but Bradshaw had been forced to postpone his visits until the small neighborhood stir over the animal's death had quieted down.

Mrs. Mortimer was jackknifing herself at the waist to touch her toes. The exercises apparently worked, for her body was firm and straight with no telltale middle-aged roll around the stomach. Bradshaw could see her large breasts beneath her outstretched arms. He had to take in a large gulp of air, the sound frighteningly loud in his ears. He exhaled carefully, expelling his breath in small bursts.

He felt a warmth of anger at Mrs. Mortimer. At first he had anonymously sent her religious tracts carrying a wide range of admonitions against a life of sin. Lately he had been mailing her handwritten notes specifically pleading with her to end her adulterous ways. He had once even followed her and her date of the evening. He had watched them plastered together, dancing at a roadhouse outside the city, and then followed them to a motel, where he had sat in his car for two hours waiting for them to come out. They had not, and he had to leave, as he was assigned to night duty at the pharmacy that week.

Mrs. Mortimer, flat on her back, now raised both legs straight in the air, balancing her upper torso with her hands on her hips. Bradshaw's fingers tightened around the limb. He wanted to put them around Mrs. Mortimer's throat and scream at her to repent. Maybe his next note should be to her husband, telling him everything.

Bradshaw peered closely at the luminous dial of his watch. It was difficult to make out the time. He wanted to make one call at the medical center yet tonight—

an old gentleman, an octogenarian, actually. Bradshaw had overheard two nurses talking about him the other day in the pharmacy. No family. Been hospitalized for months. Doctors made only perfunctory calls waiting for him to die. Bradshaw would have to detour to his apartment to pick up his Bible and his medical bag.

Mrs. Mortimer was on her feet, finished with her disgusting contortions. Bradshaw sat immobile as she walked across the room and turned out the light. She probably slept nude. Bradshaw didn't move from his leafy hiding place for several minutes. The lights of the room still danced in his eyes, and he waited until they were attuned to the blackness before making his way down the tree. The hand- and footholds were so familiar that he could descend strictly by feel; still, it was somewhat awkward with an erection that was almost painful. On reaching the ground, Bradshaw used his forearm to absent-mindedly adjust the bulge in his pants to a more comfortable position. Then he moved quickly across the deserted street and disappeared into the darkness.

—

Chapter XX

The man in the hospital bed had that hollow, consumed look. He had pulled the sheet up around his neck. His deep-set eyes, in concave sockets, circled the room before settling on Klement.

"But, Doc, this is my third trip in here, and I don't seem to be getting any better."

"I know," Klement said, looking down at his middle-

aged patient. "It gets discouraging, doesn't it? These
unspecified infections sometimes seem to hang on forever. I'm afraid you'll just have to be patient until it
runs its course. I think we'll try a different antibiotic
this time. Did you get any relief from your symptoms
with that last one?"

"Jeez, Doc, I don't know; it's hard to tell. I felt a
little better for a while, but I'm still sweatin' like a hog
at night. I got no appetite. And that damn cough . . .
The day before I come in here, I hacked up some
blood."

"That doesn't necessarily mean anything, Mr. Trumbull. If you cough hard enough, you can bring up a
little blood."

"This was more than a little, Doc. This was quite a
bit." The man ran a hand across his forehead, brushing
back strands of black hair flecked with gray.

Klement was reading the man's bed chart. "Hmmm,
yes. Perhaps we should get a few more X rays. But,
really, Mr. Trumbull, everything is being done than can
be." He hung the chart back on the bed. "I'll stop by
and see you tomorrow." Quickly he turned and left the
room.

"Thanks, Doc," he heard the man call after him. He
didn't answer.

Klement whistled tunelessly to himself as he walked
down the corridor.

"Hey, Klement! Oscar!"

He turned, to see that he was being followed by Grayson Merrill. "Oh, hello, Grayson." Klement stopped
and leaned against the wall. Merrill followed him, out
of the way of the traffic. Klement was a little surprised.
He and Merrill were on a cordial first-name basis, but
that was all. They certainly weren't friends. Merrill was
a surgeon principally known for fixing hiatus hernias.
As far as Klement knew, the only other thing he did
was play tennis. A short, wiry guy, Merrill bounced on
the balls of his feet when he walked. He always seemed

to be in a hurry. Klement almost had to put his chin on his chest to look into Merrill's eyes.

"Ah, Oscar, I've been meaning to have a little chat with you. . . . How's it going?" Merrill asked.

Klement eyed him carefully. "Fine, fine." Why the sudden interest in his welfare, especially from a guy like Merrill, who was just another medical-center white coat as far as he was concerned?

"I've been meaning to say for quite a while"—Merrill hesitated—"I mean, I wanted you to know that I am one guy who thinks you've been getting shit on around here."

"Oh?"

"Yeah, I know how it is. Hell, we've all made mistakes. I just think it's a shitty deal that they're making you the scapegoat. You don't goof up any more than the rest of us. These goddamn professors think this game is an exact science."

Klement was taken aback. Merrill's approach had been so unexpected, Klement suspected his motives. But the man seemed sincere enough.

"Why, thank you for saying that, Grayson. Ah, it's nice to know that maybe somebody is in your corner."

"Don't mention it. I know it's a little rough on you now, but it'll pass. I just wanted you to know how I feel. I was hoping I'd run into you someplace."

Klement didn't know what to say, but he was pleased. He wanted to add something besides his gratitude. "Tell you what, Grayson, maybe we could have dinner sometime. I mean, Joan and me and you and, er . . ."

"Mary Beth."

"Mary Beth, of course. What do you say?"

"Sounds super." Merrill broke into a smile. "Just great. We'll hoist a few and exchange gripes about the medical center. Well, I gotta run. I'll give you a call—soon."

Klement watched Merrill bustle down the corridor. He noticed absently that the doctor was wearing sneakers below his hospital coat. Klement had a warm feeling at this moment. He suddenly realized that he had no close men friends, had had no one since college, no one he could confide in, seek advice from, get close to. Joan hadn't filled that role in a long time. He walked slowly away. *Damn good guy, that Merrill; perceptive, too. Wonder how he ever fitted in with the rest of these assholes around here? You know,* Klement told himself, *Merrill may be just the guy to fill that surgeon's chair if I get my own hospital.* He would feel him out when they went out to dinner. *Trustworthy type, too, I'll bet. Wouldn't always have to be watching your back with him around.*

Charlie Rogers had watched the chance meeting from a nurses' station not far away across the corridor. He couldn't overhear the exchange, but the smiles on both Klement and Merrill told him it had been amiable. It figured that if anybody empathized with Klement, it would be that sappy Merrill. As a surgeon he would have made a superior bricklayer. Fortunately, Merrill never tackled anything that wasn't taught in the third year of medical school.

Rogers saw Klement disappear inside an elevator at the end of the hall. He wondered if Brailey had seen him since Krueger started putting him through the paces. The bastard sure looked his old perky self. As the elevator doors closed, Rogers ground his teeth together. "That guy should step in front of a truck," he said under his breath.

It was the tenth night in the sleep lab. Oscar Klement was relaxed but impatient to get to sleep. The nervousness in the room this night belonged to Aldair.

"But, Dr. Klement," he was saying, "we were doing so well. We were moving along at a gratifying pace."

Klement looked indifferently at the stooped, loquacious psychiatrist. "Hey, look, Aldair——"

"We were just beginning to get at the root of your problems," Aldair interrupted. He was bent at the waist, his upper body hovering over Klement's reclined figure, as though its movement would add persuasive emphasis to his contention.

Klement saw it as almost comical. The long, thin neck on the bobbing torso gave Aldair the appearance of a bespectacled crane tentatively picking its way across hot sand. Klement looked up, his face mildly agitated. He lay comfortably and felt almost at home in the sleep room. The restrictive wires were now but a minor annoyance.

"Aldair, I appreciate what you're trying to do, but I'm not sure what good it does for me to lie here and tell you about a lot of crap that happened twenty years ago."

Aldair was holding his notebook prayerfully with both hands. "The analysis will have a lasting effect, Dr. Klement, don't you see?" he said with forced patience. The sight of Klement's lips tightened skeptically prompted him to press home his point. "The progress is often slow, and it is difficult for the patient to measure it, but I can see it, I assure you. It is imperative that you continue. What has been accomplished is very encouraging, and to stop now would waste everything I—that is, we—have done so far." The words tumbled from his mouth one atop the other.

"I don't have that kind of time, Aldair," Klement broke in. "Besides, the deal with Krueger was that I'd come in for a couple of weeks for sleep therapy, for the drug thing, and damn it, it's working."

Aldair turned his head to the side. A grunt came from his lips. His voice was a capitulation. "Yes, it's working too well." An indulgent smile dawned at the corners of his mouth. "The wonder drug is working. It has reduced your anxiety. You don't feel the need to talk. You are calm, and you think everything is all right."

Klement's impatience grew. In his most sarcastic tone he said, "Tuck me in and turn out the light, Aldair. We'll talk some other time, OK? Yeah, I'm feeling good; what the hell's wrong with that?"

Aldair looked down at his wired patient. "But don't you think we——"

"No, I don't. Look, Aldair, I'm tired, sleepy." He turned his head on the pillow, looking away, adjourning the meeting.

Aldair stood wordless for a moment, looking down at Klement. "Very well," he said, starting toward the monitoring booth, "I'll start mixing your I.V."

"Make sure you mix it right," Klement called out. "Last night I woke up. I thought I was dreaming."

Aldair stopped and turned. "Are you certain?"

"Well, I'm not positive." Klement's voice was muffled by the pillow. "I woke up so damn sudden. But I thought . . . I could swear I was dreaming."

Aldair blinked behind his thick glasses and regarded Klement's back. Then he turned and entered the monitoring booth.

Chapter XXI

At the medical center, as at any teaching hospital, the afternoon hour of five is significant. That is when assistant, associate, and full professors, along with the attending staff, flee to their suburban enclaves and the house staff takes over. From that hour until eight o'clock the next morning, the medical center belongs to the residents and interns. Medical-school professors and chiefs, while not paid as well as their counterparts in private practice, do have shorter working hours and no night calls. It is an advantage they exploit.

During the day, most of the routine decisions are made by the attending staff and professors. That's when the treatment programs are outlined, surgical decisions are made, antibiotics are selected, and X rays, lab studies, operations, spinal taps, and bone-marrow exams are carried out. And since ninety percent of the decisions made in a hospital are routine, the system works for the majority. It works especially well for the professors, who can leave at five o'clock, confident there is someone watching over their patients.

Unfortunately, many people become suddenly and critically ill during the night. Then the decisions fall to the house staff—the residents and interns. The average medical professor or attending physician is in his fifties, while the average intern or resident is in his mid- to late twenties. Plenty of enthusiasm remains within hospital walls at night, but less experience; thus it often happens that many of the critical life-and-death decisions are made by those with the least experience—a fact that accounts for the public's charge that hospitals are run for the convenience of the physicians and not the patients. Another reason the young house staff is in complete control is the unwillingness of any of them to admit they need help. Owing to their small number, everyone knows everyone else, which breeds a competition among them and an arrogance that each chief resident can handle any crisis that arises on his particular service.

Thus, the gastroenterology residents handle G.I. bleeders, bowel obstructions, and perforations; the hematology residents, the bleeding hemophiliacs. Neurology residents treat the epileptics, pitting their wits against the dreaded seizures. Acute infectious diseases, from meningitis to pneumonia, fall to the resident of the infectious-diseases service. Late-night emergency

surgery is done by surgical residents, while anesthesi-
ology residents keep the patients asleep.

This night had been a quiet one for Joe Burns,
though not by accident. Four years of residency at the
medical center had taught him the art of delegating
work (some called it sloughing off). Burns was coast-
ing on the downhill side of his long training period and
was feeling rather good about himself. It was now the
month of May; in a little less than two months—July 1,
to be exact—he would be finished, he told himself, and
residents would then start doing his scut work for a
change.

It would be a high-water mark for him. God, what was
it—thirteen years? Four years of pre-med, four more
of medical school, a year of internship, and a four-year
residency in internal medicine and cardiology. Thirteen
years! And now, finally, in less than eight weeks he
would be an internist-cardiologist.

Ironically, even while Burns counted the days, he
still hadn't decided where he would practice. He had
been offered a position here at the medical center, an
assistant professorship. Lots of prestige, but no promise
of riches, Burns knew. Ironic indeed, he thought as he
finished his nightly rounds, that after thirteen years he
should now have so brief a time to make up his mind
about his niche in the medical world, a niche that he
would probably occupy for a lifetime.

He started and ended his rounds in the usual place,
at the coronary-care unit, partly because the CCU was
his home base, but primarily because the handling of
cardiac arrests was his responsibility. He was the leader
of the shock team that answered the "Code MAX"
calls. Code MAX was the chilling summons that galvanized Burns's crew into sudden movement. It told him
that somewhere in their building a human being was
suffering a life-threatening cardiac arrhythmia or arrest.
The hospital's paging operator would intone "Code
MAX" and then follow with the floor or room number.

It was the signal that meant Burns and his team members went to work, on the run.

Each team member followed a disciplined procedure that now had become almost automatic. Each cardiac emergency also served as another rehearsal for the team, which, as a result, had become a finely tuned machine. Their emergency runs were now crisp mechanical exercises. And they were fast. They converged on the stricken patient like rain-soaked commuters catching the last bus to the suburbs. Each lifesaving task was carried out by about a half-dozen people and with a minimum of talk. Burns had experienced emergency runs where literally nothing was said by anyone during the first several minutes.

Burns loved the coronary-care unit. It had an atmosphere of hushed expectancy. He likened it to something an uncle, a former World War II carrier pilot, liked to describe to him—the exciting tension before the shipboard Klaxon blared. "Pilots, man your planes." All that could be heard in the room was the blips from the cardiographs and the hissing ventilators. When someone did speak, it was softly, so as not to miss a heartbeat. Burns loved the action.

So it was this night as he and one of the team nurses talked of their future together—or lack of it—while each held one ear cocked for the commands of the paging system.

Burns had just been stunned by Nurse Stephanie Copaulis's refusal to marry him. They were in the "conference" room, a euphemism for the coffee and meeting area adjacent to the CCU. It was used mainly for a haven from the quiet tension of the cardiograph blips. The stark green walls of the small room seemed to be closing in on Burns. He ran his fingers through his coarse, wavy hair.

His affair with Stephanie had begun over a year ago, starting in the usual doctor-nurse manner, not very dissimilar from the liaisons of other couples whose job pressures threw them together: the executive and the secretary, the airline pilot and the stewardess. In the pressure cooker of the cardiac-care unit, with death a constant specter, sex became an affirmation that one still lived. The beleaguered Russian defenders of Stalingrad, Burns remembered reading, had thrown themselves into a last, desperate sexual orgy when they were told there was no hope of rescue from the German encirclement.

He had in fact "inherited" Stephanie from the previous chief cardiology resident. Incredibly, despite her intelligence and wit, she had accepted it as the natural course of events. Just last week the assistant cardiology resident had asked, "Burns, you bastard, you going to will Stephanie Big Tits to me when you go?" Two other jealous residents had leered, and Burns had found himself bothered and strangely angered. He had been screwing Stephanie in his usual casual manner, but his thinking lately had undergone a remarkable change. The thought of passing her on to someone else now was intolerable. Did that mean he loved her? He thought it did. The completion of his residency was a watershed. It was time to marry and get on with things.

Their affair had been so casual he did not know quite how to bring up the subject. Most of their time alone was spent either making love or laughing. He had mentioned marriage only jokingly at first, and she had parried his joke with one of her own. Tonight he had made it plain that he was serious, and he was dismayed at her rejection.

"No, Joe,," she said, not unkindly. "You're a nice guy and a terrific lay, lover, but let's face it—we could never make it on a full-time basis." When Burns opened his mouth to protest, she held up her hand and continued, "We've had some goddamn good times, and I like you; but, Doctor, I don't know if you've got the time to love anybody." Then, after a pause: "And I don't know if I have the capacity."

His broad face was a question mark. He was surprised at the sinking feeling in his stomach. No more—is that what she was saying? Now he really wanted her. The physical memories almost brought tears to his eyes. Standing almost as tall as Burns's five-ten, Stephanie was magnificently endowed above the waist. Her hair was a soft blonde—belying her Greek heritage—so expertly dyed that it had been only a few weeks ago in bed that Burns had discovered its jet-black roots.

"Look, Steph," he implored, "give yourself a little time. I don't think you yourself even know how you feel about me. Steph, I love you. I mean, I really do. I——"

"Hush, lover," she said, taking a quick step forward and reaching under his white hospital coat to cup his testicles in her hand. "We can still be friends." A smile crossed her face. The color applied to her full lips passed the limits of what the head nurse would think was decorous.

"Goddamn it, Steph——"

He stopped in midsentence. The cool, detached voice of the paging operator came from the speaker above their heads: "Dr. Cunningham, 407 North. Dr. Cunningham, 407 North." They relaxed and looked at each other again. Others of the CCU team had left several minutes ago when they had ascertained the personal tone of the conversation.

"Look, Steph," Burns started again, "let's talk about this later." He could think of nothing else to say.

"Yes, Joe, let's do that."

They looked at each other for a moment without speaking. Burns was sitting on the edge of a white utility table. A college jock, he had the subtle agility of an athlete and was balancing his fullback's body with one foot off the floor when the paging operator intruded on both their thoughts. He had never met her, but her voice was as familiar to him as that of the girl who had just refused his offer of marriage.

The operator had called him constantly these past few years: to the telephone, to direct him to call a certain floor, to hurry to the emergency room. She was the unseen foster mother of them all. She commanded with a firm, authoritative voice that was smooth, unhurried, and never hesitant—except this time. "Code MAX . . ." she began.

At those words, both of Burns's feet came to the floor, and Stephanie tensed. Then there was silence, a paging phenomenon that Burns had not heard in all his years at the medical center. The location of the emergency hadn't come. Instead, they were able to hear the operator *sotto voce* over the open mike: "I've never heard of that . . . that floor. Where?" Burns and Stephanie stood on the balls of their feet, poised for the words that would send them to the trouble spot.

"Code MAX. Code MAX," it came again, now with more authority. "Uh, the sleep-therapy clinic, second floor of the neuropsychiatry building."

Burns and Stephanie were out the door even as the operator, following hospital rules, twice repeated the message. The two were now joined by the other team members, who poured from the door of the coronary-care unit. Burns could see that some were puzzled by their unfamiliar destination.

"The crash cart's ready," one of them shouted at Burns. "Let's go."

It was obvious to Burns that he was expected to lead them. "Where in hell did she say?" he heard one of the team members puff behind him. Despite their desperate situation, Burns was forced to smile. It was doubtful that any of them had ever been in the neuropsych building. He knew he never had.

In their momentary directionless confusion, no one had thought to run ahead and open the elevator door. Burns felt foolish as hell pushing the "down" button, but there was no other choice. The fragile crash cart could not be taken down the stairs. Waiting for the elevator, the team members peered sheepishly at one another. The finely tuned machine had ground to a halt. Though the hotshots had responded to hundreds of cardiac arrests, they now found themselves left temporarily impotent by the mere logistics of getting to the site of the emergency.

It was only seconds later that the elevator arrived and they were able to descend to the ground floor. They spilled out the front door in a rush. It was another block to the neuropsych building. Everybody was at a dead run, cohesion sacrificed to the expedient of speed. Behind Burns, several team members had carried the crash cart down the outside front steps of the hospital, completely forgetting the wheelchair ramp only twenty feet away.

Burns was still in the lead—barely—when he chugged, gasping, to the main entrance of the neuropsych building. A young lady in a light-blue receptionist's uniform, her face ashen, was holding the door open. The team followed her down the hall to a rickety elevator, which groaned and creaked as it lifted at a maddeningly slow pace to the second floor.

Burns took only a moment to take in the surrealist surroundings of the sleep laboratory. He stared down at the bed as the cardiac team gathered around him. The scene immobilized them. The man in the bed had arrested; that much was obvious, but nothing else was like anything they had ever encountered before. Familiar was the waxy-colored body, wet with perspiration, and the man's pupils were dilated and staring straight ahead, but there were a dozen wires snaked around his head and gathered together at a point above the bed where they disappeared into the wall. Aldair stood rigidly at the other side of the bed, his eyes, magnified enormously by his thick glasses, riveted on the still male form. His outsize hands dangled from tiny wrists beneath sleeves that had shrunk from too many washings in the hospital laundry.

Burns looked stupidly at the wired man, remembering the TV reruns of Frankenstein movies he had seen as a boy. The stunned team members in turn looked at Burns for some kind of signal.

"What in hell is going on here, Aldair?" he asked.

Aldair looked up, the color of his face matching that of his coat. "I don't know," he said lamely. "I mean, he was OK when he came in here. I have no idea what happened."

"He's already got an I.V. running," said one of the team nurses.

"What's in it?" Burns asked Aldair.

"It's nothing. I mean, it's just a five percent dextrose solution in water. It con . . . con . . . contains a . . . a medication," he stammered.

"What kind of medication, for God's sake?" *Christ, psychiatrists!* Burns thought. A *real* doctor would have used abbreviations to save time.

"Well, it's a new drug. It's being used here in the sleep-therapy clinic. It's for people who——"

"Damn it, man, we don't have time for lectures."

"Well, it's called amitrypton," Aldair said dazedly, "and it's for——"

"Pull it," Burns commanded the nurse, "and start I.V. ringer's solution wide open." He yanked the stethoscope from his pocket and bent over Oscar Klement's chest, desperately listening for heart tones. "Any pressure?" he asked.

"None," came the reply.

"Pulse?"

"None."

Burns reached under Klement's hospital gown with his stethoscope and encountered the tapes and wires. "What in hell?" he muttered to himself. "Steph, cut this goddamn gown."

She snipped the string tie around Klement's neck and with one motion ripped the gown down and off his arms.

"Jesus, EKG leads," Burns said. He looked around the room. "But where's the cardiogram machine?" He looked at Aldair. "Where do all these fucking wires go?" The last question came out as a shout.

"In the next room," Aldair replied. "We monitor them from there."

"What does it look like?"

"What does what look like?"

"The EKG, for Chrissake! What does it show? Ventricular flutter? Fibrillation? Standstill?"

Aldair stared at Burns uncomprehendingly. "Well, you see, we in psychiatry—that is, I don't read EKGs very well. We're interested only in the brain waves, the EEG."

Burns thought he would jump out of his skin. The sparring with Aldair had taken only seconds, but he felt as if he'd already been in this room half of his life. "Was it a straight line?" Burns reduced the questioning to layman's terms.

"No," Aldair said. "I think it was kind of a wavy line."

"Kind of a wavy line? Goody." Burns ripped off the chest leads. "Switch this monitor on and grease up the paddles," he commanded. "We'll get our own EKG readout."

He turned his back to the bed and grabbed the paddles from the lifepak monitor-defibrillator. He held them upside down as Stephanie poured electrode paste on their round, glistening surfaces. The mayonnaise-like material oozed out of the plastic squeeze-bottle.

"Is the ringer's solution running OK?"

"Yes," the nurse told Burns, "wide open."

"Then, give two amps bicarbonate."

"Already started one," she said. "Are your paddles ready yet?"

Burns didn't reply. Even at this moment he was placing each paddle in its carefully preassigned area over the heart. The team members all turned to stare at the monitor at the foot of the bed.

"Vee fib," Burns said. "Let's zap him."

Stephanie carefully pushed two large buttons on the monitor in sequence. "OK, it's charged," she said calmly. "How much do you want?"

"Three hundred-watt seconds. He's a big one."

Burns, paddles still in place on Klement's chest, began inching his feet backward, away from the side of the metal bed. He looked quickly down at his feet to make sure the floor was dry. He had been burned—literally—once before. Each team member followed his example.

"OK, everybody, here we go," Burns announced. He gently brushed the trigger and looked around. "Aldair," he shouted, "get your hand off the bed!"

Aldair, standing at the head of the bed, seemed to be leaning against it. He was staring at Klement, seemingly not hearing Burns. One of the nurses grabbed him from behind under each elbow. Aldair stumbled slightly as he retreated to safety. Burns pressed the trigger.

Klement's body heaved under the paddles, his back forming an arch over the bed. The massive contraction of skeletal muscles seemed to bring him to convulsive life.

Burns wheeled to look at the monitor oscilloscope behind him. "Hot damn!" he said. "Sinus rhythm. Look at that beautiful pattern."

The eyes of the team were glued to the monitor.

"Give him another amp of bicarb," Burns told the I.V. nurse.

"I already did."

"Got a blood pressure?" he asked Stephanie.

"Sixty over forty."

"Not very good." Burns frowned. "Pulse?"

"Barely. It's really thready," Stephanie informed him.

"How are the pupils?"

"Still dilated," she said.

"Is he breathing on his own at all up there?" Burns asked the new anesthetist nurse. He couldn't remember her name right now, but she had done a hell of a job on the endotracheal intubation, slickly sticking the curved tube down the throat into the windpipe in the first thirty seconds of their arrival. She had not suffered from the temporary mesmerization of the rest of the team.

She stopped bag-breathing Klement for fifteen seconds. "No," she told Burns, "no spontaneous respirations."

"Things should be better," he observed, "considering."

"Considering?" It was Stephanie.

"Considering we've got such good electrical function. Hell, he's in a steady sinus rhythm at ninety a minute. You can't beat that."

As if to mock Burns, the evenly spaced blips were interrupted by one appearing too soon, followed by two more rapid premature blips, a pause, then a resumption of the steady blip pattern. Burns, the paddles still in his hands, had his back to the monitor. "What are they?" he asked.

"Ventricular," Stephanie answered quickly.

Burns's eyes were locked on the monitor. Ten seconds later another premature ventricular contraction occurred. It was quickly followed by three in a row.

"Get out the lidocaine," he ordered. "A one-hundred-milligram bolus straight in the vein and two grams in the I.V. bottle."

"Two grams?"

"Yeah, I'm a natural pessimist. I think we're in deep shit with this one." Burns watched the premature contractions occur after every second or third natural beat. "What's the lidocaine situation?" he asked over the sound of the popping of ampules, his eyes never leaving the monitor.

"The bolus is in," he was told. "The I.V. in two seconds."

"Good. What's his pressure now?"

"Forty over twenty-eight."

"That figures." Burns knew the premature ventricular contractions were lethal. They were wasted beats, occurring so soon after the preceding one that there was no time for the ventricle to fill with blood. And the abortive premature beats didn't contribute to the blood pressure. Also, the irritable ventricle was very likely to fibrillate again. "Another one-hundred-milligram bolus of lidocaine," he ordered.

"Coming up."

The premature beats started to occur less often: every sixth or seventh, then every tenth. Finally they disappeared.

"What's the pressure now?"

"Back to sixty over forty."

"Something else is wrong, damn it," Burns said. "He's probably infarcted. Cardiogenic shock now."

He took his eyes off the monitor for the first time in what seemed like hours to look at his watch. Despite everything, including Aldair's hesitant answers, they had been in the room only five minutes. You never got completely used to it, Burns thought. He could feel the perspiration soaking the back of his shirt, tiny rivers of sweat forming pools at the waistband of his pants. It had been a long five minutes. He stretched, trying to loosen his tense back and neck muscles.

"Call the CCU and get him a bed," Burns said wearily to Stephanie. "He sure as hell's no rose, but it looks like he's as good as he's going to get for a while. He's at least stable enough to be moved. Transfer him to Brailey's cardiology service." He turned to Aldair, who still stood on the spot where he had been pulled by the nurse. "Whose service is he on now?" Burns asked him.

"Dr. Krueger's," Aldair answered almost inaudibly.

Burns, who had treated Aldair a little roughly, now felt a touch of pity for the stunned psychiatry resident. "This one of your experimental cases?" he asked.

"Yes."

"Well," Burns said, "I don't think this man's problems had anything to do with that. He had a myocardial infarction, a heart attack—nothing your boss can blame you for."

Aldair said nothing for a moment. He was still staring at Klement's comatose form, his expression denoting he was not at all calmed by Burns's reassurance. "Do you think he'll make it?" he asked finally.

Burns shook his head. "No, I doubt it. Even when we had the heart in shape electrically—in sinus rhythm —it still couldn't maintain his blood pressure. That's a bad sign. Not enough heart muscle left to do the job." He gazed intently at the other man, who looked right now as though he, too, might have a heart attack. "You OK?" Burns asked. When Aldair didn't answer, he said slowly, "Tell me, after you discovered he'd arrested, what did you do?"

"Well," Aldair began tentatively, "I called the hospital operator and told her to page your group."

"I know that, but then what did you do?"

"Well, I waited."

Burns didn't know what to say next. He was torn between empathy for the poor bastard—out of his element as a psychiatrist—and rage that anyone who called himself a doctor did not at least try cardiopulmonary resuscitation. Shit, most firemen and Boy Scouts would have done at least that much. A heart attack feeds on itself. A small artery becomes blocked, not enough to do any significant damage, but it screws up the electrical-conducting system. Then the pump stops temporarily, and the pressure of blood through the coronary artery is even lower, and blockage increases. Just a few pushes on the chest—sometimes a single blow—can break the fatal cycle.

Burns sighed and decided not to give Aldair a lecture. The poor shithead was suffering enough. Why chew his ass now? His chief would chew it plenty later.

Burns's thoughts were interrupted by Stephanie. "More premature ventricular beats," she informed him. "Want another bolus?"

He looked at her for a moment. He'd proposed marriage to this woman just a short while ago. It seemed like a million years. "Yeah, hundred milligrams," he told her.

Stephanie popped the ampule and was drawing in the lidocaine before Burns finished the order; but within two minutes the premature beats increased again.

"Seven milligrams a minute on the I.V. lidocaine," Burns said, "and one more bolus." He did not dare give more. Lidocaine was a potent medicine that decreased the heart's irritability. A familiar pattern now danced across the oscilloscope. Every other beat was now premature.

"Bigeminy," Stephanie said softly.

"Yeah," Burns muttered, his voice betraying a resignation.

They both fell silent for a moment as they watched the erratic movie of Klement's losing fight.

"Blood pressure?" Burns's voice was barely a whisper.

"A few beats in the low twenties."

"What the hell," he said, "turn the lidocaine wide open."

"He'll convulse," Stephanie said.

Members of the team were looking at Burns like supporters of a politician who had just fallen one vote short of election. Their hands hung at their sides.

Burns shrugged. "I haven't seen a good convulsion all week." He said it grimly with no pretense at humor.

Somewhere behind the closed door of the sleep room, they could hear loud voices and the heavy sounds of people running. The noise reverberated through the corridors of the old building. The faint whine of a siren could be heard.

A nurse went to the door. "They're here to take him to the CCU," she said.

"Tell them to wait there until he's stable enough to be moved," Burns told her.

"You're shitting, lover," Stephanie said close to his ear. "You expect him to get stable?"

"Death is stable," Burns answered quietly.

The nurse at the door turned again. "They want to know how long before he's stable," she called out to Burns.

"Not long, not long at all." He glanced over again at the oscilloscope just in time to see that the heart rate had shot up. The blips looked like the waves of a storm-tossed sea. "Ventricular tachycardia," he said. He turned around, and Stephanie handed him the paddles.

"Three hundred watts again?" she asked.

"Why not? It worked before," Burns said without enthusiasm.

Once again Klement's body jerked violently upward as the electricity raced through him. Burns turned. There was not a sound in the room. The blips had stopped. The wild, chaotic heart rhythm had been replaced by a single thin line in the exact center of the scope.

"Straight-lined," Burns said.

He decided to play out the charade. Stephanie read his mind and handed him a syringe of adrenaline with an intracardiac needle. The stiletto-like syringe gleamed under the harsh overhead light. Burns plunged the six-inch needle through the chest wall. He advanced it slowly, simultaneously pulling back on the syringe to maintain suction. The syringe began to fill rapidly with blood from the ventricle. Burns's signal to push in the massive dose of adrenaline.

He had never seen intracardiac adrenaline work. He had never heard of it working anywhere anytime before. He had never read a case report where it had worked. It didn't work this time, either.

Burns looked down at the now blood-spattered corpse and then at Aldair. He didn't know who looked worse. "Look Aldair," he said, "I'll call your boss. Take it easy. I'll tell him you did everything you could."

"Oh, God," Aldair said, breaking his long silence. "We've never had anything like this happen before." He looked up at Burns. "Never anything like this."

Burns was growing weary of the man's hand-wringing helplessness, and he was tired.

"God," Aldair said, "he's a doctor, too."

Burns turned back quickly to look at Oscar Klement's pale body. "Hey, I *thought* the guy looked familiar. Who is he?"

"A G.P.," Aldair mumbled. "He's a G.P. at the medical center."

"Was," Burns corrected him.

Chapter XXII

"Dead? How could he be dead? I don't understand." Krueger, roused from sleep, had heard Klement's name clearly, but the news had caught him unprepared and he could not easily associate death with the man he'd seen only a few days before.

"That's right—dead," Joe Burns repeated into the telephone.

"What in the world happened?"

"He had a coronary, Doctor."

"A heart attack? That's impossible." In his mind's eye, Krueger saw the steady drip of the amitrypton into Klement's veins.

"Why is it impossible?"

"Never mind," Krueger said quickly. "Uh, how can you be sure it was a coronary?"

"It couldn't have been anything else. We tried to resuscitate him. Did closed-chest massage until we could get him hooked up to an EKG. He showed a little residual vee fib, so we zapped him twice, but then he straight-lined."

"Zapped him?"

"Yeah, you know, electrical countershock. It was no use, though. He just kind of shuffled off."

" 'Vee fib,' " Krueger said haltingly, almost to himself. "That's ventricular fibrillation." He paused before asking Burns, "Where is Dr. Aldair?"

"Well, he was here, Doctor, but he's not here right now." Burns lied, his glance going to Aldair, who was sitting in a corner chair, his face still registering his shock. "He helped us work on the guy." Burns turned the conversation away from Aldair. "Actually, there wasn't much electrical activity before we zap—er, shocked him. He had probably arrested twenty to thirty minutes before we got here."

"But how is that possible? Didn't anybody notice him? He couldn't have just——"

"Well, I saw you had him wired up to an EKG," Burns said, "but Aldair said you guys don't actually monitor it. I mean, you don't have any alarm systems that go off or anything."

"But he didn't have a heart condition," Krueger interrupted. "It's only a sleep laboratory, not a coronary-care unit. We monitor the heart only because of our research interest. We've never had any kind of trouble." Krueger wondered why he was being apologetic. "Ah, to whom am I speaking, please?"

"Oh, sorry. This is Dr. Burns, Joe Burns. I'm the

chief cardiology resident. I cover the cardiac arrests for the shock team."

The phone lines hummed momentarily as neither man said anything.

"Look, Dr. Krueger—sir," Burns began, "I know this must be upsetting to you, but believe me, a lot of people die in their sleep of coronaries, and they haven't all been diagnosed as having a heart condition. This guy just happened to be in your sleep lab at the time, that's all."

When Krueger didn't respond, Burns went on: "Ah, Dr. Krueger, I might suggest that we call Dr. Brailey. This guy was a doctor, and he did die in the hospital. I think we'd better post him."

"What?"

"Post him. An autopsy."

"Oh. Oh, yes, certainly, by all means."

"Just a formality," Burns said. "We should be able to document a coronary pretty well."

"Look, Dr. Burns, your EKG was really that certain?"

"Pretty much. Anyway, your EKG printout should show all the cardiac events leading up to the arrest."

"Of course," Krueger replied, now brusquely. "Well, Dr. Burns, I trust that you will do everything your training and experience tell you to do in these matters. But please don't touch anything—I mean, as far as the sleep lab is concerned. Leave everything just the way it is. I'm coming down."

"That really won't be necessary," Burns said. "I can take care of everything here. I sent the kid in the other sleep room home. Didn't tell him what happened. The widow's on the way in. I'll handle it. We'll post him at nine o'clock this morning."

"Very well, Dr. Burns. Thank you."

"Don't mention it, Dr. Krueger. I'll get back to you as soon as we get the results of the post. Good-by."

Krueger slowly replaced the receiver. He drew the

bed covers over his slight frame and cursed silently. Krueger never used profanity aloud. *Damn it to hell! Son of a bitch! Damn, damn, damn!* "A lot of people die in their sleep of coronaries," Burns had told him. *But that's during REM sleep, damn it,* Krueger told himself.

The clicking of the clock radio next to his head grew louder as he lay in the darkness chewing on his frustration. To lie awake in the middle of the night was nothing new to Krueger. He was an insomniac himself. He could imagine the jokes around the sleep lab if that were to become known. Truth was, he rather enjoyed insomnia. After three or four hours of sleep, he awoke refreshed, his mind turning over slowly with renewed vigor. He often used the occasion to read or write. Some of his most productive ideas came in those quiet predawn hours.

This time, however, his alert brain was muddled by the anxiety brought on by Burns's call. So Klement had died in the sleep lab—*his* sleep lab. Krueger found himself bitterly resenting the dead man, who had thrown his orderly study into confusion. *How could you, Klement, you bastard?*

Krueger regarded Klement's death as a personal affront. The research was his monument. He had set up the laboratory. He had arranged the layout, the monitoring room bisecting the sleep rooms; he had assembled and trained the staff, taking Aldair under his wing, counseling him, affording him the opportunity to participate in something truly momentous. Where the hell had Aldair been when all this happened? Why hadn't *he* called him instead of this Burns fellow, who spoke in an alien tongue? *Vee fib; zapping . . .*

Krueger suddenly sat upright and reached for his trousers. The answers, he told himself, would not come to him in bed.

* * *

The headlights of his car hit the side of the neuropsychiatry building, and Krueger was amazed to see that not one light shone from any of the windows. There was no other car in the lot. He had expected to see people milling about. The outside door was locked. Fortunately, he had thought to bring his key. A three-quarter moon in a cloudless sky made it easy to see the keyhole.

He walked quickly to the monitoring room, not bothering to turn on any lights along the way. The building was more foreboding than he had ever remembered it. He switched on a light in the monitoring room, the clack of his footsteps still echoing back at him from the outside hall. He walked into each sleep room and switched on the lights, squinting at their brilliance. He was utterly alone. The bed in one of the sleep rooms was a mess, blood spots spattered on the sheets. Klement's room, he surmised. He walked back to the monitoring room and looked through the one-way window into the other sleep room. Although the bed had been used, the bedclothes were tidy. *My teenage narcoleptic,* he reminded himself.

Back in Klement's room, he gazed at the two I.V. bottles hanging on their poles at each side of the bed. One of the bottles was marked "lactated ringer's solution." The second bore the inscription "5 percent glucose in water with one gram (1,000 milligrams) of amitrypton." This one he lifted from its pole and took with him as he strode quickly back to the monitoring room. There, noticing that both the EEG and EKG printouts were still in place in the machines, Krueger sighed. "Ah, thank God." Then he walked hurriedly to his office on the third floor.

Krueger put the I.V. bottle and the electrocardiogram printout on a shelf but threw the electroencephalogram paper on his desk. He sat down and bent over the EEG printout. He had been prepared to study it in his usual methodical manner, slowly turning the pages as he followed one line at a time, but now he found himself ripping at it as he would an unexpected telegram. Since the recordings were printed on a continuous sheet, there was more than thirty feet of paper about eight inches wide. It had been folded into booklet form in such a way that each page of the "book" represented ten minutes of Klement's brain electricity.

The first five pages registered theta waves, 13 to 15 cycles per second. Klement had been wide awake for 50 minutes. Nothing unusual in that, Krueger told himself.

On the sixth page—at the 53-minute mark—the waves began slowing to 8 to 11 cycles per second. Alpha waves finally, he noted. Though Klement was still awake at this point, alpha waves were a prerequisite for sleep. They represented the relaxed state of mind before the subject drifted off.

Krueger turned the page and saw that at the 62nd minute, only 9 minutes after alpha, Klement had entered stage-one sleep and was quickly descending into deeper sleep. By the middle of the page—at the 65th minute—he had dropped to stage-four sleep, and the brain wave had slowed to 1 to 3 cycles per second. At the 69th minute, 7 minutes after Klement had fallen asleep, Aldair had penned a notation on the EEG tracing: "amitrypton started." Krueger's fingers trembled slightly as he turned the page.

At the 71-minute mark—only 9 minutes after sleep had been achieved—Klement had rapidly ascended from his deep, stage-four sleep and had entered the REM period. Unbelievable, Krueger thought excitedly. Instead of the normal 90 to 100 minutes until the first REM period, Klement had had no more than 9 minutes. Krueger had never witnessed the recording of such REM pressure.

The EEG recording of the eye movements was wild.

The so-called REM-density pattern told a story of racing eye movements—a 33-rpm record played at 78 speed. Krueger's breath quickened. Klement's brain was playing out no ordinary dream. Its electrical conduits had gone mad. That marvelous human computer was smoking, short-circuited by its frenzied nightmare. Krueger's mind had lapsed into the present tense, and he was with Klement during his last moments on earth. He began turning the pages more quickly, looking for some relief, wanting an end to Klement's ordeal.

The REM had started exactly at the 71-minute mark—at the beginning of the eighth page. Krueger followed the chaotic lines as he turned page after page: the ninth page, the tenth, the eleventh . . . My God, Krueger almost shouted to the empty office, why didn't it end? Each page was 10 minutes! REM periods almost never lasted beyond 20 minutes. By then the dream would be over, the person descending into deeper sleep, never to remember the dream; or he would awaken with a nightmare.

At the beginning of the seventeenth page, at exactly the 160-minute mark, the REM sleep period ended and the EEG showed an "awake" pattern. Klement was awake! The eye-motion monitoring revealed that he was staring straight ahead, his eyes probably bulging from their sockets. Incredible! The REM period had lasted from the 71st minute to the 160th minute. Klement had endured an 89-minute nightmare—and then awakened!

The brain wave registered an "awake" pattern for almost a full minute; then the cycles began to slow. It was not an orderly slowing, however—no gradual changes from stage one to two to three and then to deep sleep; rather, it was a steady momentum of dying brain waves, slowly undulating, and eventually six unbroken, even lines transcribing their nothingness on the moving paper. From the wild, tumultuous lines that shouted of REM nightmare to the clean symmetry of the quiet message of brain death.

Krueger exhaled openmouthed and heard the thump of his heart. He slowly took off his glasses and wiped the perspiration from his eyes with his thumb and forefinger. His vision blurred, he stared at the bizarre tracings before him. He shook his head. "Oh sleep! it is a gentle thing, Beloved from pole to pole," Coleridge had written. No gentle dreams here, the tracings told Krueger. Klement had been awake for a full minute, his eyes wide and staring, gasping as the crushing chest pain squeezed the breath from his body. Had he known he was dying? Probably. No one had heard him cry out, apparently. Maybe death had been preferable to an 89-minute nightmare.

Krueger sat marveling at the astounding length of Klement's last REM dream. It was probably the longest ever recorded. It would make a good case report for any journal—except, he thought sardonically, that amitrypton was supposed to suppress that very thing.

His eyes wandered from the EEG tracings, the paper now snaking from the desk and across his lap down to the floor, to the shelf where he had placed the EKG printout and the I.V. bottle of amitrypton. He grabbed the cardiogram printout and spread it across his desk, brushing the EEG printout to the floor.

Can't read these things. Need a cardiologist. Brailey? No, not at four o'clock in the morning. Ah, of course— Burns. He picked up the phone and dialed the medical-center switchboard. "Operator? Please page Dr. Joseph Burns. Have him call me at this number."

He hung up the phone and looked down at the mystifying lines of Klement's heart action. Two minutes later the phone rang.

"Dr. Burns?" Krueger asked expectantly.

"No, this is Miss Copaulis. Dr. Burns is busy right now."

"I must speak to Dr. Burns," Krueger told her impatiently.

The woman did not say anything immediately, but Krueger could hear muffled voices in the background. Then she came back on the line: "He can't come to the phone now. Who is this?"

"This is Dr. Krueger, chief of the psychiatry department. Tell Dr. Burns this is important."

Again came the indecipherable muttering on the other end, then: "Dr. Krueger," the woman said, "Dr. Burns says to tell you he's busy with something important, too. He's in the middle of a cardiac arrest."

"No, no, that's over," Krueger said uncomprehendingly. "That's precisely what I wanted to talk to him about."

There was silence on the line. Krueger was not sure, but he thought he could hear someone laugh.

"Dr. Krueger," the woman said again, "Dr. Burns told me to tell you that yours wasn't the only cardiac arrest of the night. We get two or three every night, and if you'll be patient, he'll call you back and talk to you about yours."

There was a click in Krueger's ear. He experienced sudden embarrassment at his gaffe. At the same time, he thought, that woman, nurse, whatever she was, was certainly impertinent.

Chapter XXIII

Krueger paused outside the door marked "Pathology," not at all eager to enter. He hadn't been in an autopsy room since he had been an intern more than thirty years ago. He remembered his last post mortem. He had hated it every bit as much as the first. He knew they were necessary, but he had always imagined himself white and lifeless on the table while an unfeeling pathologist cut away at the only evidence of his earthly existence. As an atheist, he had never considered soul, although, when pressed for an answer during those philosophical collegiate gab fests, he would say he was an agnostic. He wondered if atheists in operating rooms outnumbered those in other professions. Medical and surgical residents in training were required to follow their patients to the end, and this room was frequently their epilog. The residents had to witness the autopsies, perhaps as a last, macabre retribution by those they had failed. A psychiatrist's failures, thought Krueger, kept their counsel or died by their own hand, leaving him blameless.

Psychiatry residents were spared this ghoulish exercise the day they entered their residency. And atheist Krueger had said a prayer of thanks for that. The reminder of his own mortality was probably the paramount reason for his revulsion—that and his natural fastidiousness, he admitted to himself. He even detested the physical aspects of his sleep research—the patients lying in the sleep rooms, the EEG and EKG wires, the intravenous tubing coiling from the human veins. It all made him uncomfortable. When he had first started the sleep studies, he would walk into the patients' rooms in the morning to interview them, collecting the brain- and heart-monitoring printouts personally. Recently he had been having the residents perform these chores, instructing them to bring the printouts to his office. Now he would rarely see a patient between the time of the initial interview and the end of the two-week amitrypton therapy, when he would conduct the follow-up interview.

He was still shaken by Klement's death. Having viewed the blood-spattered disorder of the sleep room, he was ambivalently grateful that he had not been present when death occurred, despite his frustration and determination to get to the bottom of the untimely death. He would have been utterly helpless. A small guilt returned even now as he recalled the day in a midwestern department store where he had gone to browse during a break in a dull psychiatry convention years ago. A woman had started giving premature birth smack in the middle of the antique-furniture department, while frantic clerks had wrung their hands and screamed the age-old plea: "Is there a doctor present?" Krueger had been indistinguishable from the other stunned spectators that day, and he had scurried away from the morbidly curious shoppers and his Hippocratic oath without identifying himself. He had always hoped that everything had turned out all right.

Now he had to witness Klement's autopsy. Only the memory of that horrifying brain-wave printout, an indictment of his new drug, kept him from turning away from the pathology door. This trip was indeed necessary. Krueger straightened to his full five-foot-four-inch height and turned the doorknob. The stench of an invisible wall of formaldehyde struck him full in the face. He tried to breathe shallowly as he took a tentative step into the room.

Even his earlier autopsy experiences had not quite prepared him for the view. Klement lay starkly exposed on the narrow metal table, clothed as at the moment of his birth—a wooden caricature of a man. An elongated sink—a trough, really—was anchored beneath him to catch his blood and bile. The room was otherwise bare except for a number of glass bottles shelved along the wall. Krueger knew they were the receptacles for internal organs.

He felt the blood drain from his face, and his head seemed detached from his body. He was hyperventilating, and he made a conscious effort at breath control. He was puzzled at the depth of his reaction, but then it struck him: He was alone with the body. Remembering the medical-school autopsies, he realized that always before the room had been filled with people —students, interns, and residents crowding around the corpse like skittish nephews at the funeral of a long-forgotten uncle, making small talk to allay their anxiety in the presence of death, not to mention the anticipation of the hard questions soon to come from the pathology professor.

He jumped as Dr. DeWitt Hanson entered the room, smiling. Hanson gave Krueger a little wave as though hailing a taxi. An ill-kempt little man, thought Krueger, forgetting for the moment that Hanson topped him by at least three inches. A doctor who worked only after other doctors were found wanting. What possessed him? Krueger marveled. Did pathologists venture out only at night?

"Well, now," Hanson observed cheerily, "I don't believe I've ever seen you in this part of the hospital before."

Krueger started to introduce himself, but Hanson waved off the handshake.

"Oh, I know you, Dr. Krueger." He was slipping

on a pair of rubber gloves and a filthy rubber apron. He turned his back to Krueger, gathering his instruments. "You published all that stuff on tranquilizers. Made quite a name for yourself some years ago. Understand you're messing around with sleep now, that sort of thing."

"Yes, that sort of thing." Krueger volleyed Hanson's slight sarcasm back at him. "Look, Doctor, could we get on with it? I'm a little pressed for time."

"Why not," Hanson replied congenially, "although *he's* in no hurry," he said, jerking a thumb in Klement's direction. Krueger supposed that was what passed for humor among pathologists.

Hanson barely broke conversation as he turned to the corpse and made a swift incision. Like a pianist playing a glissando, in one motion he laid Klement open from the top of the breast bone to the pubic hairs. Heart, lungs, intestines suddenly all lay exposed. The membranes covering the viscera glistened wetly as the covering shell of the chest wall fell away on either side.

There was no sound save Krueger's quick intake of air. Watching from some ten feet away, he again experienced a light-headedness. "Dr. Hanson," he said with some effort, "do you think Dr. Brailey or any of the staff will be attending the autopsy?"

"No, why should they?" Hanson looked surprised. "It's not a charity or ward case. None of the residents or attending staff took care of him." The knife stayed suspended over the body. "I really didn't expect *you*, Dr. Krueger."

"Actually, I'm in somewhat of a hurry," Krueger said, his eyes going to the door,

Hanson, still bent over Klement, looked amused. "Can I do any part for you now?"

"I beg your pardon?"

"Any organ? Can I examine any organ first—before you have to leave, that is?"

"Well, he supposedly died of a heart attack. I suppose you——"

"OK, I'll start there." Hanson gave a little shrug and plunged his dissecting scissors into Klement's chest cavity. Snip, snip, and Hanson had the heart in his hand. It made a heavy, wet sound as he plopped it on the balance scale. Hanson's foot activated a tape recorder as he began the pathologist's litany: "The heart weighs two hundred and sixty-five grams." He snatched the heart from the scale and, with a long knife, cut it cleanly in half. Next he drew a small metric ruler from the pocket of his apron. "The left ventricle is fourteen millimeters thick at the apex," he intoned.

Krueger thought he might swoon. "I really must be going. I, uh, I have an appointment and . . ."

Hanson looked over at Krueger. "I understand perfectly, but actually, I think I can give you your answer in just a minute."

Krueger, who had started for the door, turned back. He took a few steps closer to the table. Some of the color had returned to his face.

Hanson held the human pump in his hand, rotating and examining it, tilting his head for a bifocal look. He made two more cuts. "Hmmm . . . Yes, there it is, all right—an infarct, inferior wall, pretty good-sized."

"A heart attack," Krueger repeated in a low voice, joining Hanson at the table.

"Yep. See, there it is." The pathologist split open the heart wall and pointed to a brownish area the size of a half-dollar in the middle of the beefy red heart muscle. "There's your spoiled meat, Krueger."

Krueger frowned. "Arteriosclerosis?"

Hanson didn't answer immediately. Instead, he made several more cuts through the heart wall around the "spoiled meat." With a small scalpel, he delicately cut longitudinally along what appeared to Krueger to be one of the arteries. "Interesting," he said. "The right coronary artery, the one leading to the infarct, is clean as a whistle."

The queasy feelings had long since left Krueger. "But shouldn't it be clogged with fats or cholesterol?" he asked.

"Usually, but not always. Spasm of the artery can cause an infarct."

"But what would cause the spasm?"

"Nobody knows for sure. A lot of things are implicated—smoking, taking estrogens or birth-control pills, emotional upsets, fright. It's one of those medical enigmas."

"Fright?"

"Yes, it can happen. I once posted a kid who died in a dentist's chair. Tragic, he was only . . ."

Krueger had turned away and was walking toward the door, leaving Hanson talking to himself. He was just outside the door when he turned suddenly and strode back to Hanson. "Wait," he almost shouted. "Dr. Hanson, I'd like a complete spectrophotometric exam of the blood and urine and of half a dozen brain slices."

Hanson frowned. "That will have to be done at the state 'lab, Doctor. It's time-consuming and expensive. Actually, I wasn't planning on opening the skull."

"But you must; it's crucial." Krueger's voice had now taken on an authoritative tone.

Hanson eyed him curiously. "Do you want a complete or limited spectro exam?" he asked.

"Complete," Krueger said firmly.

"Why? You suspect foul play?" Hanson's mouth turned up.

In his blood-soiled apron, the pathologist resembled a playful leprechaun turned loose in a butcher shop. He had a round face, and the only hairs on his head were a few strands that lay jackstraw fashion around each ear. That and the fact that he had a slight overbite gave him the look of a molting chipmunk.

Krueger noted that the pathologist's hands and feet were tiny. The fingers were delicate, almost feminine.

"No, no, of course not. It's just that, well, we were infusing a new drug intravenously when he died, and I'd like to know——"

"I see," Hanson interrupted. "You want all chemistry, drugs, heavy metals, and on brain slices as well as blood and urine?"

"Yes, please."

"Well, that's pretty expensive. I don't think we can get the coroner's office to spring for all that, not unless you think there's something fishy."

"Charge it to psychiatry," Krueger said quickly. "My—our department will pay for it."

Hanson nodded. "OK, you got 'em. I'll send them out today."

"When do you think you'll get the results?"

"Hell, not for weeks, maybe months. Those state-lab bureaucrats take forever, especially in a routine case like this."

"It's not routine to me," Krueger said intensely.

"Yeah, but it's not some big homicide or some *brouhaha* over food poisoning or anything like that. Those state-lab chemists, they get a lot of rush orders for specimen analysis for evidence—people going to trial, that sort of thing."

"But I can't wait that long. Isn't there some way of hurrying them up?"

Hanson's impish grin was back. "Well, sure. I mean, like in anything else, Krueger, there's always a way. This friend of mine, Wilson, he's chief of the toxicology section there. Nice guy. Now, don't tell him I said this, but, well, those guys don't make much. A couple of bottles of Scotch and a phone call or two; I'm pretty sure he'll hurry things along. I'll never forget this one case I autopsied last year. The whole medical staff thought it was a straight auto-immune hemolytic anemia. Looked funny to me. I sneaked a blood sample to Wilson. Well, it was a hemolytic anemia, all right, but it wasn't auto immune. Seems his serum lead level was through the roof. The guy's wife—and get this—his girl friend were both . . ."

Once again Krueger left Hanson talking to himself. He walked quickly from the room, heading for the nearest telephone.

"Dr. Brailey is making rounds," the secretary told Krueger. He started at the top floor of the medical center and began searching ward by ward. Finally he caught sight of Brailey leaning on a counter at a nurses' station. About a dozen interns and residents were lolling about him.

"It's not visiting hours, Dr. Krueger," Brailey said, smiling. "What are you doing here on the medical wards?"

"Looking for you. I have to talk to you about Oscar Klement's death."

"Yes, I heard. The night resident told me about it. Appears he had a coronary."

"But that shouldn't have happened."

Brailey said nothing for a moment, then: "Why not? Burns is my best resident. He seemed pretty sure. Besides, they're posting him sometime this morning. That should confirm it."

"Yes, well, I was there just this minute," Krueger said. "The autopsy showed a myocardial infarction."

Brailey cocked his head sideways. "Well, then?"

"Dr. Brailey, as you well know, Dr. Klement was undergoing sleep therapy and was receiving an intravenous infusion of my new drug, and——"

"Oh, yes. I see your concern, Dr. Krueger, but Burns assured me there was no anaphylactic shock, no drug reaction involved. If the post indicates a myocardial infarct, I don't think anyone can blame your drug."

"But that's just my point, Dr. Brailey. If he had been receiving the drug, he shouldn't have had a coronary."

The interns and residents ringing the nurses' station were now giving Krueger their undivided attention. Brailey straightened up, removing his tall frame from the support of the counter. His face softened by the hint of a smile, he looked around at the staff members:

"Dr. Krueger, you have a new drug that prevents heart attacks?"

"Uh, yes," Krueger said as he watched the bemused looks on the faces surrounding Brailey. "That is——"

"Why, you'll be famous again," Brailey cut in.

Krueger felt a rare crack in his usually stiff public composure. "But it does," he said, with enough vehemence to stop Brailey's narrowing eyes.

"And just how does it do that?" Brailey asked slowly, enunciating each word precisely.

"It prevents REM sleep."

"*What* sleep?"

"REM. That's when coronaries occur." Krueger's words floated unchallenged, and he was able to hear the squeak of a hospital cart in a distant hallway.

Brailey looked at him for a moment without speaking. "OK, if what you're saying should happen to be true, then how is it that Klement died?"

"I don't know. I'm not sure. For some reason this time it didn't work—either that or he didn't get the drug. I've seen his EEG, and it's just like that of any other addict in withdrawal. I just can't understand it. It's worked dozens of times before. He died a withdrawal death, and he shouldn't have. The amitrypton is foolproof."

"Dr. Krueger, you've got a foolproof drug that prevents coronaries? My God, you'll be the richest man in the world."

"Not foolproof, but I mean——" Krueger stopped, realizing that Brailey was mocking him. He could feel the smirks of the staff; they were breaking up soundlessly all around him. "It prevents REM sleep."

Krueger's voice trailed away to nothingness. There was a heavy silence. Someone coughed.

"Well, ah, yes," Brailey said. "You must tell me more about it sometime. Now I have to finish my rounds."

Brailey walked off, leaving Krueger and the staff to stare at each other. The psychiatrist put a hand to his chin, encountering the stubbly start of a beard. He had already put in a full day since Burns's call. Redfaced, he walked quickly away in the opposite direction, his ears tuned to any sounds of derision that might come from the nurses' station. He heard muted laughter as he turned the corner at the end of the hallway. Furious, he almost went sprawling over an empty wheelchair.

Chapter XXIV

"Get me Dr. Aldair," Krueger ordered into his interoffice phone. "Immediately."

"I believe Dr. Aldair is on his rounds, Doctor," the secretary replied.

"I assumed as much, Miss Green. I didn't ask you where he was," Krueger said icily. "I said I wanted him. I also said immediately, which means it's of the utmost importance. Page him; get him in here."

"Yes, of course, Doctor, right away."

Krueger replaced the receiver, barely able to contain his rage at Miss Green, who, after all, was innocent of anything; but she was handy. He cursed the damnable events of the past week, and he was in no mood to be solicitous of Miss Green's feelings—or anyone else's for that matter. He had been so near to success. It was unfair, almost like a vast conspiracy. In one mindless foul-up, the sleep-lab staff had brought everything to the brink of failure. All they had been required to do was follow a routine that even a chimpanzee, given a modicum of training, could accomplish. His plans, at least for now, lay moribund in the same coffin with Oscar Klement. Years of work could slide down the drain. Krueger could have had the study sketched out in a couple of weeks and, by working diligently, with no distractions, in shape for presentation within a month or so. He railed inwardly at the injustice of it all: the stupidity that had stymied him so close to his goal; the fiftieth sleep subject down in the morgue, a decaying refutation of the preceding forty-nine, all unqualified successes. Krueger's anger rose by degrees as he awaited Aldair's arrival. There were three light raps on the office door.

"Come in," Krueger commanded.

"Dr. Krueger, I understand you wanted to see me." Aldair's pleasant expression vanished as he looked at Krueger, who was hunched forward over the desk. He had never seen his boss like this, a man obviously fighting for self-control. Aldair had flexed his knees preparatory to flopping in the chair opposite Krueger, but decided against it.

"Aldair," Krueger said in a flat, menacing tone, "do you realize the import of your failure? That, because of you, one of the major medical breakthroughs of this century has been halted or seriously delayed?"

"Dr. Krueger, I——"

"Do you realize your incompetence has cost this project the precious time it needed for completion of a study so important it very well could have been the basis for the most meaningful application in addiction cases?"

Aldair opened his mouth, fishlike, but brought forth nothing.

"Dr. Aldair, the death of that man in the sleep laboratory could be the end of my experimentation. And right now—right this minute—I want a thorough explanation of your failure."

Aldair was stunned at the ferocity of the words. "F-f-failure? Dr. Krueger, whatever it is, I don't believe I deserve——"

"Just the explanation, please, Doctor," Krueger demanded curtly.

"I don't know what to say, Dr. Krueger."

"Doctor, that's unfortunate—that you don't know what to say, that is. A project of this magnitude jeopardized because of an inexcusable blunder. And your cavalier attitude——"

Aldair now became angered. "Dr. Krueger, I don't——"

"And your cavalier attitude raises serious doubts as to your professional competency. Those doubts force me to reassess your performance, to the point that recommending you for your psychiatry board is, at this time, problematical."

Aldair's head reeled. He couldn't believe what he was hearing. Four years of residency wasted? Krueger had now turned away from him, seemingly addressing the wall.

"This was a historic project, Dr. Aldair, whether or not you appreciated its significance. Forty-nine consecutive cures of barbiturate addiction. The potential was enormous: a half-million heroin addicts, over six million alcoholics in the United States alone, all cured by simply regulating their sleep. Can you grasp what that could mean in terms of social order, increased industrial productivity, familial strength? And like all great discoveries, it had been so obvious. But only I had the imagination and boldness to change sleep patterns. I and no one else!"

Krueger fell silent, his eyes on medical peaks far above Aldair's present vision. Aldair had hardly listened to his boss's monolog. He had been mapping out the possibilities of his own future, which now ranged from tending back sprains as an industrial physician to sewing up lacerations in an emergency room somewhere.

Looking at Krueger now, he realized he was expected to say something. "Doctor, I can understand what a disappointment Klement's death is to you. I'm sure there's a logical explanation."

"Of course there's a logical explanation. The explanation is that Klement did not receive the amitrypton."

"What? I don't—that is, why didn't he?"

"That's precisely why you are here now—to tell me why he never received the drug."

"But he did, Dr. Krueger. I added it to the I.V. bottle after he fell asleep, just as we always do, exactly as it says in your protocol."

"No!" The word was explosive; it left no room for rebuttal. "No, Aldair, he certainly did not get the drug. There were no traces of it in his blood or urine. I've had them analyzed, even his brain tissues. There wasn't a trace of it."

"God," Aldair said in a whisper to himself. Then to Krueger: "I tell you, I put one ampule of amitrypton in that I.V. bottle!"

"No"—Krueger cut in sharply again—"that didn't happen. What happened, Dr. Aldair, was that you *forgot* to add the amitrypton to the solution after Klement fell asleep. *That's* what happened."

"Dr. Krueger, that's impossible."

"No, Aldair, not impossible. In fact, it's a certainty. You weren't even watching Klement's encephalogram in the monitoring room!"

"But there was another patient, that narcoleptic, and——"

"And you were watching *his* EEG instead, ignoring my sleep-study patient! How could you fail to notice that chaotic EEG tracing? Of all the incompetent bumbling—forgetting a simple procedure."

"Dr. Krueger, I admit I may not have been watching Klement's EEG, but I swear, I *did* start that intravenous solution and I *did* later add the amitrypton to it."

Aldair stood unmoving, waiting for Krueger to say something else. Instead, Krueger turned to fix Aldair with a baleful stare, then swiveled his chair around to face the wall again. Aldair took that as the end of the discussion. The only sounds in the room were the muted noises of traffic on the boulevard outside the neuropsychiatry building. He backed up soundlessly a few steps and then turned and walked quickly from the room. He passed the smirking secretary and felt the heat rise past his ears as he realized that, on entering Krueger's office, he had left the door slightly ajar.

Brailey's voice over the telephone told of another setback. After everything else that had happened, it brought Krueger to the brink of despair.

"But you can't stop the sleep therapy. I don't understand, Dr. Brailey. You've agreed that the drug is perfectly safe."

"Dr. Krueger, let me say again that I'm not stopping your experiments. I'm only saying that the executive committee wants you to hold off for a while."

"But why? The autopsy confirmed that it was just a heart attack, that the therapy was in no way involved with Klement's death. It seems to me that——"

Brailey sighed. "That's part of the problem, Doctor. Klement died of a heart attack. Good God, do you realize that your night resident there—what's his name?"

"Aldair."

"Aldair didn't even know how to do C.P.R."

"C.P.R.?"

"Cardiopulmonary resuscitation, for Chrissake, Krueger. He sat on his ass for twenty minutes while the shock team was getting over there from the hospital. By then it was too late."

"I didn't know that," Krueger admitted.

"Neither did I the last time we talked. But, hell, that was the morning after Klement died. Anyway, it's hit the fan since then. It's all over the hospital about how this resident of yours stood there like a house by the side of the road."

"But Aldair's a psychiatry resident, not a cardiologist," Krueger protested.

"That's just the point. We have no control over what happens over at that sleep place; yet we're responsible because it's part of the medical center. Christ, what if Klement's widow decided to sue? She'd have us by the balls. The guy's supposedly in a hospital, but nobody knows what to do if he has a heart attack. You've got to hold off your experiments until we get some sort of format worked out, some kind of protocol written."

"How long would that take?"

"Not long, a few weeks at the most."

"I can't wait that long."

"Look, Dr. Krueger, it seems to me you've been working on this project for—how many years now? I can't imagine that a few more weeks would make any difference."

"But it would. See here, Dr. Brailey, this is most distressing. I'm not sure you have the right to interfere with what we do over here. I mean——"

"Now, you listen to me, Krueger, goddamn it. I'm the chief of staff of this medical center. Up to now there've been no problems over there and I've left you alone. But a man just died under unusual circumstances—a physician, no less. Every other department at this hospital has a regular routine approved by the executive committee, and they're expected to follow it. I'm only asking you to do what every other department is required to do—have some guidelines. You're not to do another sleep study until we draw up a protocol. Now, as far as I'm concerned, that settles it." Brailey rattled the receiver down in Krueger's ear, cutting off further protests.

Krueger drove aimlessly, his battered seven-year-old car seeming to steer itself. He had left his apartment on a sudden impulse, driven to the street by a free-floating anxiety attack. It was a sign of weakness, and he hated weakness. He slouched behind the wheel, driving distractedly. The ride was a departure from a rigid routine that had been unvaried the past several years. Recreation of any kind had not been part of his life. His relaxation consisted of poring over medical case-histories until bedtime. The last movie he had seen was *Psycho,* and he had left the theater halfway through the film feeling duped. Today he had found it impossible to concentrate on his work. The lines on the encephalogram printout told him nothing, went nowhere.

Following Brailey's phone call, he had left his office for the simple reason that he could think of nothing else to do. Now he drove slowly, unmindful of the fact that he was guiding his car in repetitive circles around the same block. He took casual notice that he was in a neighborhood of high-rise apartment buildings for the elderly and trendy clothing shops and record stores catering to the young adult. It was a neighborhood that symbolized the paradox of present-day urban renewal. The residents, however, seemed to peacefully coexist.

The drive served to ease his tension somewhat, but his frustration at the imposed delay of the sleep studies still rankled. It brought back again his bitterness at the patronizing attitude of the hospital staff toward him. At no time had he felt like such an outsider. It reminded him of past days in California, where the staff of the state hospital had preferred to discuss the diversions afforded by the temperate climate than participate in any of the programs he had tried to initiate.

The fact that he had no friends—no acquaintances, even—outside his professional life made for a lonely existence. However, Krueger was not one to indulge in self-pity, considering it a wasteful emotion that sapped the energy. He had long since been reconciled to the fact that the price of achievement came at the expense of close personal relationships. Still, there were times such as now when he would have welcomed discourse with a confidant, putting his feelings before another, withholding nothing.

Krueger turned the little car sharply into an open space alongside a pocket park he had driven past several times already. He sat there for a moment taking in the scene. A light afternoon rain had freshened the grass. The park was a tiny oasis between a small hotel and a string of shops. It was almost dusk, and the few street lights in the park had answered the call of approaching darkness. People, young and old, were strolling idly on the sidewalks or sitting on benches that dotted the landscape. A few of the younger ones lolled on blankets. The muted notes of disco music from one of the shops made their way through the open window of his car.

As he watched the casual activity in the park, his thoughts returned to California. His "exile" as a staff physician at the state mental hospital there had very nearly been his undoing. Nothing really had been done for the patients. They were restrained, straitjacketed or confined in padded cells. If suicidally depressed, they were given shock treatments. If maniacally schizophrenic, they were put in insulin comas. In either case, the patient emerged benumbed and confused, but docile.

The other staff members were not much more animated than the patients. The two groups had seemed bound together in an unspoken common futility, the patients by the chronicity of their illnesses, the staff by their inability to help. Each group, the keepers and the kept, walked through their daily roles as though they would be there forever. Most would be.

Krueger's futility had been compounded. He had introduced group therapy, in those days a new and innovative method. It had failed. Staffers and patients would not attend or contribute. Occupational therapy, staff conferences, and journal-club meetings had come to the same end, so that Krueger himself had finally despaired of any improvement and become totally depressed. When he began to have suicidal thoughts, he knew it was time to leave. And so, though it meant wasting years of training, he had accepted a biochemistry Ph.D. fellowship at Stanford University.

Then, just before his departure, he had discovered the drug.

He had come across it quite by accident. He had found an unopened carton labeled chlorphenothiozine. Staff members, who had worked only with nineteenth-century opiates and barbiturates, couldn't tell him what it was; neither could the hospital administrator, except to say that it was a new drug available for "clinical trials."

The drug had been the beginning of a new life for Krueger. Within a month he had published his first scientific paper—"Thirty Institutionalized Chronic Schizophrenics Treated with a New Drug and Released to Home Care." Psychiatrists around the country, Krueger remembered, were slow to embrace the treatment. Devotion to long-term analysis had blinded them to the possibility that a mere drug could be so effective. He smiled as he recalled the reaction of one: "Too simple," the man had said haughtily. But Krueger had been the first to comprehend that these new tranquilizers would revolutionize psychiatry, and his ensuing fame had led Brailey to offer him the job at the medical center. So his discovery had also served as his "parole" from the suffocating stasis of the mental hospital.

But California was ancient history, a slice of life

from so long ago that it was as though it had happened to someone else. And now he had another drug—almost. He was close, so close.

The tempo of life in the park seemed to be picking up, he noticed, as nighttime neared. The scene was one of contentment, almost pastoral, and Krueger felt a need to become part of it. He got out of the car and walked slowly down the short flight of concrete steps that led to the recessed park area.

Two young men, dressed in shorts and sneakers, jogged past him, talking earnestly as they matched strides in almost military fashion. Colorful sweatbands held back the hair from their faces. Krueger strained to pick up the kernel of their conversation. Girls, perhaps? Certainly their unlimited futures. A stooped lady of ancient vintage sold tiny bouquets near a statue that marked the center of the park.

Krueger had never visited this section of the city, although he drove through it regularly in his unyielding routine. Many of his trips were late at night when, being the last to leave the sleep lab, he bent purposefully over the wheel, looking straight ahead in his rush to get a few hours' sleep before returning to his work. There was a certain ruefulness now in the thought that he was frequently the first to arrive at the neuropsychiatry building and the last to leave.

He sat down on one of the benches next to a well-dressed man in his late sixties, maybe early seventies. A retired banker? Former stockbroker? A widower of means whose visits to the park were part of a regular holding pattern before joining his wife in some manicured cemetary plot? A folded newspaper lay unread in the man's lap.

Krueger cleared his throat. "Ah, the rain was a Godsend, wasn't it? Just the thing to break that humidity." He was unabashed by the banality of his remark.

"Certainly was, certainly was," the man replied. He turned to Krueger, shifting his weight on the bench, and waggled the newspaper for emphasis. "It's a rebirth, a reaffirmation of life. You can smell the grass growing." He smiled warmly, and Krueger noted a pair of eyes of a shade of blue not usually given to advancing age. The hair was white and abundant above an intelligent face. The suit was dark blue and looked expensive. A tasteful maroon tie set off the white shirt.

"Yes, yes," Krueger responded eagerly. He was desperate to keep the conversation going. "Yes, ah, a rejuvenation."

The man crossed his legs and put his arm on the back of the bench. He pointed his rolled newspaper at the apartment building across the street. "That's where I live. When I first moved there, I used to sit in my apartment and watch the people here in the park. I did that for the longest time, until one night I said, 'Hey, what am I doing up here?' I decided to come down and join the fun." He looked pleasantly at Krueger. "I've met a lot of interesting people here."

"Yes, yes, I imagine you have." Krueger smiled at his newfound companion. "Uh, I hope you won't think I'm presumptuous, but I've been playing this little game trying to guess what you may be like—your background. I hope you don't mind." The man smiled an invitation. "I have you down as a widower, a retired banker or businessman playing the stock market, maybe."

The man laughed deep in his throat. "Oh, no, no, nothing like that. Tool and die maker. Saved my money. Never married. I play classical records instead of the stock market." He looked at Krueger intently. "OK, how about you?"

"How about me?" Krueger challenged good-naturedly.

"Let's see. I see you as a professional man—a lawyer or a certified public accountant. No, maybe a scientist. You have a scientific look about you."

"That's pretty close. I'm a psy—a doctor." Krueger

smiled again, enjoying the game, thoroughly enjoying himself.

"Married, of course?"

"Uh, no," said Krueger. There was a momentary pause as he looked around the park at the strollers and idlers. He turned to the man again. "Coincidentally, I'm a lover of classical music myself. I suppose one could call me an *aficionado*."

"You don't say?" The man seemed to study Krueger. He rubbed the rolled newspaper slowly across the thigh of his one leg. His hand went from the back of the bench to touch Krueger lightly on the shoulder. "I have an idea. How would you like to come up to my place? I have some beautiful recordings, most of the masters. We could talk and . . ."

Krueger did not reply. He was distracted by two young men walking past the bench. Both wore hip-hugging trousers and colored undershirts. One, his hair cut extremely short and brushed straight back, held a small radio to his ear. They were holding hands. Krueger looked back quickly at his bench companion, suddenly acutely conscious of the hand on his arm.

The man's lips were compressed, and a disapproving frown had narrowed the bright-blue eyes. "The new breed," he said, "out of the closet, flaunting themselves. Insensitive punks. Indiscreet, utterly without class." He swung his eyes to Krueger, who felt the man's grip tighten. "Give us all a bad name."

Krueger gave a start and jerked his shoulder away as though it had come in contact with a hot stove. Bouncing to his feet, he said, "Excuse me, I have to be going. Excuse me," and started to walk away.

"Wait!" the man called after him. "Why are you leaving?"

Krueger, at a half run, bounded up the steps to the street level and didn't look back until he was in his car. The man was still seated, now little more than a silhouette in the descending darkness. The white of the newspaper shone dimly against the dark-green bench.

An hour later Krueger, to his total amazement, was in a roller-skating rink making lazy, if somewhat shaky, ovals on the hardwood floor. He had turned impulsively into the rink's parking lot, puzzled at his lingering anger over the encounter in the park.

Roller-skating was the one physical activity in which he'd been adept as a child, and after a few tentative steps tonight when he thought he would fall on his face, it was all coming back to him. He easily crossed one skate over the other as he negotiated one of the four turns required to complete a circuit of the floor. Young skaters zipped around him on either side. They now paid him scant heed after first casting curious glances at his formal skating costume of suit and tie.

The activity gradually served to erase earlier events of the evening. Krueger intentionally skated until he was tired. He felt sweat droplets run down his neck and into his collar. He let himself coast the length of the rink, then collapsed on one of the long leather "rest" seats that ringed the rink's perimeter. He stuck his wheeled feet straight out in front of him and dabbed a handkerchief on his face and neck as he watched the skaters sweeping around and around in time to the recorded organ music. The revolving multicolored lights threw a patchwork of rectangles on their clothing. Their laughter bared brilliant teeth out of ghostly faces. Krueger inhaled deeply against the weight of his exertion. He wondered what would be the reaction of the medical center people if they could see the stuffy head of psychiatry in such an unlikely setting.

Two girls, no more than sixteen, were standing next to him. Their heads were almost touching as they talked secretively of some trivia. They moved their skates alternately in place and giggled almost continuously. *Atrocious posture,* Krueger observed. *Their spines will be deformed by the time they're thirty, giving them a permanent slouch and protruding abdomens.*

The girls sat down next to Krueger, who took notice of the striking appearance of the one nearest him. The blonde hair had a natural sheen. Her pink skin encased a body that had the breasts of a woman and the smooth fat of a baby.

She saw Krueger watching her and grinned with sensuous lips. "What's happening, partner?"

Krueger ignored the flippant disrespect for age fashionable with today's teenager. He smiled back at her. For the second time this evening he felt the need for conversation. "Do you come here often?"

"Whoa, partner. Where'd you learn that line, on the late late show?"

"Pardon me?"

"What I mean is, don't start somethin' you can't finish." Her friend laughed.

"I don't understand."

"What I mean, partner," said the girl with the baby fat, "is, are you sure you can still get it up after all that exercise?"

The other girl rose from the seat and pulled the blonde girl to her feet. They were both laughing as they skated away from him. Krueger felt the burning of his face, and he bent quickly to tug at his skate straps.

Cretins. They should be charged for the air they breathe. He walked to the checkout counter in his stocking feet. He would go back and talk to his cats.

Chapter XXV

The return address on the envelope was "State Department of Health." Krueger opened it without enthusiasm, knowing it was only written confirmation that the specimens contained no amitrypton. Wilson had already telephoned him that news last week. The call had come just before he had vented his fury at Aldair. Krueger's rage had still not entirely subsided. He was well aware of the petty nature of his psychiatry colleagues. He had already submitted an abstract of his paper that indicated fifty cases. When they realized there were only forty-nine in his presentation, they would pick him apart for his discrepancy, especially when he would have to admit that his one failure had died of drug withdrawal. Telling them of the absentee amitrypton would not mitigate anything. In the presentation of a paper to the World Health Organization, especially one as new and controversial as this one, his data would have to be unimpeachable. He had already added Klement's name to the printed abstract as a "cure." Krueger was committed, and someone would certainly learn about the death. Good God, what if they asked to look at Oscar Klement's EEG?

Krueger winced at the implications of his deceit as he extracted the state lab report from the envelope. His eyes went to the signature on the covering letter: "George Wilson, M.D., Ph.D., Director of Toxicology, Department of Health."

Wilson wrote: "As per our telephone conversation, no traces of the drug amitrypton were found in the samples of blood, urine, and brain tissue sent to this facility. Enclosed you will find the results of the mass spectrophotometry examination."

Krueger scanned the report swiftly. He resisted the urge to throw it into the wastebasket. Someday, he told himself, he might be called upon to document the claim that there were no traces of his drug in Klement's body. He quickly ran his finger down the computer printout that Wilson had sent. It included some eighty items. He routinely noted that sodium, potassium chloride, carbon dioxide, blood sugar, and blood urea nitrogen were said by the report to be within normal limits. There was no evidence of drug ingestion, except for a small trace of acetylsalicylic acid, a little aspirin.

Slouched in his chair, Krueger continued his perfunctory reading of the report until the word *reserpine* leaped out at him from the middle of the page. He was jolted to the edge of his chair and reached for the telephone. As he dialed, he looked back twice at the printout to make sure he had read it correctly.

"Department of Toxicology, please," he asked the voice that answered his ring. He picked up the report while waiting for the connection. The paper vibrated in his shaking hand. Yes, there was no mistake—reserpine, and a high blood concentration at that. How in God's name would Klement have had any of that in his——

"Dr. Wilson here." The voice brought Krueger back to the phone.

"Dr. Wilson, this is Dr. Krueger at the medical center. You may remember, we spoke earlier in the week about some samples you analyzed for me."

"Dr. Krueger, of course. Yes, I wouldn't have forgotten you. I want to thank you for the nice gift. It's my favorite Scotch. And, my goodness, a whole case."

"Oh, that. Yes, well, I wanted to show my appreciation for your, uh, expediting the analysis and phoning me the results. I know how busy you people are down there."

"Did you get the written report yet?" Wilson asked.

"Yes, it's in front of me right this minute. As a matter of fact, that's the reason I'm calling. I was surprised to see there was a high level of reserpine present in the blood and brain samples. When we talked earlier, you didn't say anything about it."

"You didn't ask, Doctor. As I recall, your main concern was amitrypton."

"Yes, I know," Krueger said. "But, well, as I say, I hadn't expected——"

"Wait a minute," Wilson interrupted. "Let me dig out the report so I can follow along with you from my end." There was a thump in Krueger's ear as Wilson laid the receiver down on his desk. He was back in a few moments. "Yes, you're right, Dr. Krueger. There was reserpine present. Sorry I didn't mention it when we talked. Didn't see any significance in it, really. It's non-toxic and legal. The spectrophotometer just picked it up incidentally, like the aspirin."

"Dr. Wilson, there couldn't be a mistake, could there? I mean, it's so totally unexpected. I wondered perhaps about double-checking."

There was a lapse of several seconds before Wilson responded. "Now, Dr. Krueger," he said slowly, "each chemical analysis is not only double-checked, it's triple-checked. These are computer printouts. Each analysis is done automatically three times and the computer prints out the average. Furthermore, our laboratory is one of the finest and is recognized for its accuracy."

Krueger had stopped listening. His eyes had gone to a shelf across the room. Standing behind his desk, with the phone to his ear, Krueger stared at the I.V. bottle he'd taken from the sleep lab that night. He was recalling Aldair's words: "I *did* add the amitrypton to that bottle." As cowed as he had been at the tongue-lashing, Aldair had been firm on that point.

The bottle was now a shiny puzzle—containing what? Perhaps not what it said on that label!

"Yes, yes, of course," Krueger cut in. "I certainly didn't mean to imply that your department isn't capable, Doctor. Quite the contrary, it's renowned for its thoroughness and accuracy. Actually, Dr. Wilson, I really wanted to ask another favor of you, if I may. I'd like to mail you an I.V. bottle, one thousand cc's, for analysis, plus a couple of smaller vials. I'll get them mailed out today. I'll be sure to package them very carefully."

"Dr. Krueger," Wilson interrupted, "this is very unusual. These kinds of requests usually come only from district attorneys or a county coroner."

"I was about to say, Dr. Wilson, that I would pack them very carefully so that favorite Scotch of yours is in no danger of breaking, either." Krueger let that hang for a moment. He could hear Wilson's breathing.

"Ah, it's obvious this is very important to you, Doctor."

"Very."

"Well, we'll do our best, of course. Naturally, we can't move your analysis ahead of some others."

"Naturally."

"But I'll see if I can't push it along a little bit."

"I certainly would appreciate that, Dr. Wilson."

"I only questioned your urgency because reserpine is such a common drug, you know. I was taking it myself for a little blood-pressure problem. Had to give it up—too many side effects."

Krueger smiled into the phone. "I'll wager I can tell you what kind of side effects. Did you have nightmares?"

"Hey, yeah," Wilson said. "Did I ever have nightmares! They were beauties."

"Yes, I thought so. They're very common with reserpine."

"Hmmm, interesting. Well, Dr. Krueger, I'll phone you the results as soon as I get them."

"I certainly appreciate your cooperation, Doctor," Krueger said. "I'll be waiting for your call."

Krueger replaced the receiver on its cradle. He removed his glasses and rubbed his eyes. *Reserpine, reserpine . . .* and then aloud: "Reserpine." He pulled Klement's medical chart from the filing cabinet behind his desk and studied the lengthy questionnaire Klement had completed his first night at the sleep lab. He quickly scanned to the part of the questionnaire that inquired about drugs known to affect REM sleep. Klement had admitted only to alcohol and Seconal. Krueger recognized the bold "No" in Klement's writing adjacent to the various kinds of reserpine drugs.

Of course, he wouldn't have been the first drug addict to lie. But a physician! Why would he? And why reserpine? It was not even considered addictive. It had been introduced back in the 1950s as an antihypertensive agent, and its effect on increasing REM-dream pressure was realized only when blood-pressure patients began complaining of nightmares.

It didn't make sense. But, then, nothing in this case had made sense so far. Stupid fool that he was, Krueger thought, Klement still didn't deserve the hell he had suffered during those final moments. Reserpine on top of the Seconal withdrawal had had a compound effect. It was all in the frenzied brain-wave printout. Klement's heart could not stay ahead of the nightmares, given the added load of the reserpine. It had proved to be the trigger finger of the execution.

Krueger walked out of his inner office, Klement's medical chart in hand. "Miss Green, cancel my office hours this afternoon. I'll be busy; I'll be at the pharmacy for a while. And get me another one of those packing cases—just like last week, only bigger. And get lots of Styrofoam. Also, take that I.V. bottle—the one on the shelf in my office—and pack it very carefully, but don't seal the box. I'll be bringing back a couple of vials from the pharmacy. I want them to go to the state health department lab, too. Pack them together, first-class mail."

"Yes, Doctor."

"Oh, yes. What was that, uh, that whisky we sent Dr. Wilson?"

"Chivas Regal, Doctor."

"Yes. Send him another case of that, also. Charge it to the psychiatry department again."

Krueger started out the door, then noticed he was still carrying Klement's chart. "One more thing," he told his secretary. "Get Mrs. Klement's phone number. It's here somewhere, I'm sure." He tossed the medical chart on Miss Green's desk and walked out.

Chapter XXVI

The journal had that well-thumbed look. Joan Klement recognized her handwritten notes in the margin of the article. Some paragraphs had been underlined. The article was by Frederick Snyder of the National Institute of Health:

> The existence of distinctly mammalian sleep and rapid eye motion in the opossum (she read) assures us that these conditions had been fully established prior to the divergence of marsupial and placental evolution at least 100 million years ago. These phenomena—deep-sleep cycling with REM sleep—were not only established at a very early stage of mammalian evolution, but were

especially prominent then. Therefore, it is appropriate to ask how the unique characteristics of mammalian sleep, including REM, might have enhanced the likelihood of survival of our earlier furry forebears. First, consider the competitive position in which the earliest mammals existed. Paleontologists tell us that they appeared very soon in reptilian evolution, almost as soon as the dinosaurs. Yet over the 100 million years or so that these ferocious reptiles overshadowed the earth, our mammalian predecessors remained small, furtive, insignificant creatures like the opossum or the hedgehog. The only conceivable way they could survive was by virtue of a few new biologic assets.

Yes, Joan said to herself, new biologic assets, the sentinel hypothesis of REM sleep—that cycling between deep and REM sleep that allowed mammalians, especially primitive ones, to maintain a certain vigilance during the REM period, even though they were dreaming. She drew in on the marijuana cigarette, sucking the smoke deep inside her, and resumed reading:

I suggest that the dream has such functions; that whatever may be the function of the dream in man, its function in lower animals is to awaken it in the presence of danger and set it in action, even while still asleep, the process by which it will be able to meet danger in the appropriate manner.

Joan flicked the ash from her joint. This was the fascinating part. The arousal occurs between the sleep cycles. Sleep isolates the animal from environmental dangers and is divided into short sections, between which the animal has the opportunity of reacting, if need be, to external stimuli. She looked up from the journal. She remembered the rest of the sentinel hypothesis now. Animals, during REM sleep, were able to awaken on "preset cues." A mother could sleep undisturbed through the familiar roar of a train and yet awaken to the soft voice of her baby. And she might even incorporate the external stimuli—in this case, the crying—into the content of her dream. Joan turned to the summary:

> Thus, REM sleep is protective of the organism by two mechanisms. First, there is environmental surveillance during the REM period; and, second, the autonomic arousal of the REM state makes the organism more alert if awakened during it, whereas, if awakened during deep sleep, the organism is physically sluggish with impoverishment and blocking of thought content.

Joan threw the journal on top of a stack of similar magazines on the floor. The joint had burned down to the point where she was barely grasping it by the tips of thumb and forefinger. She stretched from her crosslegged position to stub it out in the large glass ashtray. It joined the remains of two others.

If awakened from a deep sleep, it would certainly take longer to escape the predator. But awakening from a dream, you were primed; your autonomic nervous system had the adrenaline pumping. She smiled. Talk about predators! Those were the times many an unsuspecting woman found herself confronted in the middle of the night by the male arousal and erections of REM sleep.

She thought briefly of Oscar. Too much arousal? Too much REM? Maybe. Adrenaline prepares you for fright or flight. The human heart can take only so much autonomic discharge. If the adrenaline gets too high . . . Joan felt a little giddy. The euphoria produced by the weed had overtaken her.

She had heard rumors that someone had made a

mistake and not given Oscar any of the drug that stops the REM rebound. That was probably why Krueger wanted to see her. She knew that his secretary had been calling around looking for her.

So Oscar had died of REM sleep. Well, what the hell. If sleep had allowed mammalians instead of reptile dinosaurs to dominate the earth, as the article said, Oscar was a small price to pay. Joan laughed aloud. She would indeed prefer reptiles to some of the humans she knew.

She heard chimes and looked up, annoyed. Someone was ringing her doorbell. She muttered an expletive. She had gained a sense of contentment these past days that she hadn't had in years. She jealously guarded her solitude, spending hours reading, coming and going as she pleased. She had come to resent the doorbell and the telephone.

She padded on bare feet to the door, threw it open, and found herself looking into the eyes of Ty Bronson.

"Hello, Joan." There was a moment of awkward silence. "I thought we might have a little chat. Are you busy?"

"No"—she dragged out her response—"just reading about reptiles." Her face was expressionless. She considered telling him to go away, but turned and allowed him to follow her into the living room. She sat down without inviting him to do the same. Bronson took off his coat and then, holding it folded in his arms, sat in a chair opposite her.

"Well . . ." he began, surveying the disarray of the room before looking back at her. "Joan, it's about the accounts receivable. Ah, I felt we should talk." His circumspect eyes were in constant motion, his capped-tooth smile devoid of warmth.

"Accounts receivable?"

"Yes, you know, the money owed us by our patients."

"Oh, so that's what that means."

His eyes narrowed. "Yes. Well, Joan, it's really just

a technicality, something the lawyers and accountants should work out."

"Then, why are you here? Why don't you let them handle it?"

"Well, there is this technicality—a discrepancy, actually."

"Discrepancy?"

"Joan, I know this sounds phony. I mean, it looks like I'm trying to, well, promote myself. What I mean is, I am here to ask you for a favor." He paused and looked at her. She did not respond. "Have you seen the books from the clinic?"

"Briefly."

"Then, as you may know, we grossed almost a million last year—nine hundred and eighty thousand, to be exact."

"Yes?"

"Now, almost fifty percent of that was spent on overhead—paying off the building, the equipment, the nurses' salaries, and that. You understand?"

"I think so."

"Yes, well, the rest went into the professional corporation—almost half a million. Out of this, Oscar and I each drew a salary. I might say that both the salaries were quite low."

"Oh?"

"Sixty thousand, to be exact. Now, as you can see, the corporation actually earned far more than that."

"Then, why didn't you pay yourselves higher salaries, Ty?" Joan said, smiling sweetly. She had allowed herself to slide lower, her shoulder blades and buttocks her only contact with the chair. She saw Bronson's lips tighten.

"Well, Joan, that's where these things get very complicated. It has to do with pensions, profit-sharing plans, and the tax structures. You wouldn't understand. It——"

"Your salaries are taxed and the corporation isn't," she cut in."

"Yes. It's a form of tax shelter, all perfectly legal; you don't have to worry about that."

"Oh, I'm not worried, Doctor. I must say you live very well on only sixty thousand a year." She had straightened in her chair, the smile gone from her face but not her voice.

"Yes, well, we——"

"And Jeffrey. What about your son, Jeffrey? He seems to do pretty well, also. My, my, a sixteen-year-old making twenty thousand a year. You can buy a lot of rock records for that kind of money."

Bronson moved forward on the edge of his chair. Joan saw him tense, his hands unconsciously twisting the fabric of his overcoat. Ah, little Jeffrey—a carbon copy of his father. Joan was briefly jolted by the memory of her first years of marriage when she was told that she couldn't have children, but knowing Jeffrey Bronson had compensated her for her loss. She at least could never be accused of spawning such a narcissistic little shit.

"Now, listen, Joan, Jeffrey earned some of that money. He stopped in after school and——"

"And what about your wife? Did she stop in after school, too? I see the checks were made out to her maiden name; otherwise the IRS would probably wonder why so many people with the same name were on the payroll, wouldn't they?" Bronson's jaw was working furiously. "Isn't it amazing, Ty, how dividing the income among several people can keep you in a lower tax bracket?"

"Goddamn it, Oscar did it, too." Bronson spit out the words, literally. A small bubble gleamed on his lower lip. "We worked it out together. We both took out the same amount."

"Yes, I know. Oscar approached me about doing the same thing right after he started practice. You'll never find any payroll checks endorsed by me ending up in our bank account."

"I know that," Bronson snapped. "Oscar told me how uncooperative you were."

"Don't waste any sympathy on Oscar, Ty. He found ways. I've spent the last few days going over the clinic's books. God, Oscar's mother is so senile she thinks Teddy Roosevelt is still president, but the old girl can endorse checks." Joan laughed explosively, a high, shattering sound. "The dutiful, solicitous son regularly visited his poor mother in the nursing home with a handful of checks."

Bronson studied her for a moment, the agitation again showing in the way he worked his mouth. "All right, Joan. I suppose that because you wouldn't help Oscar out, you feel you can be condescending with me. Well, don't patronize me. You're no saint."

"Yes?" Her smile was angelic.

"Well, I'd just as soon not repeat the gossip."

"How good of you not to repeat it, Ty. By the way, did anybody ever tell you that you say 'well' all the time?"

"Don't mock me. You've been——"

"I've been screwing that psychiatrist I work for, right? Is that what you were going to say? You're right, Ty, and I'm ashamed. He's about as gross as you are. There are all kinds of whores. You should know all about that."

"Well . . ." He stopped. "I mean, you've got no call to denigrate me, Mrs. Klement."

"Please don't call me that." Joan smiled.

"Just because my wife helped me out a little by endorsing a few checks . . ."

"I certainly wasn't criticizing your wife. She'd be fine if she weren't married to you. You've put her down to the point where she'll even help you steal, poor woman. God, no wonder she's such a nebbish." Joan pulled out a cigarette paper and started to roll another joint, looking up coyly to see Bronson's reaction. He was breathing heavily. She giggled very quietly, almost to herself.

"Well, I guess I've heard and seen enough," he finally said. "I came here with good intentions. I was prepared to make you a generous offer for the corporation. I shouldn't even have to buy you out. Just a couple more months and I'd have——"

"You'd have it all to yourself, right? Oscar died at the wrong time—or in the nick of time, depending on your viewpoint."

"Poor Oscar." Bronson shook his head. "He had his faults, but he deserved better than you. I've a good mind to——"

"Wrong again, Dr. Bronson; you don't have a good mind at all," Joan said evenly. "And not only that, but fate stepped in. Oscar died just before you could become a full partner, didn't he?"

Bronson stood up. "You think you can sell his practice to someone else, don't you? Drive me out, get another doctor in there. Well, I'll set up shop across the street. Those patients know me; they'll come to me."

"I'm dissolving the corporation." Joan's eyes followed the marijuana smoke as far as the ceiling.

"What?"

"You heard me: I'm dissolving the corporation."

"When?"

"Now."

"But that's ridiculous! What about the accounts receivable?"

"I canceled them."

"You *what!* That's thousands of dollars that people owe us, for work we've already done."

"I know. We went through the list and sent everybody a notice to forget the money they owe—a little gift from you and Oscar, the two concerned and trusted healers. Kind of a Christmas present in May. Don't you feel just a superwarm glow right now, Ty?"

Joan looked out the window. Bronson could probably kill her right now, she thought, except that wouldn't be the expedient thing to do, and the chicken-shit always did the expedient thing. She waited a long time for him to speak, still not looking at him. When he finally did, his voice had a whipped modulation:

"What about my contract?"

"Ah, yes, your contract. It will be honored. The clinic's fiscal year begins July first. That's when the corporation is officially dissolved. There's plenty of money to pay you a couple months' salary, with a lot left over. After July first you're out. Incidentally, I canned your wife today. Your kid, too. God, that felt good. My attorney said it was probably illegal, since they also had contracts to July, but I told him I didn't think you'd contest it."

She turned to face him again. Their eyes locked for a moment. Then Bronson put his coat under one arm, turned abruptly, and walked toward the door.

"Would you be so kind as to show yourself out, Doctor?" Joan called after him.

Chapter XXVII

"I'm sorry I didn't recognize you, Dr. Krueger, but you can't be too careful these days. Even hospital pharmacies are getting knocked off. Read about one the other day in the papers—pharmacy in a big hospital— two guys posing as doctors."

"Yes, yes, I understand," Krueger said impatiently, putting away his identification card and following the young pharmacist to the back of the pharmacy.

"Here's where we keep the experimental stuff," he told Krueger.

Although Krueger didn't know him well, he had always had an unreasonable dislike for the fellow, a pimply-faced and sleepy-eyed nose picker by the name of Beshaw or Bradley, something like that. Krueger's eyes followed the pointing finger of the young pharmacist down the closetlike corridor. Shelves ranged on either side. Above the entrance was a large sign: "Drugs Not Approved by FDA." This aisle was at the extreme rear of the pharmacy, tucked out of sight like the back counter of a newsstand where the dirty books are kept.

Krueger had no idea there were so many experimental drugs. Almost half the shelves were the province of the "Department of Oncology," a sign noted. Krueger wasn't surprised. *Cancer researchers don't have to beg drug companies for money,* he thought. *If they can't get it from the medical center, the government will support them—underwriting them for playing around with apricot pits and tinkering with sound waves.*

The bottom shelf was devoted to the psychiatry department. Krueger squatted down, and his eye immediately located the box of amitrypton vials. He picked three of them at random and put them in his pocket. He stopped at the pharmacy door on his way out. "Next time you'll know me," he told the pharmacist. It was almost a question.

"Oh, yes. Yes, sir."

"I guess my chief resident, Dr. Aldair, usually comes over and picks these up."

"That's right, Doctor, but I haven't seen him lately."

"No," Krueger said, slowly drawing out the word, "we've stopped using this drug for a while."

"Yeah, I heard. Since that doctor died."

Krueger managed to hide his irritation, but not his

surprise. "I didn't realize hospital news got around so quickly."

"Oh, yeah. Everybody knows what's going on with everybody else."

"Young man, were you working that night?"

"Yeah, I was here."

"I see. And Dr. Aldair must have picked up the amitrypton then."

"Sure did."

"You say you haven't seen Dr. Aldair since then, but you did see him that night? You're certain?"

"Yep. He came by to pick up an ampule of that drug you've got there."

"Tell me, I wonder if you would mind showing me some reserpine?"

"Glad to. Tablets or injectable?"

"Injectable, please."

The pharmacist disappeared for half a minute, then returned with several small glass containers and handed them to Krueger.

"Thank you," Krueger said. All of the tiny containers fitted comfortably in one hand. Pulling one of the amitrypton bottles from his pocket, he laid it next to the reserpine ampules. "Quite a difference," he said. The amitrypton vial dwarfed the reserpine ampules.

The young pharmacist seemed not at all surprised by the statement, acting as if people came there every day to compare the sizes of drug containers. "Yeah. Reserpine is in two-cc ampules—poppers." He seemed eager to show off his knowledge. "Lookee here." He took the reserpine ampule from Krueger and broke it cleanly. Throwing away the glass top, he showed Krueger the filled ampule. Krueger watched him pour the contents into a sink and throw the ampule into a wastebasket. Krueger looked again at the amitrypton, which came in a nondisposable vial, sealed with a rubber cork that had to be punctured with a needle.

"Thank you, young man. You've been very helpful."

"No problem, Doc. Anytime."

Reentering his office, Krueger interrupted his secretary, who was packing the I.V. bottle into a large whisky case. She had sheathed it in Styrofoam, per instructions, and it was nestled between the bottles of Scotch.

"Good, good," Krueger said, bending over her. He took two of the three amitrypton vials from his pocket. "Here, Miss Green. We will be sure to get those off in the mail today, won't we? First class, remember."

"I'll do it right away, Doctor."

Krueger walked into his office and closed the door. He stood there for a moment, going back over the scene in the pharmacy. Was it possible? Had someone wanted to do away with Klement? Ridiculous! But that reserpine couldn't have just found its way into his body. Krueger began pacing slowly in front of his desk, then moved to the window, looking at the medical center without really seeing it. One thing for sure, he told himself: Aldair couldn't have "accidentally" picked up the wrong medication.

Krueger felt the beginnings of a headache; the first pain was creeping over his right eye. On the other hand, who hated Krueger himself enough to take this method to scuttle his project? Who cared enough? Most of them at the medical center had shown their ignorance of his work by their indifference to it. Somebody would have had to take the trouble to find out that reserpine increased REM pressure.

Of course, he had not checked out the source yet, either. The odds were a million to one, but there was always a possibility of a slipup by the manufacturer. He would mail the remaining vial in his pocket to the Monarch company for analysis—today.

Krueger sat down at his desk and stared at the telephone. The last possibility, of course, was that Klement had lied. It was the most probable, he told himself. It was the one he wanted to believe. He reached behind him and pulled *Pharmacology and Therapeutics* from the bookcase. He wanted to refresh his memory. His finger followed the small type under "reserpine." Yes, a half-life of almost a week. Very cumulative drug. Almost fifty percent of the dose would be present a week after it was taken. If given over a long period of time, it would take weeks to excrete. Krueger buzzed the intercom.

"Yes, Doctor?"

"Miss Green, did you get Mrs. Klement's phone number for me yet?"

Chapter XXVIII

Krueger looked at his watch: five-thirty. He would try Klement's home again. He had been calling all afternoon without success, so he was startled when Joan answered after one ring.

"Mrs. Klement?"

"Yes?"

"This is Dr. Krueger, from the medical center. I'm not sure if you remember me."

"You were treating my husband, Dr. Krueger. Yes, of course I remember you. What can I do for you?"

"The reason I'm calling, Mrs. Klement, is that I'd like to talk to you about your husband—that is, if I may."

"My husband? What about him?"

"I'm quite interested in his habits, in anything unusual that might have happened before he died."

"I don't know that I understand."

"Well, for example, had he had any chest pains or heart symptoms? Had he been taking any medicine?"

"I don't know of any heart symptoms, Doctor. If he had them, he certainly didn't tell me. As far as medicine or pills are concerned, the house is full of them."

"It is?"

"Doctor, you were treating my husband. You certainly were aware he was taking pills. It should be no surprise to you that barbiturate addicts have pills hidden in every available nook and cranny. You ask if I have pills? I've got pills in drawers, in candlestick holders, under the sofa cushions, in the garage, even in the refrigerator—everywhere but the medicine chest, actually." Her voice was light. Kreuger momentarily wondered how to proceed.

"Yes, of course." He finally recovered. "That is most common. Tell me, Mrs. Klement, have you thrown them out—the pills, I mean?"

"No, not yet. I'm waiting until I'm sure I've collected them all."

"Mrs. Klement, I would very much like to see them. I'm very interested in tracing your husband's death. It would be most helpful if I could examine them."

"I don't really understand, Doctor, but you're welcome to them. I certainly have no use for them. I don't think you'll find any surprises, though."

"Perhaps not. However, would it be too much of an imposition if I stopped by tomorrow?"

"I'm sorry, I won't be home."

"Oh. Well, then, the next day, perhaps?"

"I won't be home then, either. You see, Doctor, I work every day."

"You do? I see. What would you suggest, then? As I say, I'm anxious to see them. It could be important to my work, and——"

"Look, Dr. Krueger, if you're really that interested, stop by now and I'll give you all the damn pills I have. I have a sackful of them."

"If it's not too much trouble . . . I don't want to bother you at a time like——"

"No, it's OK, really. Come on over." She hung up abruptly.

Joan sighed as she replaced the receiver on its hook, trying simultaneously to balance a glass of Chablis and a cigarette. She shrugged. She had to get rid of the pills anyway. She supposed Krueger was a little shocked at her demeanor: probably not the response he had expected from a grieving widow. She crossed the foyer into the living room, her eyes going to Oscar's picture on the mantle over the huge white fireplace that occupied most of an entire wall. Clear of eye, resolute jaw, regular features. Joan had forgotten when the photograph had been taken, but it was long ago.

She sat on the floor and turned the page of the newspaper she had been reading. She first had to shove the Scottish terrier off the page. She poured herself another glass of wine from the decanter on the coffee table. The dog had worshiped Oscar. That made two of them, she thought.

Krueger guided his VW down the quiet boulevard that was flanked on both sides by expensive homes set on spacious plots. Mrs. Klement had hung up on him before he'd remembered to ask the address, and he'd had to get it from Oscar's office file. For a recent widow, he thought, she'd certainly been uncommonly flip on the phone. Of course, he hadn't followed the usual amenities, either. He hadn't even proffered condolences, so eager was he to rummage through a dead man's unused drugs. She had been terse, and he couldn't blame her. He now regretted his abrupt manner on the phone, but he admitted to himself that he couldn't wait.

She had said that she worked. It could have been by necessity. Addicts often die broke. Then too, doctors, even rich ones, had bad judgment when it came to money. That thought was dispelled a minute later as Krueger spotted the house—a two-story white colonial set on at least an acre of ground, obviously expensive, almost ostentatious. And then he remembered Brailey's description of Klement as being the local medical Midas. Krueger turned his car into a curving driveway that made a 180-degree circle to an exit on the same street. A concrete arm of the drive led to a four-car garage at the side of the house.

He killed the engine behind a new Continental and sat for a moment admiring the columns that supported a second-floor porch, which looked out over a brilliant green lawn and well-kept shrubbery. Krueger promptly lost any concern over the widow's financial plight. He mounted the eight brick steps to the front door and knocked, half expecting to be greeted by a black butler.

Instead, the door opened to reveal an attractive, if somewhat disheveled, woman about Krueger's height, barefoot and dressed in a pair of midcalf slacks and a red shirt, the tails knotted at her navel, like some grape picker.

"Dr. Krueger?" Joan motioned him with the wineglass to enter. "Come in."

Krueger stepped into the impressive foyer, his quick glance confirming that the interior of the house matched the elegance of the outside.

"I have the pills for you."

She turned on her heel, and Krueger followed her into the living room. A cluttered living room, he observed—stacks of books and papers all over the floor.

Joan turned to him and drained her glass. "Have a seat," she offered. "I'll be right back." And she was gone.

Krueger realized he hadn't uttered a word. He didn't know exactly what he had expected, but it wasn't this.

Nothing about it suggested a scene of mourning. He was still standing when she returned carrying a large grocery bag. Its glass contents tinkled with her walk.

"Mrs. Klement," he started lamely, "I want to tell you how sorry I am about your husband. It was, uh, most unfortunate."

"Yes," she said. She held the bag at arm's length under Krueger's nose. "Here." The bag must have contained fifty bottles.

"I mean, he was a fine doctor and will be missed very much." Krueger knew he was botching it; his solicitude now seemed very out of place. He thought he saw the ghost of a smile.

"I suppose he will be missed by some people," she said. "Look, Doctor, please don't think me heartless. It's not that at all. I'm just not one who shows her emotions very much. I've had the time to come to grips with Oscar's death. But you don't have to spare my feelings. I was under the impression that he wasn't a very good doctor at all. Those things have a way of getting around, you know. Besides, I was closer to him than anybody."

"Yes, of course, Mrs. Klement. I just meant . . ." A very practical woman, Krueger thought, and, unlike her husband, open and honest with herself. "Well," he continued, "when people are sick—that is, addicted to drugs—they're not really themselves." Krueger eyed her closely.

Joan returned his gaze. Her smile became more pronounced. "Dr. Krueger, that is very nice of you to say, but, if you'll forgive me, that is a cop-out—a convenient rationalization. I don't argue that people like Oscar are to be pitied, but it's a handy excuse. I think that if I wanted to be considered brilliant, I'd choose to become an alcoholic or an addict. You see, then when I couldn't perform, people could excuse me by saying I was just not myself, to use your words. I've known a lot of alcoholic doctors about whom it was said they were geniuses if only they didn't drink so much. I've seen a lot of those geniuses who turned out to be incredibly stupid when they were sober."

What manner of woman was this? Krueger asked himself. Even so, he allowed himself a faint smile. Wanting to change the subject, he looked around the room at the pile of books, the scattered newspapers. She followed his glance.

"I'm afraid I'm just a terrible housekeeper. Oscar was certainly right about that, at least."

Krueger realized he still held the bag of pills. He sat down on the couch and emptied the bag on the rug, more to divert his attention from her than anything else. She made him strangely uncomfortable. He fingered the bottles, reading labels. The pills were all the same, he saw: Seconal—red devils, all of them.

Catching the scent of perfume, he raised his head quickly, almost colliding with Joan. He found his face only inches from hers. He gulped audibly. She leaned back with a slight smile. She was sitting Indian style on the floor in front of him.

"They're the same," Krueger said to her. "They're all Seconal."

"Yep, that's what he took."

"Didn't he take anything else?" He waited while she took another sip of wine, then watched in astonishment as she allowed the dirty little dog to drink from her glass.

"Like what? Isn't this enough?" Joan asked.

"Is this all he took? Seconal?"

She thought about that for a minute. "Yes, that's it. I'm positive.

"But isn't it possible he was taking some other kind of medicine?"

"I don't think so. No, I'm quite sure. Of course, you must know, Doctor, that Oscar didn't really confide in me about his habit."

"You're quite certain that he didn't have high blood pressure? That he couldn't have been taking a drug for hypertension?"

"No, no. I'm sure I would have known about that. Of course, anything's possible, I suppose. Doctor, what in hell is the big mystery? I really don't understand your consuming interest in these pills. I mean, you were treating Oscar, weren't you? You certainly have his medical history. He died of a heart attack. It happens every day. Are you blaming yourself for Oscar's death?"

She was clearly upset now, Krueger saw. For the first time she transferred her attention from him. She stared out a back picture window that overlooked a radiant flower garden and patio, then looked back at him.

"I'm a little out of sorts, Doctor. You must forgive me. I've had a bad day. But I'm not one of your patients, you know. I've told you all I know."

Krueger hesitated, unsure of how much to tell her. "Well, to be frank, Mrs. Klement, it's a little more than that, than a heart attack. It's——"

"Your sleep therapy? Your experiments?"

"You've read about my work?"

"Some."

"I'm afraid, Mrs. Klement, you would have to understand what I've been attempting to do with the experiments."

Joan rose to her feet and looked archly at him. She smiled. Her earlier mood had returned. "Ah, Doctor, you are attempting to break addiction, stopping the withdrawal symptoms, the nightmares, the sweats, and the nervousness by decreasing REM pressure with a new drug." She clicked off the synopsis without taking a breath.

"Mrs. Klement, I was not aware that you had that knowledge. Your husband must have told you. I gave him some pamphlets that explained it in lay terms."

"My husband?" She chuckled pleasantly. "No, Doctor, I pretty much know about it already, from my work."

"Oh?"

"Yes, Doctor. I'm a psychologist."

"Why, I had no idea. I mean, I guess I didn't think about it. Your husband never mentioned it."

"I work at the Morrison Clinic," she replied. "I do much of their testing. That is, I did."

Krueger knew of the clinic. "Well," he said, "perhaps I should be calling you Doctor."

"Not yet, but that's coming. Now that Oscar . . ."

Krueger waited, but she didn't finish the thought. "You say you *did* work," he said finally. "Does that mean you've resigned?"

"You bet I did. Gave them my notice the day after Oscar died. I work my last day next Monday. Got my master's, so I should be able to get my doctorate in three years. *Then* you can call me Doctor."

"So you are going away."

"Yes, to the university, as soon as I get matters straightened out here—the house, Oscar's affairs, and everything. You see, there's no place around here to get a doctorate."

Krueger, not knowing what else to say, bent over, shoveling the Seconal bottles back into the bag. "Well, I must be going. Thank you for your time, Mrs. Klement." He got to his feet quickly. She was now leaning against the fireplace. The dog was on its hind legs begging more wine. "It was a pleasure meeting you," he said awkwardly. He felt a little foolish standing there with the grocery bag of pill bottles rattling against his leg.

"I'll see you to the door, Doctor."

"Don't bother."

Krueger hurried toward the door, but Joan was right behind him, reaching in front of him to turn the knob. She said nothing in response to his "good-by," and he walked briskly down the steps to his car. He felt that she was watching his departure, but when he turned, he saw that the front door was closed.

A puzzling woman, Krueger thought as he drove away from the house—a most puzzling woman indeed. Krueger didn't like puzzles. He liked everything orderly.

Chapter XXIX

"We can't get a handle on the guy, Doctor."

It was an admission Brailey had dreaded hearing. His face wrinkled in frustration as he looked at Anson Woolridge, the huge, shuffling chief of security of the medical center. Unlike his subordinates, Woolridge wore no uniform, though he had worn one for twenty years before retiring from the state police force. Like most state policemen, he had retired too early to raise petunias and too late to get into another line of work. Many were like Woolridge, drawing a good salary at a soft job while also collecting a sizable pension. They usually settled down as security guards at hospitals, colleges, or small manufacturing plants that generally needed little security. Woolridge felt out of place here in the upper reaches of the medical center. It was rare that anyone summoned him from his subterranean office between the pathology department and shipping and receiving. There he made out weekly shift schedules, drank coffee, and told slightly embellished stories about his investigative acumen with the state police.

"Goddamn it, a dozen people have described this loony," Brailey nearly shouted. "The guy seems to be walking around here with impunity. He's becoming the joke of the staff, except it's not funny."

Woolridge turned his hands toward Brailey in supplication. "Doctor, that description could fit a thousand guys in this town. Most of the patients he's talked to have either been all doped up or so sick they thought the guy came to them in a dream. And he picks his spots. He'll pull his act and then not show up again for a week."

Brailey was not going to be put off. "Look, Woolridge, so far this guy is just an annoyance, but we've got to stop him before he goes any further. Now, what are you doing about it?"

Woolridge hesitated, wondering how to placate the chief of staff. "Well, Dr. Brailey, I recommend we call in the city police and———"

"No, no. Christ, Woolridge, what in hell do you think we've got *you* for? We don't want to go public with this goddamn thing. I don't think the guy's even committed a crime, but at the very least it's causing talk. Pretty soon it's going to be common knowledge. At the worst we're going to face a damage suit."

Woolridge had a pliable oval face that seemed unsupported by bones; it changed shape like a beanbag. He worked his hands on his beefy knees. Brailey took note that he wore the same mottled-green tweed suit that he always saw him in, an attire that was incongruously out of place for the season. It clashed with a bright red tie that was of a hue only slightly more vivid than Woolridge's face at the moment.

"Well," Woolridge began timorously, "I've got my men walking the wards at night, Doctor, instead of remaining at their stations. I've been making spot checks myself."

Brailey mumbled a dissatisfied "Hmmm.".

Woolridge finished lamely, "This is a big place. People comin' and goin' at all hours. But we'll get him; don't you worry about that." The smile he tried to turn on Brailey never came off. A fly buzzed over the top of some papers on the desk. In the vacuum of the room, it sounded like a power saw. Woolridge's watery gray eyes went from the fly to Brailey. The chief of staff, he saw, was unconvinced.

"All right, I leave it to you," Brailey intoned with finality. "I want an immediate report when you catch up with the guy, soon."

Woolridge couldn't wait to reach the cool sanctuary of his cavelike office. Even as he rode the elevator down, he found himself scratching his chest under the bulky tweed jacket. This whole thing was giving him a rash. These high-and-mighty doctors were just like a captain he'd had in the state police. Fuckin' dictators, they were. He'd tell 'em to jam this job, except he had tailored his whole life around that second salary. He'd like to see Brailey do any better.

Maybe he'd better stop at the pharmacy and get some more ointment for this goddamn rash. Some breath mints, too; his breath smelled like a poolroom, from all the cigars he'd smoked last night. K-e-e-e-r-ist! Brailey should catch the guy if he was so smart. Haw, Brailey wouldn't know the guy if he bumped into him!

Chapter XXX

The intern was suturing a laceration on the scalp of a drunk who had been hit in a bar fight, and he wasn't being gentle about it. He hadn't used any Novocaine, and the drunk yelled with every stitch, which gave the intern a perverse satisfaction.

He was roughly slipping the needle through the epidermis again when the intercom came to life with a voice from the ambulance. It was heading in, the voice informed him, with an overdose, a young female.

"Christ, not another one," the intern muttered to himself. They came out of the walls after midnight. "How soon'll you get here?" he asked into the intercom. He could already hear the siren.

"E.T.A. at zero four hundred," came back the voice.

Those cowboys watch too many television shows, the intern thought. *A goddamn certificate that says they've completed advanced life-support training and they think they know it all.* "Vitals?" he asked of the two-way radio.

"Pulse fifty-two; blood pressure ninety over sixty; temperature ninety-seven point three."

The intern waited vainly for more. "Well? What about respirations, for chrissake?" The most important sign in overdose.

"Oh, yeah. Just six a minute. You want us to intubate her?"

"No, at six per minute she'll keep till you get her here."

The intern remembered that the last two endotracheal intubations performed by emergency medical technicians had resulted in broken teeth, and on one of them they had put the airway in the esophagus. He turned to the nurse who had been helping to hold down the drunk. "Better get a ventilator ready. Get a vein open with five percent and start lavaging as soon as she gets here. When the stomach's pumped out, I'll intubate her. Sounds like she'll have to be ventilated. Get arterial gases, and when they start the I.V., have a spectro drug-screen drawn."

He could hear the drunk moaning under the sterile drapes. The man still needed a few more stitches. *The hell with him; he can wait.*

Even half-dead, she's beautiful, the intern thought as he looked down at the girl. He almost never noticed physical appearances, so attuned was he to a medical evaluation of the patient's countenance. He noted her cyanotic lips, her shallow and infrequent respirations, her slow pulse; but he also took note of her full bosom, her natural blonde hair, her unblemished symmetrical legs. The eyes were bright blue, the dilating pupils seemingly staring at him as he lifted the lids. Damn good looker, really sharp.

The emergency-room nurse entered the office. "Spectro turned up Seconal, Valium, and Tofranil," she told the intern.

He turned and nodded.

"Pretty little thing," the nurse added. "How old is she?"

"I'd guess nineteen," he answered. "Maybe she'll reach twenty. We'll put her in intensive care tonight. Transfer her to psychiatry when she wakes up."

"Miss Piotroski?"

"Yes?"

"I'm Dr. Aldair. I assume you've been informed that I'd be seeing you."

The blonde girl looked up from her pillow. "Oh, you must be the psychiatrist. They said that as soon as I was feeling better, I'd have to talk to you." She laughed as she said this.

Attractive girl, he thought. She was smiling and had her makeup on—a good sign. Typical overdose: young, narcissistic, not really all that depressed, no deep-seated psychopathology. Probably a situational thing. Aldair had seen hundreds like her. They had one thing in common: they always called someone who could save them, and it usually worked. They got the attention they sought.

Aldair, as usual, was direct. "Did you really want to die when you took those pills?"

A tear formed suddenly at the corner of each eye. "I don't know. I mean, I really don't know what I wanted."

"Yes, I understand. That's very common. Do you mind if I pull up a chair? You're too pretty for me to be sitting on the edge of the bed, and I think I'm going to be here for a while."

Marlene Piotroski, who had been near death forty-eight hours ago, absolutely glowed.

Aldair filled out his consultation report quickly. At the bottom he wrote, "Reactive depression secondary to marital maladjustment and status post partum." He marked her prognosis as "excellent." Rushed to the altar by an unexpected pregnancy, the girl had fallen apart after the birth of her child. Ignored by her teenage husband except for sex, she was left with the care of the baby, whom she began to resent. Put in motion was the hostility-guilt cycle and the crying jags for which well-intentioned doctors had prescribed a merry-go-round of antidepressant drugs and sleeping pills. She had admitted that her consumption had doubled in recent months.

Aldair's pen stopped in midair, poised over the blank space that called for "Disposition," and he quickly reviewed his interview with the girl. Then he wrote, "Outpatient psychotherapy in the psychiatric clinic." He knew those words probably meant that he was finished at the medical center and he would hear of his banishment immediately.

Chapter XXXI

Krueger parked his car half a block from The Happening, the cocktail lounge where he was to meet Klement's widow. He would have preferred a site other than a bar, but he couldn't very well protest, since he had been the one who asked for the meeting.

The Happening lay near a line that divided the city from the suburbs, at least five miles from Krueger's office. He had overheard hospital talk that it was a singles' bar, although frequented only rarely by unattached personnel from the medical center. He was so eager to see Mrs. Klement again that he did not care where they met. She had aroused his curiosity to the point where it was imperative that he learn more about her. She could be the key. His circuitous inquiries, most of them indiscreet, had been fruitless.

He had called the wife of one of the medical-center staff physicians, a woman he had treated a while back for depression, with the explanation that it was merely a follow-up call. The woman was speechless inasmuch as Krueger hadn't seen her in almost five years. With little transition from his "routine" medical questions, he had blurted out, "How is Joan Klement doing these days since her husband died?" He supposed he had left the poor woman absolutely bewildered.

He had even gone to a monthly meeting of the county psychiatric association in hopes that he would run into the Morrison brothers. The "chance" meeting was obviously contrived, and the Morrisons had moved suspiciously away from him at the first opportunity. "Actually," Sam Morrison had said, "we don't know too much about her personal life or that of her late husband. She pretty much kept to herself."

Now, walking toward the cocktail lounge, Krueger was forced to admit that Morrison had been right. No one knew very much about the widow Klement. She seemed to have no friends. She had even refused to join the medical auxiliary—and *all* wives joined the medical auxiliary. "Her only interest is in that job," was the way one doctor's wife had put it.

Krueger stopped in front of the building and collected his thoughts. Yes, her job. She was a psychologist, and she seemed to know quite a bit about the physiology of sleep. When he had finally called and asked her point blank if he could meet her again "to talk about her husband's death," to his surprise, she had been receptive, even cordial.

"Sure, come on over," she had said. Then: "No, wait a minute. This place is a mess. The movers are due here any minute. Do you know a bar called The Happening?"

So, following her directions, he was here. He pushed open the double doors under the candy-striped awning and took a few tentative steps into the dark bowels of the room. He blinked into the gloom, his eyes trying to adjust to the quick transition from bright sunlight. He could make out a circular bar off to his left. About a half-dozen quiet drinkers stared at themselves in a gigantic mirror. A green-vested bartender leaned indolently against the cash register. An undercurrent of voices was barely discernible, a testament to the lounge's slim patronage at this early hour.

A half-moon of artificial-leather booths ringed the wall to his right opposite the bar, and it was in this direction that Krueger edged, taking care not to stumble down any unseen steps in front of him. It was a phenomenon of places like this, he thought, operating as they did on a minimum of electrical output.

"Dr. Krueger, over here."

Joan was seated in a booth, her face white over the thin cylindrical lamp that adorned the table. How anyone counted his change was something Krueger could not fathom.

He made his way to her, holding his hand in front of him as a divining rod, much as a blind man's cane gropes for a curb. He heard her low laugh.

"Part of the charm of the place, Dr. Krueger. Inhibitions are as hidden as the furniture."

"Yes, yes," he stammered, "I see what you mean." He sat heavily across from her in the booth. "Well," he said self-consciously, clasping his hands in front of him and looking around the room, "this seems to be a, um, very nice place."

Joan smiled broadly at him. "And now, Aaron, what's on your mind?"

She had called him Aaron. Nobody had called him by his first name in years. It sounded alien to him, as though it belonged to somebody else. This woman was an enigma. Her unexpected familiarity was no more surprising than her appearance. Gone was the disheveled, sloppily dressed woman who had confronted him in her home. Her dress was black, a tasteful, unadorned cocktail frock that did wonders for her. She was a very attractive woman, Krueger appraised, even beautiful. Her hair had been professionally done, framed close to her eyes; it accentuated her high cheekbones, yet was fashionably casual. The table light accented highlights that made it appear to change from black to lustrous purple.

"I asked to meet with you, Mrs. Klement, because——" A waitress slid a glass of white wine in front of Krueger. He opened his mouth to decline, but Joan cut him off:

"Drink it; it's good." She was softly commanding in a tone that assumed it would be obeyed.

"Really, Mrs. Klement, I don't drink. I mean, I just never——"

"Oh, for Chrissake, you had a bar mitzvah, didn't you?"

"Well, yes, but that was——"

The light bounced off her perfect teeth. "Well, you had to toast everybody, right? So don't tell me that you've never had a drink."

"Yes, but that was a long time ago."

"Look, we're here because you wanted to talk about my husband's death, isn't that right?"

"Yes, but——"

"So I say to myself, OK, and I get all dressed up and come over here to meet you just as you requested. I went to a lot of trouble, and I don't like to drink alone." She leveled a steady gaze at him.

Krueger found his fingers curling around the stem of the glass. Could this woman possibly have had anything to do with the death of her husband? She was a chameleon, presenting an aloof intelligence one moment, a child's brash candor the next. He lifted the wine glass slowly to his lips.

"*Shalom*." She smiled.

Krueger laughed at the way he had been benignly intimidated. "You are a very formidable person, Mrs. Klement."

"Call me Joan. Formidable? No, not really. It's mainly an act; you must know that. Psychiatrists know everything about a person before the person does, isn't that so?"

"I wish we were as omnipotent as you give us credit for. In fact, we are all actors to some extent. I resort to a little acting myself now and then."

"From what I hear, Aaron, *you're* the formidable one. They tell me you scare everybody out of their wits at the hospital, what with your reputation and all."

"My reputation?"

"The tranquilizer work, all that."

Krueger paused before saying, "That was a long time ago." He absent-mindedly took another swallow of the wine. "But I'm flattered that you even know about it."

"Oh, I read the journals."

"Well, that's been a long time ago, too. I haven't published anything in years." His eyes scanned the room again, avoiding her stare.

"That bothers you, doesn't it?"

Her question pulled his eyes back to hers. "Yes," he admitted. "Yes, it does. Ah, do you come here often?"

"Not much anymore. There was a time . . ." Her voice trailed off, and this time it was her turn to inspect the room.

"You're a mysterious woman, Mrs. Klement," Krueger boldly observed.

"Oh?"

"Yes. Before my research days, I was in private practice. I've always prided myself on figuring people out; but I'm afraid I've failed where you're concerned, and no one else seems to know." Krueger stopped suddenly, the embarrassment plain on his face.

Joan laughed. "So Dr. Krueger, you've been prying into my life? Do you always plumb the private lives of the widows of your patients? Why, I wouldn't be a bit surprised to find out you're a lecher lusting for my body."

"Why, Mrs. Klement, I assure you . . . I mean, I wouldn't want you to think . . . I would never . . ."

"Just teasing, Aaron." Her smile was back. "So," she said, "what about you? Since you couldn't find out about me, what about you? What dark secrets are you willing to share?"

A waitress stopped by the table, and Krueger didn't protest when Joan ordered more wine.

"I'm afraid I don't have any," he replied. "I have my work, and that's about all. Oh, I like classical music, but I don't get much time to indulge myself."

"No secret life? No other world to retreat to?"

"I guess my work is my retreat."

"From what?"

Krueger didn't answer at once. Then he said, "But we came here to discuss your husband."

"So we did, so we did. Look, I think I know why you're so hellbent to talk about Oscar. I've heard that he didn't get any of your drug that night, to prevent the withdrawal. So I assume that's the reason you came to the house the other day, because you were worried that I'd cause trouble, sue you or something." Her mouth still held the smile. It forced attractive crow's feet to gather at the corners of her eyes. "You don't have to worry. I would never do anything like that."

"No," Krueger said, "I'm sure you wouldn't."

"Then, why are we here? Why are you calling my friends, my employers? Are you on some kind of guilt trip over Oscar's death?" Her voice was gently mocking.

"Mrs. Klement"—Krueger took a deep breath—"this is difficult for me. It wasn't just that we didn't find my drug in your husband's body. We, well, we found traces, actually a high concentration, of reserpine."

"Reserpine?" Her mouth went from a smile to form an O. "That's a catecholamine depleter, aggravates REM pressure. So *that's* why you wanted to know if Oscar was taking any blood-pressure medicine!"

"Yes. You see, that would explain a lot. It might even account for his death. If he was being given a——"

" 'Being given'! Oh, wow! At my house the other day I thought you might be testing the legal waters. Then today, when you called, I thought you might be interested in me. And I guess you are. You're interested in finding out if I slipped Oscar some reserpine. You're maybe interested in putting me in jail." Her laugh was abrupt and guileless.

"Oh, no," Krueger said quickly, "not at all. It's just

that, well, I just have to know. This project, you see, is my life. The whole thing depends on finding out what really happened." Her open demeanor had cowed him.

"Well, Aaron, my friend, I'm not going to tell you." Joan smirked. "You're only going to have to do some more detective work. Do a little more probing, my psychiatrist friend. I've always been intrigued by psychiatrists, and you're the most famous one I've ever met."

It was the second time in days that Krueger felt foolish in her presence. "Mrs. Klement, I'm afraid I've misjudged you. I mean, I'm sorry I even asked you to meet me. You're making fun of me, and I don't blame you. I'm sorry to have taken up your time." He started to rise, but her strong hand on his forearm held him in his seat.

"Oh, sit down, Aaron. Have another glass of wine. We've got that foolishness out of the way. Have another drink and tell me about yourself."

He looked into her eyes for any flippancy that might remain. "Tell my life story?" She seemed attentive. "I doubt very much if you'd find it interesting." He waited for the smile that never came.

"Try me," she said. Her fingers glided on the top of the table and came to rest lightly on the back of his hand.

Krueger looked at her hand, and she withdrew it slowly.

"I have a little secret," she said. "Call it a confession. I have followed your career."

"What?"

"Yes, in a way." Her smile was back, this time tender and shy. "I was sitting in the audience when you gave a guest lecture. It was some years ago, actually. I was a sophomore psych major at the time. I can even remember the subject—the treatment of chronic schizophrenics with a new drug and how you were able to release them to home care."

Krueger shook his head slowly. "You are amazing. I'd almost forgotten about that."

"You were at a mental hospital in California and——"

His head moved more vigorously as he interrupted: "You sure you want to hear about all that?"

"Absolutely."

He spread his arms on the table, his lips compressed in embarrassed amusement. "Where do I begin?"

"What about the drug—your discovery?"

"Yes, the drug; it saved my life."

Krueger's words were a muffled reminiscence, and Joan had to lean forward to catch them. Her silence was respectful anticipation.

"You would have to have been there to know what I mean," he continued. "I came to California from private practice in New York, and it was a different world. You can't appreciate mental institutions as they were in the fifties. It was depressing, and not much of a challenge."

"Then, why did you leave New York?" she asked.

He looked down quickly, as though his eyes might mirror his thoughts. Because, he thought, the California job was for beggars, and that precisely described his bargaining power at the time. He sipped from the wine-glass—a stalling gesture—and avoided her eyes. "Well, I . . ." He looked up, wondering if she could see the pain. "It's not really something I want to talk about."

"Forget New York," she said quickly. "Tell me about your discoveries."

He shrugged. "Luck. Most discoveries are like that. I had given up on the state hospital—on psychiatry even—and accepted a fellowship in biochemistry. But, just before I left, I found an unopened carton of chlorphenothiazine. It had been there for months—sent to the hospital for clinical trials. The FDA hadn't approved it, and the hospital administrator had been afraid to try it."

"But not you, Aaron." Joan smiled and raised her glass in toast.

Krueger smiled back. "Well, anyway, I had read where it had a calming effect on monkeys; so I began dosing schizophrenics with it. The results were quite dramatic."

"And then you came to my school and awed me." She smiled again.

"Well, it didn't happen quite that quickly. But, to make a long story short, I gained a measure of notoriety and was offered the job here."

"That's how the drug saved your life," she said.

"Professionally, anyway," he acknowledged.

She had been studying his face. "And personally?"

He said nothing for a long moment. "Come to think of it, I haven't had much of a personal life. In fact, I'm afraid to admit that my work has occupied my time to the exclusion of everything else."

"Everything?" Joan asked over the top of her glass, and then, when Krueger gave no indication that he was going to answer, she hurried to break his solemnity. "Well," she said, "you should be proud of what you've done—damned proud."

"It's very nice that you should say that, Mrs. Klement."

"Nice, hell, it's got nothing to do with nice. You should remind yourself of your accomplishments. You deserve to be complimented. And call me Joan, damn it."

Krueger cast his eyes downward. A warmth crept across his face. He didn't know whether it was embarrassment or the wine. He looked up again at her. "Very well . . . Joan."

Her laugh was an infectious schoolgirl's giggle. It forced a grin on Krueger. The grin grew to a chuckle. Then he threw back his head and laughed. He suddenly felt very relaxed.

Chapter XXXII

It was the first time Krueger had ever been inside Aldair's tiny office. The room was barely large enough to accommodate a small desk. Because of the annual change of tenants, the chief psychiatry resident's office was in a continual state of disrepair.

Aldair was not surprised to see Krueger. He had been expecting him ever since he'd filled out the chart on Marlene Piotroski, the overdose patient. He was caught off balance, however, when Krueger sauntered in casually, wearing a smile of sorts, and sat down on the stiff wooden chair in front of Aldair's desk. Aldair had started to rise but instead remained seated. He read Krueger's expression as the calm before the storm, and he decided to get it over with quickly. "You're here about that overdose—right, Dr. Krueger?"

"Yes. Well, partly."

Aldair waited for the explosion, but none came.

"Why do you want her to receive out-patient psychotherapy?" Krueger asked softly.

"I simply felt it would be best for her. She's been taking too much Seconal—and other substances—but it's not a deep-seated addiction; more habituation than anything else, due to some marital problems. She's not really very——"

"You are aware that all patients admitted with any history of substance abuse or overdose are to be referred to me as sleep-study candidates?"

238

"Yes, I'm aware of that, Dr. Krueger." Aldair steeled himself for the outburst that had to come now.

"And you realize that this is the main source of patients for my study?"

"Yes."

"Then, why did you disobey departmental orders?"

Aldair drew a breath. "For two reasons. The first I've already told you: I felt she should have psychotherapy, not any more drugs. She's being drugged enough by her private psychiatrist and her obstetrician."

Any remark about drugging patients was a definite insult to Krueger, and both of them knew it. Krueger said nothing.

"The second reason, I guess, is obvious. I figured I had already lost my residency, that I was finished here, so I thought to hell with it." He sat back and watched Krueger cock his head to one side. *I have nothing to add,* Aldair thought. *It's your move.*

"Yes, I can appreciate that, Dr. Aldair. I have given this, uh, misunderstanding between us some thought; and, actually . . . actually, some of it was my fault. In fact, I owe you somewhat of an apology. You see, I've recently learned that you did in fact start the amitrypton that night. The fault, Dr. Aldair, was not yours."

Krueger went on, ignoring Aldair's openmouthed stare. "Now, about that overdose. She had been abusing Valium and Seconal, and she *must* be part of the study." His eyes bored into Aldair's. "So, if you would go ahead and arrange for her to be in the sleep lab at the appropriate time, instead of the, uh, out-patient clinic, I think there will be no problem with your residency—no problem at all."

Aldair, popeyed, closed his mouth and nodded dumbly at his professor.

"Good, good," Krueger said, turning and walking to the door. "Good."

Chapter XXXIII

Krueger swore as he used a handkerchief to blot the blood from his hand. Never a heavy user of profanity, he had found recently that cursing occupied an increasing share of his vocabulary. The cat had sunk its claws into him just as he had pierced the animal's hind-leg vein with an amitrypton injection. "Damn it!" he said. "Damn bastard cat." He threw the cat back into the cage and slammed the door. The cat, bouncing off the rear of the cage, stood stunned, glaring at Krueger. Krueger glared back.

Here he was back in the animal lab, puttering, marking time. He stuffed the handkerchief into his rear pants pocket and sucked at the wound. He hadn't injected a cat in months—it had not been necessary since the drug had been proven safe for humans—but Krueger forced himself to do something just to keep busy. He had gone to his office precisely at 6:30 A.M. and had spent about a half-hour staring off into space before finally deciding to walk down to the animal lab. He hadn't even planned on injecting the cat but had done it impulsively after walking aimlessly around the laboratory for several minutes.

He glanced at his watch: 10:00 A.M. It seemed as though an entire day had passed already. On a normal day he would be reviewing the EEG of the previous night's sleep patient. He kicked one of the cages, setting off a chorus of screeching.

Damn! His hand was still bleeding. That crazy cat

had inflicted more than a scratch. He rummaged through the lab in search of a bandage. Finding none, and holding the handkerchief once more to his hand, he started up the stairs back to his office and almost ran into Frank Riley on one of the darkened staircases.

"Riley, what are you doing here?" Krueger had expected to be hearing from the drug-company man but had thought that it would be by telephone.

Riley looked haggard, his eyes red-rimmed. "I've been looking all over for you," he said. He stuck out a hand in greeting, but Krueger showed him his own, bleeding member.

"Let's go to my office. I want to fix this." Krueger, though in a hurry to stanch the flow of blood, slowed his pace up the stairs to match that of the heavy Riley, who wheezed along in his wake. It was the first time he had seen Riley since the cocktail party. Krueger had left hurriedly that night without talking to him at any length.

As the research coordinator for the Monarch Corporation, Riley was the "overseer" of money the company granted to experimental projects. At first Krueger had resented him, regarding the man as a corporate Philistine, meddling in what Krueger jealously considered a purely personal endeavor; but over the years—Krueger had known Riley since the tranquilizer-research days—Riley had been helpful. He had been able to pry funds out of his company almost anytime Krueger had asked for them. And he had been patient when the study had taken longer than predicted. He had once been a good research physician himself, though Kreuger had never gathered sufficient nerve to ask him why he had retreated inside the corporate world.

Riley had a certain alcoholic gregariousness. Maybe the booze had driven him out of research, Krueger conjectured. Whatever the reason, his background made him the ideal buffer between manufacturer and scientist. Kreuger even harbored a certain admiration for the way

Riley, drunk to the eyeballs, could articulately discuss an intricate research project and then turn to someone else to spin a humorously smutty story. He could emerge from a night of drinking and, nursing a monumental hangover, meet Krueger at the start of the day to discuss his project.

Riley leaned against Krueger's inner-office door, his chest heaving with the exertion of the climb. "Damn, Krueger, you got somethin' against elevators?" He moved ponderously toward the desk, at which Krueger was now sitting, covering his wound with a bandage he had taken from a drawer. "You got a paper cup or something?"

Krueger motioned toward an alcove cut into one of the wooden bookshelves. "There's a coffee cup over by that percolator."

Riley took a leather-bound flask from his inside coat pocket and poured a generous amount of the amber liquid into the cup. "Got any water round here?"

"Out in the hall—a drinking fountain next to the stairs."

"The hell with it." Riley returned to the desk and sat down. Raising the cup to his mouth, he took three gulps, his eyes closed. When he opened them again, they were watery. He made a face. "You know why I'm here, Krueger?"

"I assume it's about that vial I sent you."

"You're damn right it is. Would you be so goddamn kind as to tell me what in hell is going on around here?"

"I'm not sure just what you mean."

"What I mean is, I want some answers. I caught the first plane out here to get them. For starters, why did that doctor die in your sleep lab?"

Krueger noticed that Riley had changed pronouns. In the past it had always been "our" sleep lab. "Oh, you know about that? Well, he had a heart attack."

"While he was getting our drug, for Chrissake," Riley said. "Or *was* he getting it?"

Kreuger was fully prepared for the question. "You've had it analyzed, then, the sample I sent you?"

"I sure as hell have. And, goddamn it, do you know what was in it?"

"Yes," Kreuger said calmly. "Reserpine."

Riley's face froze. "How in hell did you know that?"

"I had two other vials analyzed at another lab."

"You *what?*"

"Yes, I wanted to see just what——"

"Jesus, how could you have been so stupid?" He cut Krueger off as he started to speak. "What lab did you send them to?"

"Uh, the state toxicology lab."

Riley looked at Kreuger for a moment, took another pull from the cup, put it on the desk, and buried his face in his hands. "No, say it isn't so." His voice coming through his hands had a strangely distant quality. After a while Riley looked up, leaned back, and dangled his arms over the sides of the chair. "Krueger, Krueger . . . Why didn't you just send it to us?"

"Well, I wanted to check. You see, the autopsy blood samples that showed reserpine had already been sent out to this state lab, and since they were familiar with my, uh, problem——"

"God," Riley said, talking to the ceiling, "why me? Look, Krueger, do you understand that you sent it to a state crime lab—a *crime* lab? You might as well have sent it to Ralph Nader." He extended his arm toward Krueger, his palm turned upward in a gesture of helplessness. "How did you get the coroner to order the analysis?"

"Oh, there was no coroner. There was never any coroner on the case, Frank. A friend of mine at the state lab ran the samples for me."

Riley brightened. "Really? Well. Well, that's the first right thing you've done in this whole mess."

"Riley, I don't appreciate your sarcasm."

"Don't pout, Krueger. Tell me more about this friend of yours." Riley refilled his cup from the flask.

"His name's Wilson," Krueger said. "He's a toxicologist, nice fellow and, well, just a friend. He analyzed the samples and phoned me the results."

"No written report?"

"No. He sent a written report about the autopsy blood sample—that's how I found out about the reserpine—but there's nothing in writing about the two vials I sent him."

"You sent him a couple of vials. Did you send any others anywhere?"

"No, I took only three of them at random out of the pharmacy. You got the other one."

"Christ, Krueger, if this guy Wilson told you those vials contained reserpine, why in hell did you send one to us?"

Krueger doodled with a pencil a moment before answering. "Because, Riley, I wanted to see if you people had made the mistake, if you had accidentally filled the vials with reserpine instead of amitrypton." He sat a little straighter in his chair. "Besides, what harm could it do?"

Riley pulled his sweating corpulence closer to Krueger's desk and pointed one finger toward the ceiling. "First, Dr. Krueger, there is no chance that we could accidentally put reserpine in those vials. We don't even make it; there's none of the stuff within five hundred miles of our plant. Second"—Riley held up another finger—"the harm, my good doctor, is that it's just about finished this entire project."

"What?" Krueger felt as though a very large rock had settled in his abdomen.

Riley slouched back in his chair, looking exhausted. He was peering over the rim of the cup, taking small, measured sips of the whiskey. "Look, Krueger," he said wearily, "we've known each other a long time. I understand what you've been through. Hell, I know what it's like to be on the verge of something big and have it blow up in your face, believe me. You get that single-minded, determined . . ." Riley was beginning to slur his words. "I've tried to protect you; I've been in your corner. Look, do you know what I'm saying?"

"Yes, I understand."

"Well, my friend, Dr. Krueger, despite the fact I think you're a brilliant guy—that you've got a great thing going here—despite that, this time you've gone too fucking far." Riley drew out the obscenity, pronouncing each syllable distinctly. "Too far to cover your ass." .

Krueger could see that Riley was clearly drunk now. His intake this morning was probably only bringing to full flower the dormant alcohol still in his bloodstream from the night before. "I've pushed things too far," Krueger prompted him.

"Yeah, too far. Jesus, yes! I'm beginning to line up on the company side, Krueger. This goddamn sleep project has cost thousands. We set up an animal lab for you, hired technicians, bought equipment, hundreds of those goddamn cats, keep a feet—uh, a *fleet*—of biochemists busy sending you different drugs. You finally get one that works, and before you can get one goddamn paper published—after ten years, thousands of dollars—fuckin' guy dies before the drug is approved. Jesus!"

Krueger began to protest: "Yes, but, Riley——"

"You know what that means? You *know*, Krueger? I'll tell you what it means. The FDA moves in and stops the project cold. Those fuckers stop development of a drug if somebody farts sideways."

"Yes, but Riley . . ."

"If somebody farts sideways! And then, with my boss kicking my ass around the block for sticking with you all these years, you send us one of our own ampules—*our own drug*—and it's got the wrong fuckin' stuff in it."

"Riley, it doesn't have to be the end. I know that——"

"Jesus." Riley was now addressing the carpet.

"Riley," Krueger began again, trying to get his attention.

"Where's your can, Krueger?"

"What?"

"Your can—where's your *can?* I gotta pee."

"Just outside, in the hall, other side of the receptionist's desk."

Riley started for the door, swaying only slightly. "Just like to know what in hell is going on around here," he mumbled. "Jesus!"

Krueger watched him leave, then got up and walked slowly around the desk. His eyes went to the coffee cup. It was still one-third full. Krueger was sorely tempted.

Chapter XXXIV

Krueger had been waiting in the chief of staff's office for almost an hour when Brailey had phoned his secretary to say he was "held up on rounds." Having seen Krueger fidgeting impatiently, she had guided him from the waiting room into Brailey's inner sanctum. Now he sat in Brailey's chair behind the massive oak desk, wishing he could get up and leave. *My time's as valuable as his*, he told himself. "On rounds." Brailey couldn't confine himself to administration as did most chiefs of staff. He was on the clinician's ego trip, playing doctor.

Suddenly Krueger sensed someone else in the room, and his anger turned to embarrassment as he looked up at Brailey towering over him. Krueger hadn't heard him enter the office. Why did he feel guilty, caught sitting in the man's chair? He rose quickly and shuffled out of Brailey's way.

"Nice to see you, Krueger," Brailey said with a hint of a smile. He collapsed heavily, reclaiming his chair.

"Yes," was all Krueger could think to say. He moved to another chair on the other side of the desk.

"Sorry I'm late," Brailey continued. "Making rounds, you know." From Brailey, nothing ever sounded like an apology. "You said it was important."

"Yes, we're ready to resume sleep therapy."

Brailey, who had been trying to unlock the center drawer of his desk, looked up sharply. "We? Who's we? We just sent you the protocol yesterday."

"Yes, I know," Krueger said.

"Well, then, if you've read it, you know there are quite specific guidelines that must be followed before you can start up again."

"Yes. The guidelines have been met precisely. We are ready to start."

Brailey made no attempt to conceal his surprise. "When?"

"Tomorrow night."

"Are you serious, Krueger? My God, man, the requirements in that protocol are pretty stringent. You have to have an R.N. who can read EKG monitors and do C.P.R. You need an E.M.T. who has passed the advanced life-support exams."

"Yes, I know. Both have been done."

"You got that good a nurse and emergency medical technician?"

"Yes." Now it was Krueger's turn to show the trace of a smile.

"What about all the monitoring equipment? And I don't mean your goddamn brain-wave printouts; I mean cardiac monitors, defibrillators, a drug cart. We listed all the necessary drugs and——"

"Done," Krueger said crisply, "all of it."

Brailey paused. He was shaking his head. "You've done all that in twenty-four hours? You've set up a complete nurses' station just to monitor one patient?"

"That's correct, Dr. Brailey."

"Ah, the drug company," Brailey said. "I should have guessed. They've still got a lot of money to throw around."

"I wouldn't say it was exactly thrown around, Doctor," Krueger said.

In fact, *thrown around* were the exact words Riley had used when Krueger had wheedled the money out of him as he drove the tipsy drug-company representative to the airport. "The last case, Frank. Please," Krueger had begged shamelessly.

"OK, one more time," Riley had said, "if I can talk the boss into it. But, Jesus, Krueger, don't fuck it up or we'll both go down with the fuckin' ship this time."

Krueger had smiled to himself. He was sure Riley could get him the money. The drug company trusted Riley.

"But the executive committee has to approve your starting up again," Brailey was saying, "and they don't meet for three weeks."

"Yes, I've thought of that," Krueger said quickly, "but you—you could call it a *de facto* meeting. I believe that's quite within the hospital bylaws when there is just one item on the agenda."

"You can't wait for the next regular meeting?"

"No."

Brailey shook his head again, the smile still on his face. "Well, I've got to admit one thing: You've done a lot of hustling. I hear you practically threatened your resident, Aldair, with disembowelment. You really not going to recommend him for psychiatry boards?"

"That was just a misunderstanding. We've settled our differences. Of course I'm going to recommend him."

"You can't wait, huh, Krueger?" Brailey slowly unwrapped a cigar and struck three matches before he was able to light it. He blew a cloud of smoke in Krueger's direction. "You've got to have your fifty cases before that meeting."

"So you know about that, too? For somone who's generally ignored around here—I might even say ridiculed—I seem to have aroused to an inordinate amount of interest in my study."

"Now, don't get your balls in an uproar, Krueger," Brailey said not unkindly. "Like I just said, I'm chief of staff at this hospital and I keep a finger on things. You must have another case ready, right? That's why you're moving heaven and earth to get on with your study?"

"Well, as a matter of fact, there is this young lady we just admitted, an overdose who———"

"I thought so," Brailey interrupted. "You've got another one all picked out." He smiled again, more broadly this time. "You can't use Klement as your fiftieth case. Can't cure a dead man."

"He shouldn't be dead. If he'd just received my drug, he'd have———"

"Good God, Krueger, you going to start that shit again? You gave a speech in front of half the staff the day after he died about how your drug would have prevented a coronary."

"It would have"—Krueger paused, then decided to use the old psychoanalyst's ploy of catching the patient off guard to test the reaction—"but he never received the amitrypton. He received reserpine instead."

"Krueger," Brailey said after a moment's hesitation, "are you saying what I *think* you're saying?"

"Well, I don't know for sure, of course. It's just

that we found it in his blood on the spectrophotogram instead of the amitrypton, and it—the reserpine, that is—is known to interfere with sleep therapy. It aggravates the withdrawal and——"

"How many people know about this?"

"No one," Krueger lied. "No one knows." His mind went quickly to his conversation with Joan Klement. That might have been a mistake.

"Well, thank God for that. Do you know what talk like that could do to the medical center? You really think reserpine was administered deliberately?"

Krueger quickly debated with himself, then decided against telling Brailey about the amitrypton vials containing reserpine. "I am only suggesting that there is that possibility," he said.

"Dr. Krueger, you're paranoid. You're a candidate for your own rubber room. Reserpine is a common drug—mild side effects, a stuffy nose, a few nightmares, maybe. I mean, Christ, if somebody wanted to kill Klement, they could do it a hell of a lot easier than that. Anyone who knew how to manipulate his sleep would know how to knock him off with something that wouldn't leave a trace. Hell, a little potassium in the vein, five or six hundred units of insulin—both metabolize rapidly and leave nothing on the spectro. A few convulsions and——" Brailey snapped his finger. "Besides, why would anyone want to do away with Klement, a greedy incompetent, a turd personally, but a nobody? Kill him? Bullshit!"

"I didn't say I thought anybody was trying to kill him."

"Then, just what *are* you saying?"

"Well, maybe to destroy my experiments, to discredit me. I know what everybody here thinks about the sleep lab—calling the neuropsychiatry building Transylvania, that sort of thing." Krueger stopped, aware of Brailey's eyes narrowing above the smoking cigar.

"Krueger, you're not only paranoid; you're an egomaniac. You muck around in that sleep lab of yours and think you're the center of the universe, on the threshold of solving the mystery of life. You complain about being ridiculed. Hell, you ask for it. You give the impression the medical center revolves around you and that sleep project. You walk around the hospital like a cross between Jesus Christ and Saint Francis of Assissi. You're trying to get back into the limelight."

At the look on Krueger's face, Brailey let up. What in hell was the use of belittling the guy? He stubbed the cigar into an ashtray.

"Dr. Brailey," Krueger managed to say evenly, "do I get to resume my sleep therapy?"

Brailey sighed. "Oh, the hell with it. I'll call the executive committee together this afternoon. You can start your goddamn project tomorrow night. But you watch yourself down there, you hear, Krueger? I don't want anybody dying down there again, natural causes or otherwise. And no more of this crap about somebody trying to knock off Klement, you understand?"

"I understand perfectly, Dr. Brailey. Thank you very much." Krueger left quickly.

Out in the hall, he almost did a jig. He resisted the urge to clap his hands. Now to get to the pharmacy and get the amitrypton, make sure that everyone knew the sleep lab was back in business again.

Chapter XXXV

She was leaving town, Joan had told him, and suddenly that seemed like an intolerable loss. Krueger guided the car down the night-shrouded street. His only other visit to the Klement home had had the benefit of daylight, and now he had to find his way by landmarks instead of house numbers.

She had called to tell him of her leaving and to wish him success. There had been a pause at the other end of the line, which Krueger had boldly interpreted as an invitation. "I, uh, would like to see you again, uh, to say good-by . . . Joan. I mean, I have some things to say, to kind of clear the air." He had mumbled like a flustered schoolboy and was relieved when she'd responded with alacrity, "I'd like that. Why don't you come over?"

Fortunately the street lights illuminated the identifying signs on each corner, and Krueger wondered why the rich always lived in meandering subdivisions with British-sounding names. He passed Marlborough Place and Whitehall Court. The snobbery seemed to extend to geometrics. No neat rectangles as in the middle-class neighborhoods; here there were separate enclaves. Every street led to nowhere, dead ends and cul-de-sacs. Krueger had already driven futilely down two of the streets. He had been to her place only days ago, but intervening events had made time an unreality. So much had happened.

Just when Krueger felt that he might drive interminably in this maze, he spotted the Klement house. It was a stroke of luck, inasmuch as there didn't seem to be a light on in the place. Puzzled, he turned into the long, curving driveway. He let the car's engine idle as he sat in front of the entrance. Moonlight played off the towering white columns supporting the archway. Damn it, she had tired of waiting and had left while he was bumbling around trying to find the place. The house looked deserted. An unexplanable sense of relief tugged at his feeling of disappointment. Maybe this was fortuitous, he thought. Maybe it was just as well he didn't see her again.

Suddenly Krueger felt like an intruder. He shifted gears quietly and was about to drive away when the front door opened. Joan stood there in the doorway, and Krueger hit the brakes so violently his head snapped forward. She was an apparition in the moonlight, her hair unrestrained and falling past her shoulders. Krueger felt a stirring. It pulled him from the car. He wanted to call an appropriate greeting, perhaps something witty; but maybe there was nothing really appropriate to the moment. His nose caught the fragrance of the backyard garden, and he thought foolishly of candy and flowers.

Joan's voice sliced clearly through the night air. "Goddamn power company's shut the lights off, switching something or other while I move." Her pragmatic, cryptic manner immediately relaxed him. He somehow felt at home. Krueger chuckled at his own foolish romanticism. *When was the last time I felt this way?* he marveled.

The moment he reached the front stoop and stood facing her, he realized she was taller than he, even barefooted, as she'd been the day he met her. She was wearing an ill-fitting smock loosely tied with a cloth belt. It served to conceal her trim figure, but Krueger didn't mind. Her face was the same, those regular features that cosmetics could not enhance. A few days ago he would have thought her slovenly. Now she looked casually, wildly beautiful—so unlike the assured sophisticate in the cocktail lounge. Krueger liked them both.

She reached into a deep pocket of the smock and withdrew a cigarette lighter, which she used to touch off the wick of a candle she held in her other hand. "Here, follow me," she said, and holding the candle above her head, she preceded Krueger through the foyer and into the spacious living room. "Just like the goddamn Girl Scouts." She laughed, and Krueger watched as she lit several other candles that had been placed in the middle of the floor.

He walked slowly around the periphery of the room, the light from the candles casting his unproportioned shadow on the walls. He realized he was looking for a place to sit down in a room devoid of furniture. Joan had sat on the floor in a circle of light amid the candles and watched him with amusement. From the corner he could hear piano music, though almost as much static as music. A small portable eight-track cassette was emitting the scratchy sound. Krueger strained to listen before recognizing it as Bach.

"I must look like one of my caged cats, pacing about like this," he said.

"A caged lion." She smiled.

He moved slowly to her and sank self-consciously to the floor in front of her.

"That's a relief. I was afraid for a minute you were going to sit on my tape cassette."

He returned her smile. "I almost did. It's the only thing in the room. It's . . . it's, well, unusual to hear Bach playing on such a small . . . I mean, for classical music, the speaker doesn't——"

"Do you like Bach?" Joan interrupted.

"Yes. Yes, Bach is my favorite, especially these two-part piano inventions."

"You know, Aaron, I suspected that. Believe it or

not, I recorded them just for you about an hour ago, when I found out the power was about to be shut off."

"Are you serious?"

"Yes. There's something about Bach that I associate with you. Want to hear about it?"

He nodded, watching the flame images of the candles in her eyes.

"Well, you see, Bach—particularly in these two-part inventions—is so, well, precise, almost mathematical. The counterpoint, the way the left and right hands take turns interweaving the themes—symmetrical and balanced."

"Some people think of Bach as too stuffy for just that reason," Krueger said, "too precise and pedantic."

"Just the novices, Aaron. We both know better. After you listen awhile—after you know it, recognize what Bach is really doing—it becomes emotional. It soars; it flashes across the sky."

"You make me sound like a contradiction. I certainly don't see myself as flashing across the sky. If that was meant to be flattering, I'm embarrassed."

"Don't be, Aaron. Yes, I think of you has having soaring potential. You've just allowed the world to see your symmetrical side, the balanced you."

Krueger emitted a low laugh that sounded false in the face of her solemnity. "That's quite a metaphor. I wonder if Johann Sebastian Bach would agree with you?"

"He would."

"How can you be so sure?"

"Well, he fathered seventeen children while he was writing all that balanced music. His equilibrium must have gotten off the track now and then." Joan uncoiled from her sitting position and lay on her side, her head propped up by one arm. "Have you fathered any children, Aaron?"

The question startled him. "Why, no. No, none."

When he'd recovered, he asked, "And you? I assume you never had children."

"No, thank God."

Then there was silence. *How little we know about each other,* Krueger thought. "Did you really play Bach just because I was coming?"

"Yes, I told you." She said it emphatically, in that open way of hers. Then her voice softened. "You see, Aaron, you can have both."

"Both?"

"Yes. You can have an inner life—a life of the mind, a cerebral existence, like you have—and you can also have the rest—a physical, sensual life. One doesn't have to be sacrificed for the sake of the other."

"And you think I have?" he said. How odd and yet at the same time how perfectly natural it seemed to him to be having this conversation with a woman he had met just a few short days ago.

"Yes, I do." Joan stubbed her cigarette out on the bare wood of the floor. The floppy belt around her waist had loosened, creating a sag in the neck of the smock. The candlelight fought with the shadows on the deepening cleavage, and Krueger could see the swelling that was the top of her breasts. "Am I right?"

Krueger's answer was low but clearly discernible in the gymlike quality of the room. "Yes," he said, "you're right."

His eyes traveled the length of her lithe body. He watched the changing highlights in her hair as it tumbled along the forearm that held up her head. The smock—the wrapper, whatever it was called—had inched to midthigh. She appeared not to notice. Krueger saw that her toenails were painted. That excited him. His eyes traveled back to her face, to see that she was smiling at him.

"You seem to enjoy staring at me," he said. A stupid remark, he thought, ventured only to break the silence.

"Does it bother you?"

"I don't know. I mean, yes. Yes, I suppose it does."

She studied him for a moment, almost clinically. The tip of her tongue snaked out ever so slightly between her teeth. She curled her legs under her, her eyes never leaving him, and started to rise. "Well, then, I suppose it's time to stop staring, isn't it?" She stood over him. "Take off your glasses, Aaron."

"What?"

"Take off your glasses."

Krueger found himself obeying without hesitation. Her next movement was so casual it belied her dexterity. The smock fell to the floor, her panties on top of it, and she was naked. Krueger was speechless. In his shock, he felt nothing. No urges gripped him. His body was as of stone, and he could do nothing to erase the surprise on his face. He had thought of this possibility, but only in a dreamlike way. Now, watching it come to life, he was transfixed. It was as though he was watching the whole scene from afar. He was outside himself, an interested observer.

Joan looked around as though searching for something. Her nakedness was startlingly white in the gloom of the room. She padded over to a window. Krueger watched as the pale light from the candles outlined the muscles in her tight buttocks. She began tugging at the heavy velvet drapes covering the window, but was rewarded with only a slight tearing sound at the top. Grasping the edge of the curtain, she pulled herself free of the floor. For a few seconds she hung there suspended, swinging on the curtain until it came away. Momentarily she staggered under the weight of the fabric and then she turned, gathering the folds of the material over one shoulder. The rest of it trailed between her legs as she made her way back to him. Messalina in her toga, Krueger thought. Or Scarlet O'Hara.

Joan stopped close to him, her thigh almost brushing his face. She stood unmoving, the dark areas of her body seeming to mock him. Her presence was overpowering. Krueger felt his leg twitch under him, and he watched as her hand came slowly toward his face. As if in a trance, he raised his hand to meet hers and pressed it to his lips. How cool and smooth, how sweet . . . Suddenly she was all that he had missed. She was a chance at life itself.

Krueger felt his arms reach for her, but she collapsed in the curtain bed next to him, entangled in the heavy material. The maroon drapery was like an open wound against her white skin. He realized he was holding his breath. Several odors assailed his nostrils simultaneously—the musty smell of the drapes, Joan's perfume, her body secretions. She turned on her side to face him, and he seized her.

He tore at his clothing, then realized that she was helping him in her unhurried way. She was looking at him. Her mouth was pursed, and a cooing sound came from her lips. Krueger's breathing was ragged. It had been so long. He knew it would be over quickly, and he didn't want that. He tried to rechannel his thoughts. It was almost too late; he had entered her. *Think of something else,* he told himself. *Listen to Bach. No, God, don't listen to Bach!* He remembered someone once telling him, "Do math problems in your head."

He was only partially successful. Joan was not a passive woman. He would have been disappointed if she were. She heaved under him, meeting each one of his charges. Then it was over, much sooner than he wanted.

"You really shouldn't smoke, you know," Krueger said as she bent over him to light a cigarette from one of the candles. One of her breasts lay lightly on his chest.

"Now, don't go playing doctor with me, Aaron."

She hovered over him, her eyes huge, her body

blocking out the meager light from the candles. He was able to make out her smile, however.

"What the hell," she said, "I'm going to die sometime." She fell back slowly to the floor and left Krueger looking at the ceiling.

"Don't talk like that," he said. His authoritative tone was that of a high-school principal. "I want you to be around for a long time."

She said nothing for a while, and Krueger finally turned his head to look at her. She didn't return his gaze, her attention being fixed at a spot beyond her lacquered toenails. He heard a sigh escape her.

"But I'm not going to be around, Aaron. I'm leaving town, remember?"

"Yes, I remember, but . . . but . . . I mean, you're still going?"

Joan turned to face him. "Now, what do you mean, am I still going?"

"After this? I mean, after what's just happened, you're still leaving?"

Her answer was almost curt. "Yes."

He rose on one elbow. "Joan, you can't—not now. Doesn't this mean anything?"

She paused, her face thoughtful as she inhaled a mouthful of smoke. "Yes, of course it means something." Her voice carried a resignation. Krueger feared, a finality. "Sex is always something, I suppose; I'm not sure what. Aaron, there have been a lot of these somethings in my life. Do you understand?"

"That's beside the point, Joan. I don't care what you've done in the past or with whom you've slept. I care about now."

"Now? Now I'm going away."

"But don't you, uh, like me? Didn't you like this?" Krueger was pleading, he realized. He didn't care. "I don't have much experience. Perhaps I wasn't as——"

"Oh, hell, Aaron, don't put yourself down. It was good, marvelous. You were warm and giving. You're probably the most honest, open person I've known. It has nothing to do with that. I simply must go; that's all there is to it."

He tried to digest the indigestible. "And I'm not reason enough to make you stay?" he pursued stubbornly.

"Please try to understand, Aaron. I guess you're *not* reason enough—not you, not any man. I'm sorry. I've been dependent upon a man—or, rather, men—for too damn long. You see what I'm saying?"

Suddenly he couldn't look at her. He lay flat on his back again to talk to the ceiling. "I suppose so, but couldn't you have both?" His voice rasped out. "That is, have a man and not be dependent on him? Share his life but have a life of your own?"

"Ah, Aaron, it's a hell of a great theory, but it never works out that way. It should, but it doesn't. They won't let you. They want you dependent on them. They need it."

"Is that so bad?" He realized he sounded petulant. "Would it be so wrong for me to tell you that I need you?"

"Aaron, don't."

"Why not? Why not, if it's true?"

"Oscar used to say that to me."

"And you believed him?"

"Of course. He meant it. It *was* true: He *did* need me."

"But that was different; *I'm* different."

"Also true. Oscar was out of control of his life, and you're too much in control of yours. One is almost as demanding as the other."

He started to reply, to protest, but she reached over and squeezed his hand to signal silence.

"Aaron, there is something I must tell you. It's the real reason I called you today, but I just couldn't get it out over the phone. I wanted to tell you that . . . that I didn't give Oscar the reserpine. I know you thought I did it, didn't you? But I didn't, I swear.

I hated him, was going to leave him, but I didn't kill him." She withdrew her hand from his, and Krueger could sense that she was looking at him. "Do you believe me?"

"Yes. Yes, I believe you."

"You see, I thought I could change him, or that he would change on his own. God, how naïve can you get! And you wouldn't change, either, Aaron. Or, if you did, it would be at my expense."

Krueger could hear his own breathing. He put a hand slowly to his forehead to brush away the last few drops of perspiration from his hairline. Even the tick of his wristwatch was distinct in his ear. He searched for a plausibly persuasive argument, but his reservoir was empty.

Joan's voice, when it came, was loud and conversationally matter-of-fact. "Oh, Christ, why am I lying here naked—wrapped in a curtain, for God's sake, and analyzing a psychiatrist?" Then, more softly: "A very nice psychiatrist, of course."

Krueger said nothing.

She got up and was dressed almost as quickly as she had disrobed. "I'm staying the night in a motel, Aaron. Can you let yourself out and find your way home all right?"

He looked up from his position on the floor, suddenly conscious of his nudity. He saw that she was holding a pair of rope-thonged sandals in her hand. "Yes, I'll be OK," he told her.

She stood there for a moment. The candles were much shorter now and their flames higher. The angle of light deepened the natural hollows in her face and made her high cheekbones even more pronounced.

"You won't reconsider," he asked, "think it over?"

She didn't answer but instead moved in slow cadence to the door. He turned his head and saw her pick up a small suitcase from the foyer. She paused at the open doorway. The sudden rush of air whipped the candle flames into flickering gyrations. It was too dark to make out the expression on her face, but Krueger could see a moon halo around her hair.

"I'll think it over, Aaron. That's all I promise." She started out, then stopped. "And, for Chrissake, blow out those candles before you leave. I can't have the place burn down before the new owners move in."

He heard the deep rumble of the engine of her sports car, and he lay there until the sound faded away to nothing. He sat up and felt himself shiver. Must be a draft someplace. He contemplated his skinned knees. Rapidly he blinked his eyes once, twice, and then squeezed them tightly closed. There was a wetness on his cheeks.

Chapter XXXVI

Krueger's wristwatch told him it was almost nine o'clock. He was perspiring as he entered the animal laboratory. Where had the time gone?

He had phoned the staff members individually, telling them of the resumption of sleep therapy, confident that the hospital's efficient grapevine would do the rest. For good measure, he had put the same notification on all bulletin boards, taking care to report that the amitrypton would be kept in the animal lab.

He placed the box of amitrypton vials on the desk located in the center of the room and looked at the familiar surroundings. The animal cages were aligned on each side of the room at right angles to the desk.

The space between the cages was barely wide enough to afford access to two persons standing shoulder to shoulder. The single light bulb over the desk was too weak to penetrate the darkness of the narrow passages.

Krueger peered around the dingy "cat lab," as the staff called it. By necessity he had spent a lot of time here, but he did not enjoy this part of the research, and he delegated much of the work to his assistants. He regarded the bodies of animals as distasteful. He could feel the eyes of the cats following his movements.

He considered the cat the least offensive of animals. Lithe and clean, it was favored by intellectuals. Dogs were too aggressively affectionate for Krueger's taste. Of course, man was still the ultimate experimental animal. A pity he could not be used.

Theoretically almost any animal could be used in the sleep experiments, but the cat was uniquely qualified. It slept twelve to fourteen hours a day—a period exceeded only by the opossum and the bat—and more than twenty percent of it in REM sleep. The cat's nictitating membranes allowed the researcher to easily follow its eye movements. And when REM pressure drove cats psychotic, the behavioral changes were much more obvious than in other animals, which might act frantic under any conditions.

The normally placid and haughty cat was an experimental Jekyll-and-Hyde. Under controlled conditions, it vented its full-blown psychoses like some child's top run amok on a linoleum floor. Screeching—in perpetual motion—it threw itself at the edge of its cage, driven mad in the interests of science. Krueger was at once both fascinated and repelled.

Pressure was induced by depriving the cats of REM sleep in the same manner as in humans, usually with Valium or barbiturates. Sometimes, though, they were simply kept awake for prolonged periods until they became psychotic. One of the techniques was to cast them adrift on small blocks of wood in a tank of ice water. The wood was so delicately sized that the cats had to stay awake to maintain their balance. The slightest weight shift, as when they fell asleep, and they splashed into the hated water. Then they would frantically scramble back aboard their precarious floating sanctuaries, safe once more until sleep overtook them again, and again, and again.

It was in this room that Krueger hoped to spring the trap, to play out the final step of his plan. The basement animal lab was the largest room in the neuropsychiatry building. With its rows of tall animal cages and poor lighting, he could safely conceal himself. He spied a surplus army cot near the door and dragged it between two rows of cages, setting it up well out of sight of the door but in a place that would afford him an unimpeded view of the case of amitrypton on the desk. Then he sat on the edge of it to wait. The scuffling noise of the caged cats provided a nervous counterpoint to his beating heart. In the blackness, the cat eyes glared down at him.

Krueger suddenly began to shake, now almost as nervous as his feline companions, for it occurred to him that he might very well be in personal danger. He jumped up from the cot and walked back into the circle of light over the desk. He would recheck the box of amitrypton; it would help to pass the time as well as shore up his weakening resolve. Opening the case, he was horrified to discover that it contained only eleven vials instead of the full carton of fourteen. God, how stupid of him! He had forgotten them? Yes, he must take time. Anyone who had the knowledge to foil his research certainly would have the intelligence to instantly spot the discrepancy. He would have to find three more vials. He left the room almost at a run.

Krueger was back within minutes, placing the three substitutes in the box, but not before dropping one of them on the concrete floor. Thank heaven, it didn't break. Breathing his relief, he retreated again to the catacombs of the cat cages. There, in the darkened recess, a shattering pain knifed into his brain. It came from his leg, which had just come in violent contact with some metallic protuberance jutting from the bottom row of cages. Krueger's shin was on fire. He bit his lower lip, his eyes watering, and did an impromptu one-legged dance for a few moments there between his psychotic pets. He sat down on the cot and waited for the agony to subside. One hand tested his damaged leg. A thin trickle of blood ran into his sock. *Damn, this better work!* he thought forlornly. He briefly considered forgetting the whole thing but chastised himself immediately. He'd rather lose a leg than his project.

He got up, putting his weight gingerly on the foot attached to the now-swollen shin, and dragged the cot as far away from the offending cage as possible. He could move it perhaps only two feet, however, so confining was the space between the cages. Krueger's mind once again turned to his mission, and he hit upon another idea. He began a hurried search for cat food, a special brittle kind he knew was kept in the lab. He found it beneath the desk and began scattering it on the floor in the general area around the door. The noise the cat food made underfoot would serve as an alarm in the unlikely event he became drowsy.

Krueger's eyes snapped open. Where was he? He was momentarily more asleep than awake. He desperately sought to reorient himself, to will his brain to identify the location of his body. Another mystery of sleep, he thought groggily. He must study it sometime. His ears likewise were sifting the sounds of the animal lab from those of his just-concluded dreams. A constant but not unpleasant humming sound forced its way past his mental cobwebs. The animal lab, that's it. Damn! Time had eluded him. How long had he dozed? Two minutes? Two hours? His eyes quickly adjusted to the dark, helped somewhat by the light on the desk, which served as a reference point. He confirmed now that the humming sound did not come from his subconscious but from somewhere in the room. It was low but distinct, a musical background to the occasional squeals of the cats, a tune from a bygone time. Krueger tried to recall it, and then he identified the notes of a favorite from the days of his youth: "If I could be with you one hour tonight, if I could be with you, I'd hold you tight."

Someone had joined him, was here now, in this room. Krueger's sphincter muscle tightened spasmodically. He eased himself from the cot and came to a half-crouch. He realized that after running his leg into the cage, he had pulled the cot just far enough to the side to block a clear view of the intruder. By cautiously leaning sideways, he could see part of the back of a head and the left shoulder of a form he could identify only as a male. Whoever it was was bent over the case of amitrypton.

As stealthily as possible, Krueger moved forward, easing one foot ahead of the other in small steps. A crunching noise froze him in mid-stride, and he forgot to breathe. He had been victimized by his own silly alarm clock. A particle of the cat food had clung to the sole of one shoe—the cat food he had spread to trap the killer. His eyes darted upward. He was relieved to see that the noise had been covered by the sounds of the cats and the humming of his visitor.

Krueger now approached the area where the illumination from the light over the desk splashed weakly on the ends of the middle rows of cages. His eyes blinked at the light and registered fully on a man dressed in a white hospital coat. His back was turned to Krueger, and he continued resolutely at his task. A reflection of light caromed off a glass ampule that Krueger could see above the man's elbow.

"Come on out, Krueger. You really don't have to play hide-and-seek."

Krueger stopped, startled into immobility, but he was

pleased to find that he was now relatively calm, in control.

"Don't be shy," the white coat said, still not turning. He resumed humming the song, which Krueger was beginning to find maddening. "I saw you asleep back there, Krueger. Did anyone ever tell you that you snore? I decided not to wake you up. You've had a busy day, little man; you need your rest."

He was six-foot-five or so, Krueger judged, a bear of a man, and somehow familiar. Krueger started to edge around the desk so he could put a face to the hulking form. Why hadn't the man turned to confront him? "If I could be with you," the white coat hummed.

Was it possible he'd made a horrible mistake? Krueger asked himself. Was he suffering a paranoid overreaction at facing the end of his research? Had there ever been any methodical plan? Had Klement's death, after all, just been an unexplainable medical accident? Or, had it, in fact, somehow been due to the amitrypton? That would certainly be the end of everything.

". . . I'd love you long, if I could be with you, I'd love you strong," hummed the white coat. He was pulling the vials from the case one by one, casually exchanging the contents. Working with two large-needled syringes, he carefully observed sterile technique, wiping the top of each vial with cotton moistened in alcohol.

Krueger, abreast of the man now, watched as he slowly drew the contents of each amitrypton ampule into his syringe and then, with a second syringe, emptied the reserpine ampules into another syringe.

No, by God, I was right! Krueger told himself. "You're exchanging the medicine," he sputtered. He had been vindicated but wondered why he felt no sense of triumph. He now faced the intruder. He knew him—somebody on the medical staff—but he couldn't put a name to the face. The deliberate, single-minded way the man was making the drug transfer was infuriating and defied reality. "You're putting the amitrypton back!"

For the first time, and still without interrupting his work, the man looked at Krueger obliquely over one shoulder. "No shit?" The big man's laugh boomed in the dank lab. The cats answered with demented whines. The laugh was as out of place in this setting as the humming. "I'm also putting the reserpine back into its ampules. It's obvious, Krueger, that all this time in this loony bin has not dulled your keen powers of observation."

Krueger was speechless. He had visualized the scene many times, from the instant he'd decided on this ruse; but at the climactic moment, his adversary was not following the script. The man methodically continued switching the two drugs.

"You don't recognize me, do you, Krueger?"

Krueger said nothing. The man's openness, his utter indifference at being discovered, had unnerved him.

"Perhaps you've been looking at EEG tracings too long. I certainly know you." The man had adopted a sad little lopsided grin.

Krueger took a deep breath. "You . . ." he began. "You . . ." The words formed in his brain too quickly for his mouth. "Why did you do it? What did you possibly have to gain? Who are you?"

There was no reply.

Krueger's earlier fears for his safety had given way to intense curiosity and frustrated anger. "You said you know me," he said. He nodded in the direction of the case of vials. "It's obvious you know of my work."

"Oh, yes, indeed I do. I've read everything you've written. Had to, you know. Fascinating stuff. I've even waded through all forty-nine of your case reports. You're quite a writer."

Krueger stared at him blankly. "But what did you possibly have to gain?"

The man looked intently at Krueger and wiped the palms of his hands on his white coat. His ruddy face was in repose, as though he were weighing a decision.

"There could be only one reason," Krueger continued. "To hurt me, to ruin me professionally—wreck my research."

"Wait," the man said, holding up a hand.

Krueger ignored the interruption. "I know everybody here laughs at me and ridicules me. They're jealous, always have been. To them I'm just the funny little psychiatrist who messes around with people's sleep. You all think you're God's angels of mercy. About the only thing you're good for is playing doctor-nursie games and trading cruel jokes about the patients. If you ask me, *you're* the weird ones." He was warming to his diatribe, taking no notice that the man's calm expression stayed constant. "Who put you up to this? Or did you——"

"Wait a minute, Krueger. You've got it all wrong. I couldn't care less about your scientific ego trip. It was that bastard, that's all it was. It was that bastard I was concerned with." For a brief moment the man looked menacing.

"You despised me because I was better than you," Krueger went on, "and that's what you couldn't stand. Somebody who's willing to dedicate himself to something nobler is always ridiculed."

"Oh, shit!" The man pointed a finger at Krueger. "Shut up, you little tight-ass." Though low, his voice was authoritatively sharp enough to silence Krueger for the moment. "If you'll run down for a minute, I'll try to get a few things through that introspective brain of yours."

The big man sat down in one of the two plain wooden chairs and propped his feet on the desk. The sudden movement made Krueger take a backward step to block the man's exit, although he hadn't the foggiest notion of how he would have physically restrained him had he tried to leave.

"I got rid of that bastard Klement, and that's all I care about. He won't butcher any more mothers or babies," the man said, "or anybody else, for that matter."

What in the world was he talking about? Krueger wondered. "I'm not sure I understand," he said. "Before I call the authorities, I——"

Exasperation clouded the man's face, but his voice remained unruffled. "Krueger, sit down," he commanded. "You're not going to call the cops, for two reasons. First, if I really wanted to, I could beat you to the door and knock the piss out of you and then feed you to your cats." He chuckled without mirth.

Was he drunk? Krueger wondered. Was this some kind of hospital prank that had turned into a macabre joke?

"Sit down," the man ordered again. His feet had come to the floor, and Krueger noted that his elbows now rested lightly on the desk, his upper body coiled. Krueger sat.

The man rested his arms on the top of the desk. His speech came controlled, a lecture. "Let me say, Kueger, that when I first contemplated this little sin of mine, I had to admit to myself that I didn't think I'd ever go through with it. Sitting up in my little obstetrics ward, I——"

"Of course!" Krueger shouted triumphantly. "You're——"

"McCallister," the man finished for him. "Yeah, that's me, the Irish baby doctor." The finger was pointing once more. "Now, if you want to know the rest, you'll keep your mouth closed for just a few more minutes." McCallister inhaled deeply. "To repeat, I didn't give a shit about your experiments, just like you didn't care about Oscar Klement. But *I* cared about him. I cared about him a lot, the son of a bitch."

Krueger eyed him warily.

"Now, why won't you call the cops? Like, what would you tell them? Answer me that, Krueger. What in hell would you tell them? That you caught a licensed physician in a laboratory with some ampules of medicine and needles and syringes? That this bad man had induced a heart attack in one of your patients and you wanted him arrested for murder?"

"What about Dr. Klement?" Krueger asked. The question was timorously posed.

"What about him?"

"Well, he's dead. I mean, after all, a man died, and you killed him."

McCallister looked at the ceiling. "Yeah, he died." He once more propped his feet on the table and clasped his hands behind his head. "I'm sorry about that, Krueger. For what it's worth, I didn't plan on the bastard dying. That's the truth. I just wanted him out of medicine. I thought, if the reserpine drove the bastard crazy, the problem would be solved. He could never practice medicine again." He looked at Krueger for some hint of understanding. "Do you get what I'm saying?"

Krueger did not respond.

"Actually, Krueger, there's another reason you won't call the cops, the best one of all, from your point of view. Your experiments are everything to you, right? Your whole life. You don't give a damn about Oscar Klement—or anybody else, for that matter, I'll bet. You have to have fifty clean cases to report, right? Fifty home runs. So you've had one strikeout. But one more swing of the bat, fifty addicts certified cured. Quite an accomplishment. And you need the fifty before the meeting in Stockholm, right? See, Krueger, I've studied up on you quite a bit. You get a bunch of cops in here asking dumb questions about a not-so-mysterious death, a common garden-variety heart attack"— McCallister paused—"you can kiss Stockholm good-by. Brailey doesn't need that kind of publicity. He'd shut down that sleep lab of yours quicker than he'd jump that red-haired nurse on Second West."

McCallister gave Krueger a few seconds to let that

sink in. "Understand now? You were too successful. You were getting Klement off the dope, and I just couldn't have that. This was my only chance. Hell, you would have cleaned the drugs out of him and he'd have been back in business. Maybe they would have kicked him out of the hospital eventually, but he would have been back doing business at some other stand the next day, probably bigger than ever. I've seen it before. The son of a bitch would have just gotten wealthier, along with the funeral directors. I didn't mean to kill him, but I'm not so sure I'm sorry he's dead."

Krueger remained silent.

"You should have seen him in action like I did, Krueger. The sad part is, out there someplace there are a lot more just like him, maybe a hundred Oscar Klements, and somebody should boot their asses out of the business, but they won't. And, hell, it wouldn't do to go around willy-nilly executing incompetent doctors, would it, Krueger?" McCallister smiled thinly.

"So what you're saying," Krueger said slowly, "is that you did it out of a sense of justice."

"Something like that. Ah, how well did you know Klement?"

"Not very well, really."

"Well, then, it would be hard for you to understand why I did what I did. I only wanted your experiment to fail this one time. I wasn't trying to sabotage your whole project. I just wanted Klement stopped. And I sure as hell couldn't count on the system. The system sucks when it comes to disciplining doctors."

"I see."

"As a matter of fact, Krueger, I think you've got a great thing going here. I wish you luck; I really do."

Krueger squinted at him and said, "I'm not sure I believe that."

"Well, you would if you could believe that I feel almost as strongly about bad doctors as you do about your research. Bad doctors don't always kill people, but their peccancy pollutes the air around them."

"What?"

"Peccancy. You know what it means?"

"Yes, I know."

"Peccancy," McCallister continued, "an evil, diseased member of the total body—something like that. Guys like Klement and his partner, that Bronson, see ten cases for every one I see. They run a volume practice that thrives on patient fear and their own duplicity. Neurotics and psychosomatics run through their examining rooms hoping to be told they're sick. Klement obliges them and treats 'em with X rays, B-12 shots, and a lot of unnecessary medicine. Then, if they really get sick, it takes five or ten good doctors to rectify the mistakes. That's where the pollution comes in. The fallout is with the residents, med students, and interns who see guys like Klement out there knocking down half a million a year and boobs like me on medical-center staffs making forty grand. You think that doesn't make an impression? Pretty soon they want a piece of the action. It becomes a kind of medical Gresham's law: The bad drives out the good."

Krueger emulated McCallister, leaning back in his chair and hoisting his feet to the desk. There were several seconds of silence as the two men regarded each other. Krueger broke it:

"My, my. Dr. McCallister, the totally principled man."

"Not at all, Krueger. I plead guilty to a little melodrama, but I'm not bullshitting you. I believe everything I've told you."

"And it doesn't bother you that you killed a man—I mean, for whatever reason?"

McCallister returned his feet to the floor and leaned toward the diminutive psychiatrist. "I suppose it will, in a way, despite what I've said. It goes against all my training. But that's *my* worry." He shrugged, and his mood brightened once more. "So, you see," he told Krueger, "your experiments not only have tremendous potential for healing; they can discipline bad doctors. You've stumbled onto something here."

Krueger's gaze was distant, his eyes befogged.

McCallister pushed back his chair and got to his feet. "Think it over," he said. "I'm a pretty good doctor, Krueger. I still think I've got a lot left to contribute." He looked down, his massive frame casting a shadow across the entire desk. "So have you, if you want to look at it that way." He walked slowly toward the door.

Krueger continued to stare at the chair McCallister had vacated.

"I'm going to get myself a good, stiff drink. I'd invite you along, Krueger, but you probably have some thinking to do. I'll be at that saloon across the street. But after that you can tell the cops they can find me in the doctors' lounge."

Krueger heard the crunching of the cat food as McCallister left the room. It was a full five minutes before he rose and looked around. The voices of his animal mental patients had sunk to an agitated mewing. He could never remember them being this quiet before.

He ran his fingers along the edge of the ampule case. Suddenly he felt exhausted, drained. He needed a good night's sleep. Maybe he could take one of the beds in the sleep lab. He wouldn't have to waste time going home. He picked up the case of amitrypton and walked slowly from the animal lab, his shoes grinding the cat food to powder.

A strange fellow that McCallister, he thought as he mounted the stairs. Something of a rogue. Krueger walked down the second-floor hall and into the sleep room. On balance, McCallister had been right about one thing, of course: The sleep research could benefit countless thousands. When viewed in those terms, the death of Klement—a vain, greedy man with no redeeming qualities—was inconsequential. That overdose Mar-

lene what's-her-name, would be an ideal subject. Krueger could use what was left of the drug on her. If he
started bright and early tomorrow, he told himself, he
could finish the study in two weeks. Then a week or so
of concentrated writing. There was more than enough
time. He could work around the clock if need be.

Krueger stretched full-length on the bed where Klement had lain, hands folded behind his head. He glanced
over at the case of amitrypton he had placed on the
floor next to the door. More than enough time, he told
himself again. He felt a weight against his eyelids. What
was that tune McCallister had been humming? "If I
could be with you, da da de dum," Krueger sang softly.
"If I could be with you, dum dum de da." Catchy.
Krueger slept more soundly than he had in weeks.

Chapter XXXVII

The police cruiser moved at a snail's pace down the
darkened street. It literally crawled around the twelve
square blocks it was mandated to patrol. It would roll
gradually to a halt at intersections, then poke its nose
tentatively around corners like some outsize beetle
nudging a leaf.

At times, Officer Harlow B. Putnam would vary the
routine, driving the route in reverse or parking for
extended periods in one location. Then he would watch
the passing traffic and listen disinterestedly to his radio
as it cracked with discordant and disembodied voices
sending others to sources of violence. The voices had

nothing to do with him. Trouble rarely visited his beat. If one were to ask Officer Putnam the reason, he would say that it was because the "spics and niggers" hadn't moved in yet. They were still penned up in their economic concentration camps on the far reaches of the city. Here were upper-middle-class homes where quiet prevailed. Oh, there was an occasional burglary, but even then Officer Putnam would merely go to the scene and wait for the plainclothes boys to arrive and take over.

It made for a boring tranquility, which suited Officer Putnam just fine. The crime-incidence graph at headquarters revealed his neighborhood to be the safest in town. It was the reason he drove one of the few one-man night patrols in the department. His partner had been reassigned during the latest austerity drive at city hall. It was just as well. The last three partners had been young studs who spent most of the time bemoaning the lack of action and the cruel fates that had cast them into this backwater where opportunities for recognition were skimpy. Officer Putnam's nostrils made a scornful noise.

His left hand steered the cruiser while his right loosened the gun belt at his waist. The young tigers would learn, he thought, when it was too late, when they found out that success came through connections downtown, departmental policy notwithstanding. Let them find out for themselves. That's what he had had to do. Four times the bastards said he had failed the sergeants' oral exam. At fifty-two years of age, thirty pounds overweight, and with recalcitrant bowels, Officer Putnam just wanted to be left alone. He could retire in three years, and he sure didn't want some hophead putting a hole in him now.

His thoughts went to the photograph on the mantle at home. Taken on graduation day at the academy, it showed new Officer Putnam as a trim six-footer with close-cropped black hair and shiny badge. Over the years, it seemed that the young man's smile grew contemptuously wider as it beamed down at him from its place on the mantle. The image brought on melancholia that had all the symptoms of a gas attack. Now Officer Putnam was stoop-shouldered and round, with an extra chin that partially concealed the knot in his tie.

He guided the cruiser past the sprawling medical center. The towering face of the brightly lighted hospital loomed in contrast like a gigantic pinball machine over the homes shielded by profuse vegetation. There was action there, all right, but generally not the kind that Officer Putnam had to worry about.

He turned down a silent street flanked by homes showing few lights and curbed the car in front of one of them. Thrusting his wristwatch into the illumination of the dashboard instruments, he saw that it was almost 1:00 A.M. In the regular cycle of Officer Putnam's nocturnal world, it would soon be time for lunch. He slouched low in the seat, the familiar night noises comforting him through his open window.

His freckled hand was moving to the radio to ask permission to break for lunch when a movement flickered in the periphery of his pale-blue eyes. His glance went to the two-story Georgian home across the street and roved over the deep lawn and stately trees. A solitary lamp shining from inside an adjoining stucco was of little help.

Nothing, he told himself—nothing but a shapeless shadow high on the roof of the Georgian, its silhouette just slightly darker than the background of the starless sky. Whatever it was, it didn't seem to be moving, and Putnam knew how the night could distort and deceive. He was unconcerned. Still, he dutifully swung the cruiser's spotlight around and moved its narrow, powerful beam up the side of the house.

It froze on a man who, by God, was hanging from the trestle. The spotlight turned his face to a slash of chalk. While Putnam was telling himself he should be doing something, the man dropped from the roof and out of the pencil of light.

Putnam threw open the door of the patrol car while shouting into the dark. "Hold it!"

The man was on his feet, scuttling almost crablike across the lawn in front of the stucco house. He dragged one leg behind him like a wounded deer. Putnam was now running across the street, his feet hitting heavily on the concrete. He veered to his right, trying to cut down the angle on the fleeing man, but he stumbled as he climbed the terrace of the elevated lawn and went to his knees. His cap came off his head. He scrambled to his feet, the sod giving way beneath him. He was already wheezing from the brief burst of activity. "Son of a bitch," he muttered to himself.

His quarry was now several house lengths in the lead, and Putnam was unable to close the gap despite the man's obvious handicap, probably an injury sustained in his drop from the roof. Putnam's hand clawed furiously for his service revolver. The holster was flopping about like a beached fish on the belt he had loosened in the patrol car. Just as his fingers closed around the butt of the gun, the limping man gave out a sharp cry and fell headlong to the ground.

Putnam closed in on him, his strides ever wider and shorter in his exhaustion. By the time he reached him, the man had flopped over on his back and was struggling to rise. Putnam dived awkwardly for him. His breathing was like a sea in his ears, but he managed to roll himself atop the man and pin him to the earth with his considerable bulk.

Up close, the man showed a thin face marked by several scratches incurred when he had dropped into the thick bushes at the base of the Georgian. Somber eyes stared out beneath lowered lids; straight brown hair fell across his face. He was dressed in dark denim jacket and pants. Putnam judged his age to be twenty-five to thirty.

Putnam reached for his handcuffs and took in a tortured breath. "Don't move," he rasped, and then, for good measure, "you punk."

At which point Officer Putnam was treated to some of the most creatively obscene vituperation he had heard since leaving the navy in '44.

The uniform of the operating room—the green scrub suit—hung like a baggy clown's costume on Charlie Rogers. The surgical mask rested loosely under his chin. The green beanie had been pushed to the back of his head.

Rogers drew deeply on the cigarette and let the smoke drift past his tired green eyes. His square jaw rested on his chest as he stuporously regarded the light-brown hairs on his forearms. Constrained for seven hours by the rubber gloves, they were matted tightly to his skin.

It was the kind of depletion of physical resources that left one numb yet wide awake. The tension of the hours of sustained concentration had gone in the blink of an eye, as it always did, to be followed by a draining exhaustion that was almost total. He glanced around the doctors' lounge. It was marked by a disorder that was almost as unique as the sterile neatness of the rest of the hospital. Cups with cold coffee littered a Formica-topped table in the center of the room. Magazines were scattered on the plastic-covered couches and chairs. Soft-drink bottles were left where they had been emptied, the rack for their disposal largely ignored.

Rogers, with extreme difficulty, uncrossed his ankles and stirred. He put his hands palm down on the couch to give impetus to his effort to rise. He came erect and groaned as he felt the constriction of knotted muscles across his upper back. A young man's game, he thought, although he was only in his mid-forties and a mirror would still show him to carry his slight, well-proportioned frame with a quick agility.

His surgical slippers whispered on the gleaming tile floor outside the doctors' lounge as he made his way slowly, head down, in the direction of the elevator, ignoring the scenes of quiet urgency that flowed about him. He had done his bit for the day.

He rode the elevator to the seventh floor and stepped out into the administration corridor. In this wing, suits and sport jackets mingled with white hospital coats. He made for Brailey's office and saw him in the hall talking to a nurse. Brailey, catching sight of him, dismissed the nurse and hailed Rogers with a lift of his head. Rogers slumped against the wall.

Brailey regarded him benignly. "There he is, red of eye, the selfless surgeon, armed with only a scalpel, doing endless battle with the grim reaper against overwhelming odds."

"Fuck you," Rogers said with a wan smile.

Brailey grinned. "Tough one?"

"Long one."

"What the hell you doing up here, then?" Brailey asked.

Rogers's shrug was exaggerated. "All the time I was cutting out about a mile of that guy's lower intestine, I was thinking of you."

"Touching"—Brailey grinned—"but we've got to stop meeting like this. Come on in. I'll spring for a cup of coffee."

"I've got coffee coming out of my ears," Rogers said. "Actually, I thought maybe you'd let me use your couch for a while."

"Whatever," Brailey said and turned to the door. He was stopped by a shout at the elevator:

"Dr. Brailey!"

It was Anson Woolridge, the security chief. Rogers heard Brailey mutter a resigned oath. Woolridge was bearing down on them, his coat open and his green tweed trousers flapping around his legs like the streamers of a parade float caught in a cloudburst.

Brailey swallowed his intense dislike for the man and put on his chief-of-staff face. "What is it, Woolridge?"

Slightly short of breath, Woolridge opened and closed his mouth a few times while Brailey waited impatiently. Then he said, "Guess what, Dr. Brailey! We caught your phony doctor."

Brailey's eyebrows went up, and even Rogers's tired face revived with interest. Woolridge was beaming. He was shifting his weight excitedly from foot to foot.

"Well, for God's sake, man, let's have it," Brailey said. "Where? Who is it?"

"You won't believe this," Woolridge said eagerly. "He's been right here all the time, in the pharmacy. A guy named Bradshaw. A goddamn common Peeping Tom. Cops caught him on a roof not six blocks from here last night. He dropped right into their arms. I had them put him in a lineup this morning, and a couple of former patients picked him out right away."

"I'll be damned," Rogers said.

"Yeah," Woolridge said, turning to Rogers. "The cops searched his apartment and found a whole bunch of porno magazines. And get this: He's been sending letters to a lot of women who live around here, telling them to repent their sinful ways and all kinds of stuff like that. Then he's been going out at night, getting his jollies peeking in windows." Woolridge, still smiling broadly, waited expectantly.

Brailey was looking at Rogers. He chuckled. "It takes all kinds, huh, Charlie?" He shook his head and glanced at the floor, then looked back at Woolridge. "So he was here all the time," he said coldly. "How many times you must have passed him in the hall, huh, Woolridge? How many times you must have ridden on the same elevator."

Woolridge's face fell. His mouth twitched nervously at the corners. "Well . . ." he began.

Brailey turned his back on him. "Come on, Charlie."

They closed the door on the crestfallen chief of security and walked past Brailey's secretary into the inner office. Rogers headed straight for the leather couch.

Brailey stood propped against the desk, his arms folded. "I'll be damned," he said.

Rogers exhaled loudly and stretched his arms over his head. He snorted, "The guy is dispensing medical advice without a license. He's also the self-appointed moral watchdog against weaknesses of the flesh, and at the same time he's got a few earthy temptations of his own."

Brailey looked over at him. "How does that square?"

"Hell, ask Krueger," Rogers said wearily. "That's his specialty. Mine's gallbladders and hemorrhoids."

Epilog

The landing gear settled into its metallic nest with a reassuring thump. Pan American flight 372, New York to London, gained altitude effortlessly as Krueger watched Long Island Sound slip beneath the wing of the 747. As the plane pointed its nose out over the Atlantic, Krueger squinted into the glare of the sun bouncing off its shiny skin. He was able to identify Montauk Point on the tip of the island. A rush of boyhood memories raced past his mind's eye.

A sigh escaped his lips. He felt overcome by a sense of relief and accomplishment. The two feelings mixed with another, that of a natural emotional letdown. Events of the past few months now seemed packed together in a timeless blur that gave them an unreal quality. He had to persuade himself that it was all over and that he was on his way to Stockholm. He reviewed the episodes and his role at the medical center. Images of Klement, Brailey, McCallister, the sleep lab flickered before him. It all now seemed like a jerky two-reel silent movie in which he had been the director. He had been so close to failure, so very close. He congratulated himself on his perseverance.

Krueger listened to the hum of conversation within the cylindrical cocoon. Three hundred or so passengers were settling back, talking in eager anticipation of three hundred or so European adventures. He was not scheduled to deliver his paper for four more days. There would be at least two days in London to do whatever he wished. He looked forward to it, of course, but he was mildly disturbed by the feeling of deflation.

Stockholm was almost anticlimactic. Then what? Brailey's *bon voyage* had been a friendly needle: "Well, I suppose that when you get back, Krueger, our little hospital here won't be nearly big enough for you anymore. You'll be too famous for us."

A fishing expedition? Krueger had replied in the same congenial fashion. "Ah, Dr. Brailey, who knows what tomorrow brings for any of us?"

But now he wondered: What of his future after Stockholm? There was still certainly much to be done in sleep studies. He had reached a goal but hardlly a pinnacle, and life was so short.

"It's all kind of an anticlimax." Krueger said softly.

"What's that, Aaron?"

"I said it all seems kind of anticlimactic."

"*Au contraire,* Aaron, my little genius. This is only the beginning. The best is yet to come. You are going to rewrite the book on psychiatry. I'll see to it."

Joan squeezed his arm, and a tingle coursed along his spine. He knew she was humorously indulging him, but he was pleased nonetheless. He smiled at her paternally.

Krueger had, of course, made no announcement that he would be traveling to Europe with the widow Klement. Still, it was no secret, and the medical center would be abuzz with the news. He didn't care. No one had made a direct reference to it except Brian McCallister, who had bumped into him yesterday outside the pharmacy. Sticking out that large hand of his, he had wished Krueger good luck and added, "You both have fun now, hear?"

Krueger smiled to himself. He felt a special kinship with McCallister, and he was no longer troubled by the secret they shared. Maybe someday he would tell Joan about it. Maybe.

He sighed again and nodded to her. "London should be fun," he said.

PLAYBOY NOVELS OF HORROR AND THE OCCULT

ABSOLUTELY CHILLING

CHELSEA QUINN YARBRO

___16766 **MESSAGES FROM MICHAEL** $2.50

EDITED BY CHARLES L. GRANT

___16554 **NIGHTMARES** $1.95

___16751 **SHADOWS** $2.25

RUSS MARTIN

___16683 **RHEA** $2.50

ROBERT CURRY FORD

___16651 **HEX** $2.25

T.M. WRIGHT

___16673 **STRANGE SEED** $2.25

JACQUELINE MARTEN

___16529 **VISIONS OF THE DAMNED** $2.25

GENE SNYDER

___16612 **MIND WAR** $2.50

ADAM HALL

___16522 **THE SIBLING** $2.50

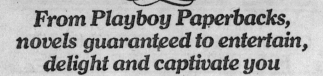

From Playboy Paperbacks, novels guaranteed to entertain, delight and captivate you

A MARVELOUS SELECTION
OF TOP-NOTCH MYSTERY THRILLERS
FOR YOUR READING PLEASURE

PHILLIPS LORE

___16587	**WHO KILLED THE PIE MAN?**	$1.75
___16694	**THE LOOKING GLASS MURDERS**	$1.95
___16652	**MURDER BEHIND CLOSED DOORS**	$1.95

MICHAEL COLLINS

___16551	**BLUE DEATH**	$1.75
___16506	**SHADOW OF A TIGER**	$1.50
___16525	**THE SILENT SCREAM**	$1.50
___16478	**WALK A BLACK WIND**	$1.50
___16593	**ACT OF FEAR**	$1.75
___16672	**THE BRASS RAINBOW**	$1.95

MARGOT ARNOLD

___16639	**CAPE COD CAPER**	$1.95
___16534	**EXIT ACTORS, DYING**	$1.75
___16684	**ZADOK'S TREASURE**	$1.95

CHARLES ALVERSON

___16530	**GOODEY'S LAST STAND**	$1.95
___16603	**NOT SLEEPING, JUST DEAD**	$1.95

MICHAEL P. HODEL &
SEAN M. WRIGHT

___16711	**ENTER THE LION**	$2.50